apman

Cover design by Dissect Designs

ISBN: 978-1-8382644-6-8

This book is also available as an eBook.

For my family

PART ONE

Festive gatherings of the Cockle family were a nightmare, that was the truth. The vying for attention, the teasing, the one-upmanship, the just-trying-to-get-a-word-in-edgeways. Oh, and the attempts to remember that somewhere underneath it all you love these people who at times you could quite happily strangle.

But Stacey never believed a family gathering, no matter how stressful or cringey, would lead her to make a decision that would haunt her for the rest of her life.

Not until this one.

Following her reckless announcement that she'd finished the first draft of her novel, Stacey grew flustered under the sudden scrutiny of all three brothers, three sisters and various in-laws and other halves. In fact, the entire room was now eerily hushed – apart, that was, from The Twelve Days of Christmas which was blaring out from the speakers on the old sideboard, where there also stood a profusion of family photos in matching silver frames, currently with tinsel draped haphazardly amongst them.

'*You've* written a book?' her brother Jack broke the silence, for once sounding not entirely certain of himself, as if he literally couldn't believe what he'd heard.

Well, she couldn't back out now. She had ten faces staring at her. 'Yes. I finished it last week.'

There was another pause. Gulping back some wine, Stacey blushed and fussed about with the naff keyring from her cracker. The yellow paper crown on Jack's head had slipped forwards over his eyebrows, and he took it off.

'And what's it about?' her sister Bea asked, raised eyebrows disappearing into her choppy red fringe.

'It's… well, it's a romance.'

Her cheeks now positively radioactive with heat, she wished she could melt into the floor and disappear.

Why hadn't she learned it was better to blend in at these family gatherings? Keeping your head below the parapet was the best way to survive, especially when you were the youngest and generally the butt of all the jokes. Why had she thought it would be a good idea to spill the beans about the romance she'd spent a year writing? Besides, if any of them did read *One Winter in Paris* – and the idea was toe-curling, since it was full of spicy love scenes – they would only use the opportunity to shoot it down in flames. The book was supposed to be only *her* baby for a little longer. Her private triumph. For the moment, at least.

But it had been hard not to bring it up. Bea had been talking about her upcoming wedding, Jack about the exciting news that he and his wife were soon to be parents. In fact, *everyone* had something positive going on, from new jobs to new homes, new partners to promotions.

'I suppose it's kept you busy,' Jack said. 'Now you're *between jobs* again.'

'Oh yeah, what happened with the last one?' Bea asked, adjusting the bow at the top of her shimmery gold blouse. 'Haven't you lost three jobs now since you graduated? And two boyfriends,' she added unkindly.

'Here it is,' her mum Faye called from the doorway of the dining room, bearing – with some difficulty – an enormous Christmas pudding on a patterned plate, flames raging alarmingly from all around it.

'Jesus, Dad, how much brandy did you pour on that thing?' Jack asked, leaping to the rescue just as her dad appeared in the doorway, looking sheepish.

Relief flooded Stacey's body as all eyes were now on the sweet inferno. Thank goodness she wouldn't have to start talking about how she got made redundant from her first job, quit the second because she hated it, and had now lost her third because the company went bust. It was far from her favourite topic. And she *certainly* didn't want to start talking about the two boyfriends she'd "lost."

Being dumped from two relationships as well as two jobs had really stung.

If only I had some good news, for once.

As Jack placed the pudding in the centre of the table, his wife and one of Stacey's other sisters were asking Bea about her hen night plans, and there was soon a reassuring hum of chatter from all around the table once more. Good. Before she knew it, it would be as if she'd never opened her mouth about *One Winter in Paris,* and it could be her secret project once again.

'Stacey, did I hear you say you've written a book?' her mum asked, placing a warm hand on her shoulder.

No such luck, then.

'Oh, yeah, it's nothing really.'

Please, everyone just leave me alone now.

'Shall I go and get some bowls and spoons?' she asked quickly, to cover her awkwardness.

'Your dad'll get them.'

'It's a romance,' Jack said.

'Ooh,' her mum said, 'is it a *steamy* romance? I like those.'

'Mum, please,' her brother said.

'What?' Faye asked, grinning and reaching behind her back to untie the novelty Santa apron she was wearing.

'When will we see it in Waterstones, then?' Bea asked.

'I— it's a bit early for that…'

'I'll tell you what,' Jack said, 'if by next Christmas you've got a publishing contract, I'll—'

'Go on, what will you do?' Bea asked, as chuckling spread around the table.

'He'll shave off his beard,' his wife suggested. Jack's facial hair was his pride and joy, and he put his hand up to it protectively.

'Now, let's not be hasty…'

'Go on,' Bea said. 'It's not like you'll have to do it, is it?'

Jack grinned widely. 'That's true,' he said. 'Okay, then. The bet is on. What d'you say, Stacey?'

In all honesty, she didn't want to say anything. Her book wasn't a bet. It wasn't supposed to be a joke.

But they all thought it was.

'Yeah, okay. Whatever,' she said.

Her mum handed her a bowl from which a heady aroma of brandy and dried fruit emitted. 'Stop teasing her,' Faye said. 'Writing is a lovely hobby. But don't let it distract you from jobhunting. There's no money in books.'

Nodding, Stacey picked up her spoon, though her stomach – already full of turkey and stuffing – had now tied itself in knots. She'd applied for so many jobs in the run up to Christmas that when she closed her eyes, she swore she could see application forms on the back of her eyelids. Writing had been the best way to escape, and yes, perhaps she had fantasised about it being a big success, seeing *her* book on the shelves. It had given her a warm glow in the midst of so much rejection. But now she felt ridiculous.

They're all laughing at me.

Then another thought sprang into her head. She didn't care one way or the other about Jack's beard, but it *would* be something to not be the failure of the family, for once. Why was she letting them make her feel ridiculous? There *were* authors who did very well, why couldn't she be one of them?

Perhaps she *could* get a publishing deal by next Christmas.

Stranger things had happened, surely?

…

Arriving back to her little studio flat later that evening she was still fired up with enthusiasm. But what should her next step be? Perhaps she could get an opinion on her story to start with – some confirmation she hadn't been wasting her time. Then she could do a little more work on her writing and see where things went from there.

Yes, that would be a good way forward. Another set of eyes would make a huge difference. And preferably the eyes of someone who didn't know her in real life, and certainly not anyone from her family.

It took less than a week to find herself a perfect online critique partner.

Her stomach full of butterflies, she sent *One Winter in Paris* off to them for their feedback, while *The Darkest of Paths* by J. M. Kirkbride landed in her inbox for her to critique in return.

And as Christmas rolled into a bleak and rainy new year with no new job yet on the horizon, she curled up under her favourite fluffy blanket to open *The Darkest of Paths,* and she began to read.

13 years later

Chapter 1

Settling back in her coral pink desk chair, Stacey muttered half-heartedly under her breath, 'I am capable, I am confident, I am creative, I am productive,' before taking a sip of a takeaway latte she'd treated herself to after completing the school run. She shuddered at the memory of the morning chaos. Ava couldn't remember where she'd left her shoes, and Teddy had a meltdown about the contents of his lunchbox. As if *that* wasn't bad enough, he'd gone on to point out that she'd forgotten to send in the permission slip for a school trip *and* neglected to get any donations on his mini marathon sponsor form, at which point she'd thought her head would blow clean off.

Letting her eyes drift to the wall above her writing desk where more positive affirmations – or what her husband cheerfully called "propaganda" – were displayed in colourful framed prints, her heart sank further. *Be happy!* proclaimed sunny yellow writing on a white background. *Squeeze the day!* said a lemon. *You are enough,* soothed a pretty pink heart. Of course, *Grant* didn't need these sorts of messages. He *was* happy, he *was* enough. But there weren't enough colourful prints, pretty desk ornaments or cute notebooks in the world to make Stacey's writing room a productive place, as the blank page on her laptop screen was testament to.

The words FIRST DRAFT were emblazoned across the top of the otherwise empty document, in an optimistic nod to the idea that not only would she complete the task of writing her new book once, but there would be further drafts to come.

In a sudden burst of emotion, Stacey straightened her back and said with conviction, 'Today is going to be the day.' But no sooner were the words out of her mouth than her phone screen lit up and she glanced down at it automatically, groaning at Bea's name on the screen.

'Bea, I'm right in the middle of something,' she said as she answered, 'can we chat later?'

'Writing your next masterpiece?' came the sarcastic reply.

Stacey's fingers tightened around the phone. *Don't let her get to you. Just rise above it.* 'Yes, actually.'

Bea had the decency not to laugh, at least, though it wasn't much better when she said haughtily, 'Andre has just been promoted.'

A movement in the corner of her vision startled her and Stacey turned, but it was only the cat, Queenie, coming to doze in her favourite spot on the window seat.

'That's great,' she said with false enthusiasm. Anything to get Bea off the phone. 'Tell him congratulations. Now, I really must be—'

'I thought we could all do with a big family celebration, maybe a holiday. As well as Andre's promotion, we've got dad's seventieth coming up, Jack's turning fifty, and there've been *two* more babies this year.'

Stacey smiled. The ever growing Cockle clan. At least most of them had mellowed nowadays and didn't treat Stacey quite so much like the runt of the litter – in fact, aside from Bea and Jack, who grated on her like nails down a blackboard, she enjoyed meeting her siblings and horde of nephews and nieces. 'That would be lovely,' she said. 'Do you have a date in mind? I can help you organise—'

'It would be our treat, of course,' Bea cut off her offer of help. 'You and Grant don't need to contribute, what with your *current situation*.'

At this, Stacey closed her eyes and counted slowly to three inside her head. She'd said in confidence to her mum that money had dried up from her book and Grant's business had hit a rocky patch, and now every one of her siblings had found out and concluded she was practically destitute. 'That's generous of you,' Stacey said. 'At least let me help with the planning, in that case.'

'Well, it needs to be *nice,*' Bea said. 'So just let me handle it all. All you need to do is turn up.'

Stacey raised her eyebrows but didn't bother to argue. 'I'm sure you'll find something perfect,' she said sweetly, but Bea was already saying her goodbyes. After she hung up, Stacey looked incredulously at the phone for a moment before placing it down on the desk. Let Bea try and score her little points; she, Grant and the kids would love to go on a free holiday – if the price was Bea lording it over her, well, she could handle that easy enough.

Her phone chimed and for a second she thought it would be a message from Bea, but instead it was an email, and it concerned something quite different to a family holiday. Snatching up the phone with shaking fingers, she stared at the screen harder, as if the email title would rearrange itself into something else. She must be hallucinating. Perhaps day after day of procrastinating had finally made her crack. After all, there was no way she could be reading this right. She rubbed her eyes and opened them again slowly. The words would have rearranged themselves now. It would be okay – what she'd seen before was surely nothing but confirmation that she was slowly losing the plot. She fixed her eyes on the screen, but the words hadn't changed.

The Darkest of Paths.

She pushed her chair back from the desk in a panic, the phone falling from her hand. The sudden movement startled Queenie, who climbed back down from the window seat, brushing past her legs, but Stacey barely noticed as she sucked in air desperately. In a sudden spasm of movement, she lunged forwards to scrabble through the powder-pink bookcase at the side of the desk – an item of furniture that was mostly for show, the spines of the books arranged in perfect colour order – to try and find what she was looking for. Yelling 'Shit!' as her fumbling hands bashed her latte, she continued her search, ignoring the hot liquid soaking the pages of her empty notebook and spreading over the desk. Her fingers found it – *Two Lost Souls* – *her* book. Slipping it off the shelf she brought it to her chest and clutched it like a shield.

Don't open the email. Just delete it. Pretend you never saw it.

But that was impossible. She couldn't pretend she hadn't seen it. Coffee was dripping off the edge of the desk and soaking into the fluffy grey rug on the floor. Seconds ticked by. Stacey took a deep breath, before placing *Two Lost Souls* down on the desk, well away from the coffee spill.

You have to read the email. You have to.

With a deep breath, she clicked.

Stacey,

I'll get straight to the point.

I know you stole my story thirteen years ago. It might have taken me a while to figure it out, but Two Lost Souls by Stacey Cockle is The Darkest of Paths by J. M. Kirkbride. That publishing deal you got, those film rights you sold, those interviews you did… you're a better actor than you are a writer. You've got away with it long enough. I want you to tell everyone you're a liar and a fake.

J. M. Kirkbride.

A sound started in her throat. As it bubbled up, she put a cushion over her face and screamed into it until her voice was hoarse.

Chapter 2

'Come on, Stacey, you've been in bed most of the week,' her husband Grant's voice was filled with concern as he placed down a mug of tea on the bedside table beside her. Receiving no response, he sighed and picked up the cold and untouched cup he'd brought her earlier and took it into the ensuite to pour it down the sink. 'At least drink something. You'll make yourself ill.'

She continued to ignore him. How could she possibly bring herself to talk to him about what was upsetting her? How could she even show her face after what she had done?

'Right, that's it,' he said firmly as he came to sit beside her on the edge of the bed. 'I'm calling the doctor. This isn't right. If you won't talk to me, you have to talk to somebody. You've been so down, perhaps they can prescribe something—'

'I'm not depressed!' she said. 'I'm not ill, I don't need to see anyone, I just…' she trailed off, suddenly exhausted, while he took out his phone.

'I said I don't want you to call the doctor,' she said, swatting the phone from his hand. It fell on to the bed beside her and he grabbed it quickly, but not fast enough to stop her spotting he had eight missed calls from his builder, Desh. Guilt washed over her. 'I'm so sorry,' she said. 'I didn't mean to take it out on you. I really appreciate everything you're doing. I just… I don't feel myself right now, but I'll try and get my head together today, I promise. Besides, you've got more important things to do than hang around here all day, by the looks of all those missed calls.'

'Nothing's more important than you.' He started stroking her hair, his warm fingers working through the tangles. 'I'm worried about you,' he said softly. 'This isn't like you. Even the kids are wondering if you're okay. And Bea called me, saying you won't answer her messages about a holiday, or something?'

'Oh, God,' she groaned, before rolling over, hair falling across her face so that she was looking at Grant through a black curtain. She tucked it behind her ear, trying to ignore how lank and greasy it felt. He didn't seem to mind what a state she looked. Grant didn't exactly look tidy either, with a couple of days of stubble – in a patchwork of dark browns, coppers and, more recently, a touch of white – and dressed in scruffy jeans and an old t-shirt.

'I told her you're unwell,' he said, 'she started asking all sorts of questions about what's wrong with you.'

'What did you tell her?'

'That it was just some virus you'd picked up.'

'Thank you,' she said. 'I'll talk to her later, or tomorrow, maybe.'

Grant got up and crossed the room to open the silver satin curtains. 'Why don't you get some sun?' he suggested. 'It's a lovely spring day. You can come down to site with me if you want, I'll show you how we're getting on.'

Chuckling as she pulled a face at his suggestion, he sat down beside her again. 'Squelching around a muddy building site isn't really your thing, I know,' he said.

'It's not that, it's just… I just need…' she put her hands over her face. She just needed Kirkbride to go away. It had been a week since their email, but the words were as fresh in her mind as if she'd just read them five minutes ago. *You've got away with it long enough.* So many years had gone by that the painful fear of somebody discovering what she'd done had faded away, almost to nothing. She'd spent years wishing she could tell her younger self not to take *The Darkest of Paths* for her own. She'd been reckless and selfish; so obsessed with getting one up on Bea and Jack that when the incredible manuscript had fallen into her lap and made her realise how awful her own first draft had been, she'd lost sight of everything else. The true author had fallen silent – they'd never replied to a message from her again. Nothing. It was as if they'd disappeared off the face of the earth. So, she'd changed their book's title and put her own name at the top. She'd found an agent, a publisher, and everything had snowballed until she was so caught up with everyone's infectious excitement about the book that she could see no way to back out. She'd tried to stay out of the limelight as much as she possibly could, wishing that *Two Lost Souls* had never taken off the way it had, but by then she was in a hole so deep she could barely see daylight. A hole so deep that she'd begun to believe her own lies.

'You just want to write a new book,' Grant said heavily, startling her from her dark thoughts. 'I know.'

'I need to, don't I?' she said guiltily. 'I know this latest project you've taken on is a money pit. If I can write something new it would change everything for us.'

He plumped up the pillow behind her and tucked in the duvet like she was a sick child. 'You look so tired,' he said. 'I know you're not sleeping. *Is* it the money that you're worried about? I know I bit off more than I can chew with this warehouse conversion, but I've got to see it through now. If we cut back on a few luxuries at home until the flats are sold, we'll be okay. You don't have to stress out so much about trying to write another book like *Two Lost Souls*. For God's sake, you've been trying for over a decade! If you can't follow it up with another book no one will think any the worse of you for it. You still achieved something most people could only dream of. I'm so proud of you, nothing can change that.'

Stacey rolled away from him, eyes squeezed tight shut, his words cutting her. *I'm so proud of you. Nothing can change that.* If he only knew.

I want you to tell everyone you're a liar and a fake. Kirkbride's words hit her anew. How could she ever do that? It would destroy her life.

'Are you listening to me?' Grant said gently. 'I'm saying you don't have to torture yourself like this. Take some time out. Figure out if there's something else you want to do instead of writing. You know I'm behind you one hundred per cent whatever you decide.'

She let out a sob as she curled up in a ball. *I just want this all to go away.* She'd thought it would be easy to follow up her "success" with a new book, a *genuine* book. Her plagiarism had started her career, plus it had bought them their beautiful house and kick-started Grant's business, but she would put in the graft now. That's what she'd told herself. That's what she *still* told herself. She'd write plenty more books, of course she would. But the years had passed.

She'd got married, had Teddy and Ava, and no new book had been written. *And now it's too late. Now I'll lose everything, even the respect of my husband.* Would Grant still love her, if he discovered what she'd done? He was so honest and kind – it would never cross his mind to lie and cheat his way to success.

'Come on,' he said, as he started tapping away on his phone. 'You need a distraction. You go to yoga with Wen on Thursday mornings don't you? Perhaps you could make it to that? I won't work late tonight, and I'll bring back a takeaway. How does that sound?'

'I don't know if I can face seeing anyone.'

'Well... I've just told her you'll go and she's coming to pick you up. You know seeing Wen will make you feel better. You can go for lunch with her after, it's not like there's much food in the fridge here.'

'You know she doesn't like being called Wen,' she said. No matter how many times she told him that her friend hated this shortened version of her name and preferred people to use her full name Morwenna, or Wenna for close friends, he always seemed to forget. Personally, Stacey loved her friend's name, especially as the Cornish name Morwenna, chosen for her dad's birthplace, was followed by Precious, after her Zimbabwean grandmother, so her name was full of meaning.

Grant grinned. 'There you go. That's some of the old Stace. I knew you'd tell me off for that.'

Sitting up, Stacey gave him a playful shove, which made his grin even wider, and a bit of lightness returned to her. Yoga and a takeaway sounded okay. It sounded doable, anyway. Perhaps a change of scenery would give her some perspective and help her decide how to respond to Kirkbride's email.

Tentatively, she swung her legs out of bed, sinking her feet into the thick carpet, and Grant put his arms around her. 'It'll be okay,' he said. 'Whatever this is, we'll get through it together.'

Chapter 3

If she'd hoped that yoga and lunch would be relaxing and carefree, she was soon to be disappointed. When they walked out of the yoga studio, Morwenna's face took on a troubled look. 'Dad's having issues with his carers,' her friend said, once they'd dropped off their yoga mats in her car and started walking to the little cafe down the street. 'I was supposed to be going on a date on Saturday – one I've already had to rearrange once – but now I'll have to go down to Cornwall instead.'

'A date!' Stacey nudged her friend. She *loved* hearing all the gossip about Morwenna's dates. If anything could take her mind away from Kirkbride, it would be hearing about this date once it had happened.

They squeezed single file through some scaffolding over the pavement. It seemed like most of the normally pretty street was having building work done. Sometimes Stacey could hear it from her house, though generally her tidy, tree-lined street was a secluded refuge from the noise of the real world. She finally took in her friend's words as they emerged from the scaffolding and fell into step side by side on the pavement. *Supposed* to be going on a date. There wouldn't be any juicy gossip for Stacey to hear next week; instead Morwenna would be driving down to her elderly dad in his dilapidated cottage. Stacey felt a pang for her friend. Though it was obvious how close Morwenna was to her father, the constant worrying about him did grind her down. She was always having to speak to his carers, help him sort out his bills, fix something or other in his house, or find tradespeople who could. Defending the nightmare dwelling, Morwenna had said her dad was born there, and, after moving back from London following the premature death of Morwenna's mother, he intended to die there. 'He's at peace in that house,' Morwenna explained. 'He says his heart feels lighter.' She had added proudly that you could see the sea from the window of the front bedroom. Hearing this, Stacey had suggested that if they did the house up and rented it out to holidaymakers, her dad could move somewhere that was easier to maintain, and make a bit of cash besides, but that advice had gone down like a lead balloon. Morwenna and her father were both romantics at heart, and the house was a part of the man's soul. Separate him from that, and what would there be left?

'You can't cancel a date because you have to go to your dad's! And I'm sure if he understood the situation he wouldn't want you to.'

'No, my *date* should understand the situation,' Morwenna said passionately, 'but I bet he won't. I've been through it all before; being ghosted when I try and rearrange things. I'm getting sick of it all, to be honest. I should just forget these stupid dating apps altogether.'

Reaching the coffee shop, Stacey made a beeline for her favourite table in front of the large window and sank down gratefully into one of the patterned armchairs, before Morwenna's mention of the weekend prodded something in her mind. 'It's your birthday on Sunday!' she said. 'We're going out that night. You can still make that, can't you?'

'No, but it doesn't matter,' Morwenna said. 'I didn't really want a massive night, anyway. I'll just… skip it this year,'

'You can't *skip* a birthday. And spending it with your dad is hardly a proper celebration.'

'I won't tell him it's my birthday,' Morwenna said as she adjusted the floral headband she wore to yoga practices. The same colour as Stacey's jet black hair, Morwenna's was as tightly coiled as Stacey's was straight and formed a puffy cloud above the headband. 'He won't have realised and if I bring it up it'll upset him that he forgot. And besides, it's not a big birthday is it, thirty-nine—'

'It's the last year you'll still have a three at the start of your age.'

Morwenna smiled mischievously. 'Jealous?'

Busying herself trying to move the table to stop it wobbling, Stacey did her best to ignore the pain blooming in her chest. Kirkbride's words hit her again with force. *You've got away with it long enough.* Forty years old and she still wasn't really a writer. The dream she'd had since she was a child had come to nothing. Not from the point of view of anyone apart from herself and Kirkbride, of course. To the rest of the world, she *had* achieved her dream, but calling herself an author – now *there* was a great piece of fiction, and one that made her heart feel like it was breaking in two.

'Let's do it the following weekend then,' she said. 'Please, Wenna, I need a night out. Things are a bit shit at the moment—'

'Grant did say you're having a tough time,' she said, placing down the lunch menu she'd been perusing. 'What's been going on?'

Stacey searched for an answer, and since the truth wasn't an option, she settled on a convenient alternative. 'Oh, Bea phoned last week,' she said at last. 'Going on about Andre getting promoted.'

'Bea? Your sister? I thought you didn't speak to her much nowadays?'

'Not if I can help it. My mum's told them all that Grant's project isn't going well and now Bea's calling offering to pay for a holiday—'

'Yeah, what a bitch,' Morwenna said with a smile.

'Oh, you know what I mean. I know I'm overreacting, she just gets on my nerves, that's all.'

'We should probably order,' she said as a large group came inside, 'otherwise I think we'll be here a while. And look, Stacey, don't let Bea or any of them wind you up. Andre works in his family's business. Of course he's getting promoted. A bit of nepotism doesn't compare to what *you've* achieved, does it?'

Stacey's stomach began to tie itself in knots. *What I've achieved.* 'Well, I—' she began, but then her phone chimed, saving her from having to come up with a reply. Slipping it from her pocket, she froze when she saw the name on the screen.

J. M. Kirkbride. They'd emailed again.

She jabbed at her phone in horror, terrified to read the words, but unable to look away.

I don't like being ignored.

'Stacey?' Morwenna said.

'I…' Stacey began to push her chair back, 'I've got to go, I'm sorry.'

'Your stuff's in my car—'

Stacey ignored her and fled from the cafe. It was half an hour to walk home, but fresh air was what she needed. Sunshine fell on her face and warmed her, but it couldn't touch the cold dread at the pit of her stomach.

Kirkbride hadn't gone away.

Chapter 4

Stacey burrowed further down into her blankets when the doorbell sounded. 'Tell them to go away!' she yelled out to Grant, whose footsteps she could hear in the hall. Sticking out a hand from her cocoon to grab her glass of white wine, Stacey closed her eyes. Why now? Why did it have to be now that Kirkbride started bothering her? Why couldn't it be after she'd managed to write something else? With another book published she'd be safer – even if he did expose her, at least she'd have something out there that was genuine. *Or maybe I should just come clean.* After all, she *had* stolen, and cheated, and lied. She deserved to pay for what she'd done, but did her family? Did Grant? *Two Lost Souls* had been so popular it would cause a huge scandal if the truth came to light – Teddy and Ava would be the children of a fake, a fraudster, and as for Grant… she downed a large mouthful of wine. Grant would never understand.

'It's not a good time,' Grant's voice filtered through the door. 'But I'll tell her you dropped by with her yoga mat.'

'She ran off earlier when we were about to have lunch,' Morwenna started to explain. 'One second she was okay, then she saw something on her phone and just left…'

Stacey sprang up from the sofa, some of the wine sloshing out of her glass and over her hand. 'Shit,' she said as she plonked it down and tried to take a step, but the blankets tangled round her legs and almost toppled her. She tore them away and burst into the hall. The last thing she wanted was Grant to start asking her what message she'd received.

'Stacey!' Morwenna said. 'I was worried about you, after earlier. You… you look terrible.'

'Thanks,' Stacey said, swaying a little, her head thick from the three – or was it four – glasses of wine she'd got through that evening. 'And you don't need to worry about me. I'm fine. I'm completely fine.'

Morwenna and Grant exchanged a look, and then a little voice from upstairs cried out, 'Daaadeee!'

'It's Ava, again,' Grant said. 'This is the third time she's got up tonight. She's so unsettled.'

'I'll go,' Stacey said, lurching towards the stairs. Her children were the one thing keeping her sane right now. Sharing a book with Ava or answering Teddy's surprisingly perceptive questions about anything and everything, were about the only two things that could distract her from the deep pain that filled her body.

'No, I will,' he told her. 'You should drink some water. Your head is going to be pounding in the morning.'

Stacey sighed. He was right; she couldn't go upstairs and settle Ava in this state. Morwenna put her hand gently on her arm. 'What's up?' she said. 'I know there's something. You said earlier that things aren't good.'

Making her way towards the kitchen, Stacey tried to keep control of her emotions, but despair overwhelmed her. *Why did I do it? Why the hell did I ever do it?* What she wouldn't give to turn the clock back.

Morwenna stopped her as she opened the fridge to grab the wine bottle. 'I'll make some tea,' she said. 'And you need to tell me what's going on.'

Staring blearily at her friend, Stacey said, 'How am I supposed to write another book like *Two Lost Souls*?' Her voice was barely above a whisper. Perhaps she should tell Morwenna. Just spill the truth out, confess her sins. Surely if anyone would understand it would be her best friend. But the words died on her lips. 'I need to write another book,' she said instead. 'And I can't… I don't know how.'

'It's a lot of pressure, I know,' Morwenna said as she started filling the kettle. Stacey slumped down on one of the stools at the kitchen island. With its duck-egg blue cupboards and marble effect tiles, the kitchen was one of Stacey's favourite rooms in the house, though at this moment she could be sitting in the most luxurious room in the world and still get no comfort from it.

'You'll find a way,' Morwenna continued. 'You set the bar super high with *Two Lost Souls*, but you can't let fear hold you back. If you did it once, you can do it again. One day something will inspire you—'

Stacey let out a burst of humourless laughter. *If you did it once, you can do it again.* Morwenna couldn't have said anything worse.

Her friend had stopped in the middle of taking mugs from the cupboard, an eyebrow raised. 'Stacey?'

Realising how bizarre her response had been, Stacey quickly tried to recover from it. 'Nothing inspires me,' she said morosely. 'I am creatively dead. And my career might as well say do not resuscitate.'

Morwenna turned on her heel. 'Then do something about it,' she said. 'Set yourself goals, find a writing group, try new things,' she paused, as if startled by her own uncharacteristic assertiveness. 'I just mean, if everything you've done so far hasn't helped, it's time to look at the situation differently, isn't it?'

Placing the mugs down gently on the kitchen island, Morwenna said quietly, 'Are you sure that's all this is about?'

Stacey shook her head, but couldn't trust herself to speak. Morwenna rushed over and started to stroke her back as a sob escaped her. 'Come here,' her friend said, and put her arms around her. Stacey let a few tears fall, but quickly pulled away, though the warm, slightly sweet scent Morwenna wore lingered in the air.

'I've run out of time—' Stacey caught herself. 'It's Grant,' she said. 'His warehouse conversion is struggling. He's taken on too much trying to turn it into luxury flats and it's costing far more than he expected. I want to be able to help him, but I can't, and I feel so… I feel useless.'

Morwenna sat down beside her. 'He'll find a way. These things usually work themselves out in the end. How bad is it, do you know?'

'He won't tell me exactly. But it's bad.'

'I'm so sorry. He's got other properties, though, hasn't he? Perhaps he can move some money about.'

Stacey folded her arms on top of the kitchen island and lay her head down on them. Yes, perhaps Grant would find a solution, but there was no guarantee. What if Grant really couldn't finish what he'd started? What if everything went completely tits up? Who would get them back on their feet again? She may have given Grant most of the money to buy his first investment property, but she was in no position to bail him out, and perhaps never would be.

'How about a writing retreat?' Morwenna said suddenly. 'A complete change of scenery, nothing else to worry about. Perhaps that would help?'

Stacey raised her head. A writing retreat. Away from any distractions, any reminders of what she had done. It made sense! Perhaps it could work, actually really work! A slow smile spread across her face as hope filled her body. She'd still need to think of some response to Kirkbride's email, of course. She'd try to diffuse their anger as much as she could, but if she could focus, get something written quickly enough that she was offered a new publishing contract, perhaps she would still have a career left to salvage. She *had* to try.

PART TWO

Chapter 5

Emerging from a grand driveway, Stacey drew in a breath as she was confronted with the elegant, double fronted house, framed perfectly by the azure sky above and manicured lawns which spread out to either side. Now *this* was the kind of place she could find inspiration. There were some cars already parked – not surprising since she was late – and she quickly joined the end of the row. Packing had taken far longer than expected. What exactly did a person wear to something like this? And, admittedly, she'd been nervous, which had made her even slower. In fact, she'd strongly considered not coming at all. Still, she was armed to the teeth with new pens and notebooks along with her laptop, and she was determined to make it work. *I have to do this. I've got no choice.*

Grant had had a look on his face at the cost of her attending the retreat, and though he said he supported her and thought it was a good idea, if she came back having produced nothing it would make for a very uncomfortable conversation. Failure was not an option. 'I can do this,' she said to herself. 'I am creative. I am productive. I *am* a writer.' She pasted a smile on her face. Yes, she would return home with notebooks bursting with ideas, perhaps even having started her first draft, and she'd make everything right.

Snapping a couple of photos of the pretty house as she stepped out of the car, Stacey sighed, her confidence already slipping. She had – perhaps unwisely – told her followers online that she was going on a writing retreat when she had booked it a few months back, so now they'd expect to hear all about it and see plenty of pictures.

Once her things were safely in her room, her hosts – a beaming whirlwind of a man called Erik, and his quiet but efficient wife Janice – directed her to the other writers, though she hardly needed their help to find them, as the sound of laughter and chatter drifted from the dining room down the hallway. Stepping inside, Stacey cast her eye over the selection of little cakes and scones that were laid out enticingly to welcome the new arrivals. The doors at the end of the room had been flung open to allow people to spill out onto the terrace, and everyone was apparently getting on like a house on fire. *Don't say that you wrote Two Lost Souls,* Stacey reminded herself as Erik and Janice bombarded her with information about timings of breakfast, lunch and dinner. *Just try and fit in.* She certainly didn't want any reminders of that book, anyway. She wanted to keep a cool head and start afresh.

'You should try the scones,' said a voice by her side once their hosts had eventually departed, having showered her with wishes for a "productive week." Dressed in an alarmingly colourful assortment of garments, of which at least one appeared to be homemade, Stacey smiled at the enthusiasm of the woman who had spoken. She could almost feel rays of excitement fizzing out of her new companion. 'They're very good and there are still a few left,' the woman continued.

'What time did everyone else get here?' Stacey asked.

'I don't know. About thirty minutes ago? I'm always late, too. I can't seem to help it. I'm June, by the way,' she added. 'I write children's books. Write and illustrate. I come here to get away from my husband.'

'Stacey,' she said. 'I guess I've come to do the same.' There was an uncomfortable silence, as each woman realised that while June's comment about escaping her spouse had been made in jest, Stacey's was somewhat more sincere. It was becoming unbearable, having Grant around to witness her constant failure. It couldn't be more obvious how stressed he was about money, and knowing that she could help him if only she could get her act together put her under so much pressure she sometimes felt she would burst. One small mercy was that Kirkbride had gone quiet, though she didn't know whether this made her more relieved, or more worried what they were planning next. *I'll put it right. Once I've got another book done, I'll make amends for the stealing.*

'Let's introduce you to the others,' June said, quickly covering the awkwardness as she bustled towards a pair in the corner by a large, overstuffed bookcase. 'This is Yasmine and Dante. I'll leave you to it; I haven't introduced myself to those two yet.'

Stacey followed her gaze, to where the youngest members of the group stood just outside the door, chatting in the sunshine with the rest of the guests. Looking to be in his early thirties, the man had a broad smile, which he directed at her when she caught his eye, while the woman – perhaps a little older than him – had a pretty heart-shaped face topped by masses of tightly curled hair. A pair of oversized glasses with bright pink frames perched on her nose, and she was too absorbed in talking animatedly to notice the new arrival.

'You look nervous,' said Dante, and Stacey turned to face him. A tall, tanned man in perhaps his late forties, he wore a checked shirt that had one too many buttons undone, and he fixed her with a disconcertingly direct gaze.

'Everyone is ever so friendly,' Yasmine told her reassuringly. 'I've never been to one of these before, but Dante has.'

'I haven't either,' Stacey said, looking at Yasmine. Striking in a copper-coloured blouse, her black hair was tied in a ponytail with a few wisps escaping to frame her face. Feeling like an imposter, Stacey muttered an excuse about wanting to grab a cake while there were still some left and headed towards the table where the remaining sweet treats were rapidly dwindling.

'Oh, Stacey, come and join us,' June said, a fresh scone in hand, as Stacey finished selecting a small slice of shortbread. 'We have a very auspiciously named writer in our midst. Not that he's enjoying making a fuss about it.'

Sighing inwardly at the prospect of coming under further scrutiny, Stacey stepped towards the terrace.

'Joel Shakespeare,' June announced, gesturing at the man who had smiled at Stacey earlier.

'The name's a curse, not a blessing,' he told her. 'I'm definitely going to be using a pen name.'

'Stacey Cockle,' she said, without thinking.

'Wait a second,' said a voice at Stacey's shoulder – the woman with the glasses and curly hair – 'you're not *the* Stacey Cockle, are you?' She paused for a moment, as if composing herself. 'The one who wrote... oh… what was it?'

'*Two Lost Souls*,' June said, a strange tone to her voice, 'that's what you're thinking of.'

Everyone's eyes were on Stacey. Well, she couldn't deny it. All they'd have to do was take out their phones, search for her name, and photos of her face would be plastered over their screens. Her heart sank as she was forced to say, 'Yes, I am *that* Stacey Cockle.'

…

'So, how is it?' Grant asked her. 'What are the other people like?'

Stacey sighed and gazed up at the ceiling in her room, enjoying sinking back into her soft king-sized bed while she held the phone to her ear.

'They're fine,' she said, reflecting back on the afternoon and evening she'd spent at the retreat. 'They're friendly, but it's difficult when I don't feel very confident right now. I just want to hide away.'

'Well, that's what the retreat is all about, isn't it?' Grant said. 'Getting in touch with yourself again. Getting your creativity and confidence back. I'm sure they can all relate to that.'

'Yes, I suppose so,' she said limply. The others were already feeling creative, that was the problem – the thing that made her even more self-conscious, more aware of how she wasn't like them. Over the course of the evening, she'd managed to find out at least a little about everyone. Yasmine – the woman in the copper-coloured blouse – was a doctor who was working on a cosy mystery series; Heidi, a loud and vivacious woman who between work and looking after her nine year old daughter self-published books for teenagers and funny short stories; Chandice, who was writing a memoir of her mother's recollections about coming to England from Jamaica to work as a nurse in the fifties; and Dante – the man with too many buttons undone – wrote self-help books. Then there was Charlotte – the woman who had asked if she was "the"

Stacey Cockle – who had been trying to complete her gothic novel for the last five years without success, and Joel Shakespeare, who was far less prolific than his namesake and described his goal for the retreat as wanting to "finally get something down on paper". The very last person she'd spoken to had been an English tutor named Tom who wrote meticulously researched historical novels. His answers to people's questions were generally monosyllabic, though he had found a rapport with Chandice, who was also more on the quiet side, and the two had chatted companionably most of the evening. During the inevitable rush of questions she'd been bombarded with after revealing she'd written *Two Lost Souls*, Tom had looked at her askance and made her feel quite uncomfortable, and she sensed that while she was the object of some curiosity, her revelation had also alienated her from a couple of the writers.

'You told them, didn't you?' Grant said.

'It was an accident; one of the writers recognised my name.'

'I guess that was always a possibility. And does it really matter? You're there to work, anyway, not to chat.'

Stacey sat up on the bed, her skin starting to prickle with irritation. It had been a long day, and she felt exhausted. 'I can't exactly *ignore* everyone, can I?' she said.

'Well, no, I know that. Look, I only want you to be happy, and after spending all this money on the retreat you'll be so disappointed if it doesn't work out—'

'Do you mean *you'll* be disappointed?'

There was a short silence. 'Just remember you have other things in your life that are meaningful as well,' he said, 'you don't have to write for people to value you. You've got me, and the kids—'

'How are they?' Stacey asked, regretting her outburst. Grant wasn't the enemy here. The retreat *had* cost a lot, it was only natural he would be concerned about how it would work out. 'You must call me when you're putting them to bed tomorrow, so I can say goodnight to them.' She'd missed curling up to read a book with Ava that evening, and after the day she'd had, a cuddle from her daughter and Teddy was all she wanted.

Getting up from the bed, Stacey went over to the window to close the heavy, floral curtains. It was a pleasant room, with a view over the gardens, which were now enveloped in darkness as the last light disappeared from the June sky, and in the corner a large free-standing bath stood invitingly, a fluffy towel draped over its side above a pair of soft white slippers. Stacey wandered over and slipped her bare feet into them, before picking up the small bottle of bubble bath and reading it absent-mindedly as Grant told her how Ava had been invited to a party while Teddy had asked at teatime why air was see-through.

'I'd have enjoyed hearing you explain that one,' Stacey said as she placed the bottle back down. Grapefruit, she could understand, but what on earth was "May Chang"? She'd have a bath soon and see if it really did make her feel uplifted and energised. God knows she needed a bit of that.

'Stacey, you know that I *do* believe in you, don't you? Just block out all the noise. It doesn't matter what other people think – this is about your journey.'

'Try telling that to Bea and Jack.'

'Oh, ignore them,' Grant said. 'Don't take the stuff they said to you on that holiday to heart. They *want* to wind you up.'

Stacey winced as memories of their time in the villa resurfaced. Though her parents, and most of her siblings, had been kind, Bea and Jack had an uncanny knack of making her feel like she was a child again.

'I know you're having a difficult time,' Grant continued, 'but perhaps opening up, telling people how you feel, might be helpful. I'm sorry I said you weren't there to chat. You *should* talk to the other writers if it helps. They'll understand what you're going through better than me.'

Once they'd said their goodbyes, Stacey reminding Grant to call her the next evening so that she could say goodnight to Teddy and Ava, she grabbed a plain sweatshirt from her suitcase and pulled it on. After that conversation she didn't feel like sleeping, so perhaps she'd go downstairs in case anyone else was still about, see if Grant's suggestion of opening up really did help.

Making her way across the room, she stopped in her tracks as she spotted a piece of white paper, folded in half, which had been pushed under her door. She frowned as she reached down to pick it up, but once she unfolded it and read the words – printed out from a computer in a large font on the crisp white surface – she had to clap her hand over her mouth to stop herself from screaming. The paper fluttered from her fingers back down to the floor, but the words were etched in her mind.

Try ignoring me now.
J. M. Kirkbride.

Chapter 6

With a moan of frustration, Stacey turned onto her front and buried her face in the pillow. *Stop thinking! Just stop thinking.*

But they're here! J. M. Kirkbride was at the retreat, watching her every move. They had figured out which room she was in and slipped that note under her door to scare her. After reading it, she hadn't wanted to go downstairs any more. She'd curled up on the bed, shaking with anxiety. How had they found out where she was? Were they stalking her now? *I posted about this retreat all over the place,* she remembered. *Why didn't I realise Kirkbride would be reading everything I say on social media?*

So, who were they? The book was written from a man's – or rather, a teenage boy's – point of view, but that had no bearing on who could have written it. It seemed unlikely to be Chandice, if she was putting together her mother's memoirs rather than writing fiction; or Dante, who wrote self-help. Both Joel and Charlotte were on the young side to have written it over a decade ago, however that didn't rule them out completely. Theoretically *any* of the writers here could be J. M. Kirkbride. It was only Joel and June whose names started with a "J" but that also meant nothing. It was probably a pen name, not a real name. It could be anyone. Anyone at all.

'Did you sleep well?' June asked her when she came down to the dining room the next morning, eyes dry and scratchy from lack of sleep.

'Not really.'

'It's being in a strange bed,' June said as she adjusted a patterned scarf tied jauntily around her throat. 'You'll be all right tonight. You're in the big room, aren't you? The one with that lovely bath?'

'Yes, I am.'

'Oh, you are lucky. I'm in the room next to you. Make sure you get yourself plenty of coffee and a nice breakfast, that'll pick you up. Need to get those creative juices going.' With a chuckle, she rushed off towards the breakfast buffet, and Stacey looked about to see who else was there. Some of the writers were sitting at tables on the terrace outside enjoying their breakfast in the morning sun, and after grabbing herself a black coffee and a plate of scrambled eggs and toast, Stacey went to join them. *I have to figure out who it is. Figure it out and talk to them, explain what I'm trying to do.* Surely, they would understand she was only trying to help her family. Once she'd got another book done, got it published, helped Grant out of the hole he was in, *then* she could make things right with Kirkbride.

I'm living in a dream world. I'm never going to be able to pull this off.

'I feel a bit guilty,' Yasmine was saying, 'leaving my husband to deal with the kids and taking a week for myself.'

'I know,' Heidi replied as she spread honey across a slice of toast, 'my partner is looking after my daughter, Daisy, this week after she pushed me to come here. I wouldn't have done it otherwise, but she insisted she and Daisy would be just fine without me.'

Stacey's unease deepened. It would be tough for Grant sorting the kids out this week at the same time as he was having so many issues with his building project. At least his mum lived nearby though, she could help out if it got too much for him.

'So, Stacey, is your next book going to be like *Two Lost Souls*?' Yasmine asked her.

Shit, what was she supposed to say to that? 'Everyone will have to wait and see,' she said, grasping at straws. Who knew what kind of book it was going to be? She still didn't have a single good idea.

'When did Lost Souls come out?' Heidi asked. 'It was a few years ago, wasn't it?'

'More than ten years ago now,' Stacey said. 'But then I got married and had kids, and things got crazy for a bit.'

'Hopefully you'll get a bit of peace and quiet here, then,' Yasmine said.

Stacey nodded and pushed her eggs around the plate with her fork. She didn't have much appetite. This was supposed to be a chance to empty her mind and fill it with ideas, but all she would be able to think about now was Kirkbride. A flicker of anger made her draw in her breath sharply. Why did they have to follow her here like this? What was their game, for God's sake? Her nerves were already shredded, but at the thought of them sat at one of these tables, casually eating breakfast, while all the while watching her and plotting, fear gripped her like a vice. She turned at the sound of voices in the dining room to see who had arrived. Joel was there, talking to Charlotte, who was hanging on his every word. Stacey raised an eyebrow. Was a romance on the horizon? They made a cute couple.

A few minutes later, Joel and Charlotte emerged onto the patio with their food and sat together at a table beside a large terracotta pot containing a lemon tree. Soon Chandice joined them, and Charlotte looked irritated at being interrupted, but did Joel look slightly relieved? Perhaps a romance wasn't on the cards, after all.

Her phone chimed, and she found a message from Morwenna. *How was your first night? What are the other writers like?*

It's ok, Stacey typed back, *I like the other writers, I just need some inspiration to strike.* Suddenly, she remembered the plans Morwenna had had for the weekend. *How was your date!!??* she added.

Oh God don't even ask. I'll tell you when you get back.

Stacey was about to insist she get the full story straight away – it had been months since Morwenna had had to cancel her last date to go and help her dad – but before she could type her reply, she was interrupted by Dante joining the table.

'Everyone feeling motivated?' he asked.

'Oh, yes,' Heidi gushed. 'My mind was *abuzz* with ideas as soon as I woke up. It's so nice to be able to dedicate all my time and energy to writing.'

'Yasmine?' Dante asked.

She didn't catch Yasmine's reply as she stuffed a forkful of scrambled eggs into her mouth and tried to swallow it.

'And you, Stacey,' he asked, his blue eyes boring into her.

'I… I didn't sleep well,' she said, as the whole table looked at her. 'But I'm hoping my brain will wake up after a bit of caffeine.'

Dante smiled widely. 'You should try putting your phone away for a start,' he said, angling his head towards the offending device that Stacey had just placed beside her plate.

'I'm trying to have a digital detox,' Heidi said. 'I can't turn the thing off in case my girlfriend needs to get in touch about my daughter, but there's to be no doomscrolling for me this week. I'm determined.'

'Yes!' Dante said passionately. 'A digital detox is what we all need nowadays. Don't you think, Stacey?' His voice took on a cloying tone.

Stacey almost choked on her eggs. A week without her phone? As if this whole situation wasn't difficult enough for her already.

'I guess it can't hurt to cut down,' she said obligingly as she slipped her phone back in her pocket. She'd message Morwenna later.

'Here's an idea,' Dante said to her, 'why don't we help each other out this morning? We could spend an hour bouncing ideas off each other. No point struggling on your own, is there?'

Stacey found herself nodding. She'd have to get through the day one way or another, and perhaps some of Dante's drive might rub off on her. It had to be better than being alone with her thoughts, anyway. 'I'll grab my notebook,' she said.

Rushing off towards her room, she almost collided with Tom – the historical fiction writer – who jumped at her sudden appearance. 'Morning,' he said, having recovered himself, before shuffling away.

Once she'd collected the notebook from her room, Stacey joined Dante downstairs, and they found a spot on the grass in the shade of a tree. *Just try to get through the day. You're never going to figure out who it is if you don't get to know the other writers.* Opening her notebook, she drew in a sharp breath. There was a sheet of paper inside, folded in half, and she opened it to find another message printed in that same large font.

I'm watching you Stacey. Come clean, or else.
J. M. Kirkbride.

Chapter 7

In the end she spent almost two hours brainstorming with Dante, but not so much because she was making good progress, more because she wasn't able to escape. When he wasn't trying to squeeze ideas out of her as if she was a ripe lemon, he was spouting the "wisdom" he was going to use to fill his new book *The Only Thing Getting in Your Way is You*. His interest in her and her writing journey was so intense that it unnerved her. Was she a case study for him? The creatively blocked, formerly successful writer? Perhaps she was the kind of person he used to get ideas for his self-help books. *Or does he have some other agenda?* The thought of Kirkbride placing their message inside her notebook made her stomach churn. *They have been in my room!* Had she left the door unlocked? It was possible; she was always forgetting stuff like that at home, much to Grant's exasperation. But when could they have done it? Had somebody snuck up there the previous evening when they were all downstairs? She couldn't recall anyone leaving for any great length of time before they all went up to bed, but then, it wouldn't have taken that long, not if they had a key or if she had forgotten to lock her door. Or perhaps it had been while she ate breakfast. That would rule out Dante, Yasmine, Heidi and June, but any of those four would have had the chance to do it the previous evening.

'Have you written any fiction?' she asked Dante innocently as they made their way back towards the house for a much needed break. 'Or has it always been self-help books?'

'I prefer to stay in the real world,' he said without hesitation. 'Daydreaming and imagining are all very well, but the real world is where you can make your mark. That's why I help people focus on concrete, achievable goals.'

Stacey sighed inwardly. That was no use. And the only goal she cared about right now aside from finding Kirkbride was drinking a large coffee and sprawling on her lovely soft bed.

...

It was a relief that most of the writers were still nowhere to be seen when she went down for dinner that evening. Well, that wasn't entirely true; Tom, Dante and Chandice were still outside on the grass working, but the others must either still be at the writing desks in their rooms or maybe taking a walk in the garden, and it was nice to not be immediately surrounded by the whole group. After a painful afternoon scribbling the odd idea down – to abandon each of them immediately – followed by staring at a blank page on her laptop, Stacey had given up the fruitless task of trying to pull inspiration from thin air, spending the time dwelling on Kirkbride instead, her thoughts dark and uncomfortable.

'How are you finding it here?' Stacey turned to see Charlotte in the doorway, clutching her laptop under her arm.

'Great,' Stacey lied, 'I've got loads done.'

'Me too!' Charlotte said, giving her a smile that seemed sickly sweet. 'A change of scenery has made such a difference.'

The three writers on the grass stood and began making their way towards the dining room, and voices drifted down the hallway too. Stacey braced herself for the onslaught of people and conversation. Part of her was glad of the distraction of dinner, but a bigger part was horrified that somebody about to sit at the table was the person whose work she had stolen. Why wouldn't they simply talk to her face to face? If she could only have a sensible conversation with them! She'd already tried emailing, asking if they could meet, but Kirkbride had so far ignored her plea.

'I hope your day was better than mine,' Joel said as he sat down beside her at the table. 'Everyone else is raving about how much they've got done.'

'There's a lot of positive vibes going on,' Yasmine said as she took the seat to Stacey's right. 'But I wouldn't say I had the best day.'

Stacey smiled a little. Thank God, not everyone here was a torrent of creativity.

'How did you find today, Stacey?' Joel asked, as he poured her some water from a large jug in the middle of the table, before filling his own glass.

'It was okay,' she said. 'I did some brainstorming with Dante.'

'That must have been… full on,' he said quietly, the expression on his face making her smile. So, he found Dante hard work, too.

'It was, quite,' she agreed.

The conversation around the table tailed off as their food arrived, and Stacey poked at the roasted squash and feta salad in front of her without much enthusiasm. Finally taking a forkful, she discovered it was tastier than she expected, and though her insides felt like they were in knots she managed to finish the whole plate.

'Even if I don't get much done this week, at least I'll have eaten well,' Joel said, running a hand through his dishevelled brown hair as plates of vanilla cheesecake topped with summer berries arrived and were duly admired by the writers.

This statement was greeted by chuckling from much of the table, and Charlotte simpered at Joel in a way that made Stacey's heart break for her. From what she could see, Joel wasn't giving any signals he was interested in Charlotte's attentions, yet this apparently wasn't deterring her. If she carried on this way it was all going to end in tears, for sure

'Stacey,' Yasmine said quietly, 'I hope you don't mind me asking, but are you okay? You seem a little stressed.'

'I'm a bit tired, that's all.'

'Well, if you want to talk about anything, people say I'm a good listener.'

'Thank you,' Stacey said. 'But I'm fine, honestly.'

'So, how about we talk through what we've been working on?' Charlotte suggested, her voice over-loud after a couple of glasses of wine. 'I'd love some feedback on *Gossamer*. I've completely rethought Euphemia's love interest. I'd got him *all wrong*.'

Stacey looked up from spearing one of the fruits topping her cheesecake. Had one of the characters in Charlotte's gothic novel suddenly acquired Joel's tousled hair and warm eyes, by any chance?

'That sounds great!' Heidi boomed, while June, Dante and Chandice agreed with enthusiasm.

'I'd love to listen,' Joel said, 'but I don't have much to contribute of my own work, not yet.'

'Same here,' Yasmine said, while Tom nodded.

'I'm not feeling great,' Stacey told the group, 'but I'll stay for a bit. I'd like to hear what everyone has been up to,' she added, with as much enthusiasm as she could muster.

...

It wasn't until gone nine o' clock that Stacey began to wonder why she hadn't heard from Grant. The kids would be in bed by now, so why hadn't he called so she could say goodnight to them? The writers were all involved in an intense discussion with Chandice, who was finding it hard to get her mum's notes and anecdotes into a logical order to write the memoir. The conversation was growing increasingly animated as more wine was consumed; nobody would mind if she slipped out for a moment to call her husband, they likely wouldn't even notice.

Stacey reached for her phone on the coffee table in front of the uncomfortable pink sofa she was slouched on. She frowned. It wasn't on. She'd charged it overnight, it couldn't be dead, and she never turned it off. Surely one of the other writers hadn't done it, trying to enforce their digital detox? Her eyes widened once she turned it back on. Seventeen missed calls from Grant, countless messages, of which the most recent showed his frustration with her.

I'm assuming you're going to ignore me all night as well as letting the kids down, so I've asked my mum to come and babysit. I'm going out with the guys. You're not the only one having a hard time right now. Call me when you can be bothered.

Stacey closed her eyes for a moment. She *hadn't* turned her mobile off. She rushed out of the room to try to phone him, but he immediately rejected her call, and she swore under her breath. Why hadn't she checked her phone earlier? She'd completely lost track of time, her mind too consumed with Kirkbride to focus on much else.

After messaging Grant to say her phone had accidentally been turned off, she sighed. He was clearly upset by something beyond her not answering his calls, but there wasn't much else she could do right now. She'd talk to him in the morning when he'd cooled off. A night out with his friends would be good for him, anyway; she was always saying he should let his hair down once in a while. It would be fine. But then her breath caught. *Accidentally* turned off? No, *Kirkbride* had turned her phone off! She'd told everyone at dinner that she was looking forward to speaking to Teddy and Ava – they all knew she was waiting for her husband to call, so Kirkbride had taken the opportunity to mess with her family. Tears prickled her eyes.

Please, let's meet up and talk about this, she begged Kirkbride once more in a hasty email. *Let me explain, at least. I want to make this right, but how can I when I can't talk to you?*

She hovered outside in the hall for a moment, but of course they weren't going to reply straight away. They were in there with the other writers, talking to Chandice. Sagging against the wall, she closed her eyes. *I'd do anything to go back and stop myself taking that manuscript. Anything.* She could take Bea and Jack laughing at her every day for the rest of her life if it only meant she didn't have to carry the weight of her lie any longer.

Suddenly completely furious with herself, she let out a low moan and balled her hands into fists.

I should post a confession online. Right now.

The thought stopped her in her tracks. Why draw it out any longer? After all, she deserved the hate she'd get, the respect she'd lose, the awful questions, and whispers behind hands.

And let's face it, she couldn't write a new book. Even if she *could*, it wouldn't be finished in time to help Grant. He needed money *now*, not several months, or even years, down the line. She couldn't help her husband. She'd always known deep down that she wouldn't be able to write a book in time for it to be any use; it had been an excuse, that's all, it was wishful thinking, and a reason to delay telling the truth.

Resolve filled her body. Things were never going to get better, not while she carried on lying. What she needed was a clean slate – but before she posted online, she'd need to tell Grant the truth. She couldn't have him finding out second hand. Yes, she'd tell him the truth, as soon as he was willing to pick up the phone to her.

Chapter 8

Jumping out of her skin at the sound of the door opening beside her, Stacey quickly slipped her phone in her pocket. Had she really been considering confessing to Grant? The idea was already beginning to seem crazy, and she felt giddy and confused. How many glasses of wine had she had?

Charlotte emerged, as startled to find Stacey lurking there as Stacey herself was to be interrupted.

'I was just on my way back in,' Stacey said. 'I needed a bit of air, that's all. It's so stuffy in that lounge.'

'Actually, I'm glad you're here,' Charlotte said, blinking rapidly a few times behind her glasses. 'Yesterday, when we met and I recognised your name…'

'Yes, I remember.'

'Then I pretended not to know the name of the book you wrote.'

'I hardly expect everyone to know,' Stacey said, her insides churning.

I can't talk about Two Lost Souls right now. I can't. I can't!

'No, I mean, sorry, I'm not explaining myself very well,' Charlotte laughed uncomfortably. 'I was a bit… starstruck, I suppose.'

'By me?'

'Well, *Two Lost Souls* is my all-time favourite book,' she said. 'I've read it so many times the pages are practically falling out. You're a huge inspiration.'

'I— thank you,' Stacey said, feeling as though she was looking down on herself from a great height. Lie after lie after lie.

It's been years. Thirteen years. I don't know how to be anybody else.

'In fact, I have your book with me,' Charlotte said excitedly. 'If I go and grab it, could you sign it? It would mean a lot.'

Stacey still felt like she was floating. She was watching herself nodding, watching herself smiling, saying she'd be delighted to sign the book. Finally, Charlotte scurried away, and she plummeted back to earth.

Who am I kidding? I can never come clean, not even to Grant. I can't be anybody else. I can't turn the clocks back.

This is who I am.

…

'It must be hard,' Dante said, once all the other writers had left for bed, 'trying to follow such a great success. Do you ever feel like you peaked too early?'

Stacey stretched out her legs on the pink sofa, kicking a couple of scatter cushions to the carpet. She didn't want to move. After signing Charlotte's copy of *Two Lost Souls,* she'd drunk so much wine that her head was thick and fuzzy, and all she wanted was to close her eyes and drift off. The babble of the writers had become soporific. They had given up trying to engage her in their conversation, and she was content with that.

I just want this whole nightmare to stop. I want to forget it all, just for a while.

'I don't wanna talk about it,' Stacey slurred at Dante. Why was he still here? Surely it was obvious she was not in a fit state for talking. The decorative ceiling rose above her head appeared to be swirling around, but when she closed her eyes, her whole body felt like it was spinning, too.

I need to sober up. I can't let myself fall apart.

'It seems like you need to talk,' he said. His voice was closer. 'Do you mind if I sit here?'

Stacey curled her legs up towards her and he joined her at the other end of the sofa. 'How did it feel when your book exploded like it did? It must have been surreal.'

'I wish it hadn't exploded,' she said.

'Really?' he leaned towards her. 'Why would you say that?'

'I don't know,' Stacey lied, uncurling herself so that she could sit, rather than lay, beside him. 'Be careful what you wish for, I guess.'

'And what do you wish for now?' he pressed her.

Stacey rubbed her face with her hands and then took out her phone, determined to ignore Dante. Immediately she was confronted with a reply from Kirkbride, sent an hour previously, before the writers had all gone up to bed. She drew in her breath sharply. Who had had their phone out earlier? But she could barely remember what had happened five minutes ago, let alone when all the writers had filled the room, talking and laughing in a wave of sound that had washed over her and lulled her into a state of semi-sleep. *I can't deal with this right now.* But she had to. She couldn't ignore them. Blearily, she scanned through the message, the words dancing around before her eyes.

I don't want to meet. I don't want to hear any "explanation". I already talk straight to your lying face every day on this retreat, and there is nothing you can say to me to justify what you did. You don't need to know who I am to do the right thing. Confess publicly to your theft. That's the only way to make this stop.

Dante was watching her closely, and though she tried to compose herself, when tears began to threaten, she couldn't help but let them fall.

...

Waking to light streaming around the edge of the curtains in her tranquil retreat bedroom, Stacey stretched out her arms and legs, luxuriating in the pleasantly scented sheets. Her fingers brushed against paper, and she grabbed it and lifted it up as she opened her eyes.

A book page.

Frowning, she placed it down to give her eyes a rub, and this time when she brought the page in front of her face, the words crystalised and she began to read.

Dropping the paper with a yelp of fear, Stacey scrabbled up into a sitting position, and as the full horror of the scene in her room reached her eyes, she let out a scream.

Chapter 9

The pages. They were everywhere. Leaping out of bed, Stacey started gathering them up in her hands, until inevitably she unearthed the book's cover. Though she knew full well which book the pages were from, seeing those words, *Two Lost Souls* by Stacey Cockle, splashed across the cover like an accusation, was more than her frayed nerves could take.

She must have screamed louder, or for longer, than she realised, because the room was suddenly filled with voices. Yasmine, June, Dante, Joel and Tom had all crowded in, probably thinking she was being attacked from the racket she'd been making, and June's heavily beringed hands were taking hold of Stacey's arm. 'It's okay,' the woman was saying gently. 'It's all right. You're safe here. You're safe.'

'How did you get in?' Stacey asked, 'I want you to go! All of you, please, leave me alone!'

'Your door was open,' Yasmine said gently. 'And the key was in the lock. You must have left it like that accidentally when you came up to bed last night.'

Accidentally? *Accidentally?* Kirkbride had done it, somehow. A wave of panic consumed her. How had she got to bed last night? Her memory was a black hole. She'd been talking to Dante downstairs in the lounge – she'd started crying, that much she could recall, but what had happened after that? She couldn't remember getting into bed, but then she was still fully dressed in the clothes she'd had on the previous night, so she'd clearly been too drunk to even get changed. She could well have left her door open if she'd been that out of it. Her cheeks flamed with heat. Everyone was gawping at her, no doubt wondering what drunken antics had caused the scene before them, and she felt like a fish in a bowl.

Dante had his phone out, as if he was thinking of taking a photo, while Tom was looking at one of the book pages, pointing to something he'd spotted. He was encouraging Joel to look too.

'No!' Stacey yelled, snatching the paper from his hand. 'This is private! All of you, go! Go away!' But as soon as her eyes fell onto the page, she could see exactly what had drawn his attention. There was writing down the edge – unusual writing, with a mixture of capitals and small letters, spaced oddly, as if the writer had been trying to disguise their handwriting, but it didn't take long to make out what it said: TELL THE TRUTH.

'Stacey needs some space,' Yasmine said quietly.

They all started towards the door, but Yasmine said, 'Tom, why don't you pick these pages up before you go, make the place look a bit tidier? And Stacey, I'll get you some water.'

'Yes, show's over,' Stacey said, trembling from head to toe as June, Joel and Dante shuffled off.

'Sit down for a moment,' Yasmine said.

'I'm not mad.'

'Nobody is saying that,' Yasmine reassured her, before placing her hand on her arm and guiding her over to the bed.

'I'm okay,' Stacey said. 'I'm just tired…'

As Yasmine busied herself filling a glass with water, Tom placed the pages he'd collected down on her writing desk and quietly slipped out of the room.

'Thank you,' Stacey said as the doctor-turned-mystery-author handed her the glass and she sipped at it.

'I'll let you get some rest,' she said, as Stacey flopped back onto the bed, exhausted. A message came through on her phone from Grant and she glanced at it.

Sorry if I sounded blunt in my message last night about going out. I should have realised you weren't ignoring me on purpose. I know you need to focus and the last thing you need is any drama. I was just stressed about work and my head wasn't in a good place. I miss you. If you're absorbed in writing and can't talk right now, I get it. I'm glad if it is going well for you. Love you xxx

…

Once all was quiet again, Stacey's nerves eventually steadied and she got up from the bed to run a bath. *I'll have a nice soak, then I'm just going to have to front it out with the other writers.* The thought of facing anybody made her want to climb out of her own skin, but there was no escaping it.

With a sigh, she left the bath slowly filling and sat down on an armchair by the window to call Grant. At least she could make things right with him; that would give her the strength to face the day. But if she'd thought hearing his voice would make her feel better, she couldn't have been more wrong.

'Wait, slow down,' she said, after listening to Grant's panicked voice for several minutes. 'You sounded fine in your message.'

'Because I didn't want to worry you.'

Taking a deep breath, Stacey let it out slowly. 'Look, it's money, Grant, not life or death. If you have to sell some of the rental properties to fund the warehouse project, then that's what you have to do. We're hardly going to end up penniless.'

'That's not the point!' Grant said. '*You* gave me the money to buy my first property and do it up, on top of God knows how many other times you've helped out with cash.'

'Well, you're my husband, and you didn't ask me to do it, I *wanted* to help you. You hated your IT job, why wouldn't I help you to do what makes you happy?'

'Because I've fucked it all up!' he said, and Stacey winced. It must be bad for Grant to start swearing. Getting up from the armchair, she held the phone between her shoulder and her ear while she opened the fancy bottle of bubble bath and poured some into the water.

'Grant,' she said firmly. 'You have not fucked anything up. Doing up old buildings is a gamble, you never know what you're going to find. Think how beautiful those flats will be once they're finished, though. They'll be selling like hotcakes.'

Finally, his voice lost its panicky edge. 'I've been so worried about telling you,' he said. 'I don't want to let you down. Especially not when you've got your own stuff going on. You don't need this stress.'

'Is this why you wanted to talk to me yesterday?'

'I just wanted to hear your voice. You're the solid one, really, Stacey. I've been going out of my mind without you here.'

Stacey's skin began to prickle and she had to sit down on the edge of the bath to stop her legs shaking. *You're the solid one.* Her eyes slipped over to the pile of book pages on her writing desk. *Is that really how he sees me?*

'You will get through it,' she told him, though it took some effort to keep her voice strong and steady. 'Even Desh never foresaw how many structural problems the warehouse would have, and he's been a builder for over twenty years. How could you have possibly known what you would unearth?'

'You're right,' he said. 'I knew you'd put it in perspective.' He paused for a moment, 'Were you in the middle of breakfast? Or writing? I should let you go; I need to get back to site anyway. See what new can of worms Desh has found,' he added, with a reassuring touch of humour.

Having said their goodbyes, Stacey sank down into the fragranced bubbles and closed her eyes. *Grant's always been a worrier.* He'd had panic attacks after Teddy was born, convinced that some terrible fate would befall such a tiny, helpless baby, even when Teddy was perfectly safe at home with the two of them. Finding out the truth about *Two Lost Souls* right now on top of everything would be the final straw for him.

I have to hold my nerve. I have to keep Kirkbride at bay, somehow, and I have to do it alone.

…

Having bathed and dressed in her favourite t-shirt – a bright pink number covered with tiny, embroidered cats that reminded her of Queenie – Stacey straightened her back and made her way quietly down the corridor. *I will deal with this Kirkbride situation. Today.* She'd have to appeal to them, get them to understand the precarious situation she was in and how their mind games weren't helping. *I just need time. That's all.* Time to find a solution that would give Kirkbride the justice they were after, without blowing her whole life – and her family – apart.

She paused at the top of the grand staircase as giggling drifted up from the hallway below. Peering over the banister, her eyes fell on Joel and Charlotte, sharing some joke or other. Dressed in a frilly white blouse, buttoned up almost to her chin, Charlotte threw caution to the wind by placing a hand on Joel's arm. Clearly emboldened when Joel allowed this small act of intimacy, Charlotte lunged forwards, going in for a kiss, and Joel dodged her advance. Stacey couldn't help but draw in her breath as she felt Charlotte's embarrassment viscerally.

'I'm so sorry,' Charlotte was saying. 'I thought…'

Joel was reassuring her in hushed tones not to worry, but Charlotte tore away from him and ran up the stairs. There was no way Stacey could avoid her, and when Charlotte realised that her humiliation had been witnessed, her cheeks turned scarlet and she glared at Stacey, eyes glistening with tears behind her enormous glasses.

'Hey, don't worry…' Stacey started to reassure her, but the writer was already storming away, and Stacey shook her head helplessly. Having the scene with Joel witnessed by her favourite author had likely made Charlotte feel a hundred times worse.

'Is she okay?' Joel asked as she met him coming up the stairs, 'I should talk to her.'

A door slammed from down the hall. 'I think perhaps she wants to be alone.'

Joel hovered on the spot, his kind eyes clouded with concern. 'About what went on in your room this morning—'

'Everyone thinks I'm crazy, I know,' she said, before she could stop herself.

'Stacey, it's a building full of writers. We're all crazy.'

Despite herself, she let out a small laugh. 'Thank you, Joel.'

'We didn't all come upstairs because we wanted to stare at you. We were having breakfast and heard you. We thought—'

'I was making so much noise you thought someone was attacking me,' she said flatly.

'That's why so many of us were there. I'm not trying to make you feel worse,' he said quickly. 'I just wanted to explain.'

'*Dante* came to stare,' she said. 'He was trying to take photos of me and all the pages, I know he was.'

'I'm sure he wasn't. No one is going to talk about this, you don't need to worry.'

'What happens at writing retreat stays at writing retreat?'

'Exactly.'

She jumped at a voice behind her. 'You going to head outside?'

Her heart sank. It was Dante.

'I think of my best ideas while I'm getting in my steps for the day,' he continued. 'Exercise is good for your *mental health*, you know.'

Stacey curled her toes, digging them into the bottom of her trainers. Of course, *Dante* was going to use every opportunity to needle her about what he'd witnessed in her room that morning; he had already been overly interested in her, now he'd be insufferable. 'Not with you,' she muttered under her breath as he passed her and started descending the stairs.

'Ignore him,' Joel said, once Dante was out of earshot.

'I just wish *he* would ignore *me*.'

Joel nodded and left her dithering at the top of the stairs. There were three more days of this retreat. How could she bear it? With a huge sigh, she turned back towards her room. Might as well grab a notebook. What else was there to do to fill the hours? If she could make some progress it would distract her at least, until she'd planned her next move with Kirkbride.

Picking up the notebook from her desk, her blood ran cold when a sheet of paper fell onto the floor. She bent down to retrieve it, unfolding it with unsteady fingers. It was one of the printed-out notes again, and the crisp sheet of A4 shook in her hand as she read the words.

POST A VIDEO ONLINE CONFESSING THAT TWO LOST SOULS IS PLAGIARISED. THAT'S THE ONLY WAY OUT OF THIS.

Chapter 10

By sheer force of will Stacey made herself carry on with the day and walked out to the garden with her head held high, notebook tucked under her arm, to immediately be waylaid by June.

'How are you feeling?'

'I'm not going to lie, I'm a bit hungover and embarrassed,' Stacey said. 'But everyone has been so kind and understanding.'

'When my sister got married, I drank so much champagne that I woke up in bed with someone I shouldn't have done,' June said, cackling gleefully. 'And now I'm married to him.'

Stacey couldn't help but smile, her eyes settling on the necklace of enormous pink and red wooden beads that June was wearing along with a rumpled linen dress. 'Thank you,' she said, 'that does make me feel a little better.'

'We were all a bit worse for wear last night,' June said gently. 'Anyone can go off the rails after a few drinks, especially if it's been a while. You have small children, don't you? I know how mentally demanding that is. You must have a lot on your plate, trying to write alongside taking care of a young family.'

Stacey nodded but couldn't bring herself to speak. *All these people – with the exception of Dante, anyway – are so kind to me. But if they knew the truth…* It didn't bear thinking about. All of them were so committed to their creative visions, so determined to get their ideas on the page. *And what am I here for? She* had no ideas for a book. Perhaps she would have, if only Kirkbride didn't occupy her every waking thought; she had no mental energy left for anything except worrying.

June smiled warmly. 'Onwards and upwards. Today is a new day,' she paused to glance at her watch. 'Well, this afternoon is a new day – afternoon – you know what I mean.'

Once June had gone, Stacey took her time exploring the paths in the rose garden, stopping to smell some of the particularly enticing blooms while she let her mind drift. *I have to ignore Kirkbride, for the moment at least. I came here to write, so that's what I'll try to do.* What could Kirkbride do to her, really? She was on her guard now – she wouldn't give them a chance to take her room key or mess with her phone, and she certainly wasn't going to get drunk again.

Sitting down on a stone bench under a rose arch, Stacey placed her notebook on her lap and pulled the biro from where she'd stuffed it down the ring binding.

Beginning. Middle. End. She wrote the headings spaced evenly down the page and underlined each three times. How hard could it really be? Stories were everywhere. Surely, *surely* she could pull something together. But it wasn't as simple as that. *Two Lost Souls* had been a dark, tragic romance – two teenagers who had fallen in love against the backdrop of a crumbling old country house, perhaps a bit like the one she was staying in right now, though this house was certainly not crumbling. She didn't write stuff like that. Stories that popped into her head weren't dark and intense, they were fluffy and bubbly. They were light-hearted escapism, fun beach reads, not something to plunge you into the depths of despair. They were the opposite of the book she'd taken for her own.

What she *wanted* to write was a book inspired by Morwenna's chaotic love life – not exactly that, of course, she'd never break her friend's confidence or risk hurting her feelings – but something along those lines, anyway. And maybe the story would feature a cat, too, she thought, as she imagined Queenie dozing on the window seat in her writing room back at home. *And if I hadn't passed Two Lost Souls off as my own work, I could have written that!* But how could she now? She could say she'd changed direction with her writing, but what if the radical departure meant her new book flopped, or worse, made people suspicious? A heavy feeling settled in her chest. Who was she trying to kid? *Kirkbride won't wait for me to write an entire book before they ruin my life. I'll be lucky to get a few chapters written before everything blows up in my face.*

She put her pen down and took out her phone. She still wanted to get the gossip about Morwenna's latest date, which would be a welcome distraction, but before she could call her friend, she found a message from an unknown number.

Tick tock, Stacey. Post a confession video by the end of the retreat, or I will make your life a living hell.

Her skin broke out in goosebumps.

I'll give you all the royalties I earn on Two Lost Souls going forward, she typed back frantically. *Just until we can work something out properly.*

Hands shaking as she tried to catch her breath, she waited for Kirkbride's reply. Surely, they would see sense. She made nowhere near as much from the book now as she had done in the past, but her offer would show she was willing to start making amends. The reply finally came through and she scanned it with mounting horror.

I don't care about the money. I care about the truth. You can't take what isn't yours and get away with it.

...

'Enjoying the gardens?' At Chandice's voice Stacey nearly jumped out of her skin, but then she quickly stuffed her phone back in the pocket of her denim skirt and tried to smile. How long had she been sat there for, just staring at her phone screen? She hadn't even heard Chandice coming.

'It's a beautiful place, isn't it?' Chandice said, even though Stacey hadn't replied. 'Especially the meadow, with all the wildlife. Have you made it that far? It's getting so warm indoors, my head felt like it was full of cotton wool and I had to escape for a while.' The woman nodded towards the bench. 'Do you mind if I sit down?'

Stacey shuffled along, and Chandice sat, stretching her legs out in front of her.

'How are you getting on?' Stacey asked, while in her mind the words she had read swirled about.

I don't care about the money. I care about the truth.

Tick tock, Stacey.

'I'm getting there,' Chandice said. 'Sometimes it's all flowing so well, and I make a great bit of progress, and then other times I have to step away for a bit – like right now.'

Stacey nodded as she stared out across the rose garden; a riot of pinks, peaches and yellows, woven through with lavender and buzzing with bees. Her stomach was churning. Everything was heightened; the floral smells, the oppressive heat, the buzzing and flitting and fluttering of insects. It was as though she was slowly imploding. *This is a nightmare. I'm inside a nightmare. I have to get Kirkbride to stop. Just for the moment. Just until I can get my head together.*

'I haven't read *Two Lost Souls*,' Chandice said. 'I'll have to buy a copy when I get home. I don't think it's my usual kind of thing, but I'd love to read it, having met you.'

It's not my usual kind of thing either. The words sprang into her mind unbidden. They were swiftly followed by Grant's advice from the night she had arrived. *Perhaps opening up, telling people how you feel, might be helpful.* 'Chandice?' Stacey said. 'Can I… can I tell you something?'

'Of course, what is it?'

'I haven't got anything done since I arrived,' she said quietly. 'I don't want to write another book like *Two Lost Souls*, but I feel like I have to.'

Chandice shrugged. 'Who says you have to?' she replied casually. 'Just do what *you* want to do. They say the heart wants what the heart wants. I think the heart *writes* what it wants to write as well.' She stood up. 'I'm going to head back. I'll try and get more done before we have another post-mortem this evening.'

'Another what?'

'You know, sitting down picking through each other's work from the day, finding the bits that are wrong.' She paused as Stacey still didn't react. 'I was making a joke,' she said, and then chuckled to herself. 'A pretty bad one, clearly.'

'Oh… yes,' Stacey said. 'Sorry, I get it. I'll see you at dinner, then, before we start working out some causes of death.'

Once she was alone, she took out her phone and stared at Kirkbride's message, but then a seed of an idea began to grow. She *had* to know who they were. She couldn't express herself properly through these impersonal messages, she needed to sit down and have a conversation, face-to-face. And if they wouldn't come out and tell her their identity, she'd have to work it out herself. The "post-mortem" that night would be the perfect opportunity.

Chapter 11

'I feel like at the end of the book Gabi's still the same person as she was at the start,' Yasmine was saying as she sat perched on the edge of an armchair, talking animatedly about a character in her book that she was having trouble with. 'I want her to have learned something.'

'I feel like Euphemia changes a lot during *Gossamer,*' Charlotte said, as Stacey gathered her nerves. The room needed to be quiet for her plan. 'To start with she's so naive and trusting,' Charlotte went on. 'She thinks she can fix Gabriel with her own goodness, but by the end she's as consumed by darkness as he is. More so, if anything.'

In the brief silence that followed, Stacey slipped her phone from her pocket. This was her chance. Opening the messages from earlier, she pressed her finger on the number that had texted her, and pressed Call.

No one's phone made a sound. Nobody took their phone out to look at it. They were all absorbed listening to Charlotte, who had started speaking once more. Stacey called the number again and raised the phone to her ear. The call couldn't even be connected! A wave of despair overwhelmed her and for a desperate moment she wanted to grab each of the writers by the scruff of the neck and shake the living daylights out of them until Kirkbride revealed themselves. How had she thought it would be so simple as calling their phone? Of course they wouldn't leave it turned on. *You're the solid one.* That was what Grant had said. *You're a huge inspiration,* Charlotte's words now; taunting her, haunting her, making her sick to her stomach. *Why did I do it? Why did I have to steal The Darkest of Paths? Why did I do it? Why, why?* She tried to will the hands of the clock backwards, as if for a crazy moment she really believed she could go back in time. But time wouldn't ever go back. Only forward. Forward to the end of the week, when she had to confess.

Tick tock, Stacey. Tick tock. Tick tock. Before she knew it, she was on her feet.

'Everyone show me your phones!' she demanded.

A roomful of startled faces turned to her. 'One of you has been messaging me, and I want to know who it is.'

'Stacey, listen—' Yasmine said.

'I am not mad!' Stacey said. 'I tried calling the number, and the phone was off. Which one of you has their phone turned off? Well?'

Nobody took out their phone to show her. Now Heidi was beside her, talking quietly. 'Nobody here is trying to upset you,' she said; her usual sunny, open face clouded with worry as she put one of her arms around Stacey's shoulders. 'Look, it's been so hot today, why don't I get you some water?'

'I don't need *water*!' Stacey said. 'One of you is… one of you is *torturing* me, and I need to know who! Show me your phones,' she said, grabbing at Heidi's, which was sticking out from the woman's pocket. Heidi removed it herself and showed her it was switched on. All of the other writers followed suit, some more reluctantly than others, and when Stacey started saying one of them must have a second phone, she found herself being led from the room by Heidi and Yasmine.

'I'll go and get you some water,' Heidi said quickly, as Yasmine guided Stacey down the corridor and towards the sofa in the large square entrance hall.

'Stacey…' Yasmine began.

'Please don't.'

Yasmine sat beside her and crossed her legs neatly. Stacey wouldn't meet the woman's eye. *Did I really just do that? I completely lost control in there!* She fixed her gaze on the gold sandal poking out from the wide leg trousers of her calm and collected companion, painfully aware that in comparison she was a dishevelled, sweaty, nervous heap.

They were all staring at me. Why did I have to do it? Why did I confront them like that?

Her cheeks were burning, and she rubbed her damp palms on her skirt.

'I just want to be alone for a moment,' Stacey said.

'Perhaps you could tell me what was in these messages?' Yasmine suggested. 'And why it upset you so much.'

'Please, I need to go and lay down,' Stacey said, getting to her feet.

'Heidi will be back in a second with some water,' Yasmine said. 'Just stay here and take some deep breaths. You're probably dehydrated—'

But Stacey couldn't bear to stay another minute, and before Yasmine could say anything further, she'd dashed away up the stairs.

...

With an effort, Stacey uncurled herself from the armchair by the window in her room. Although she was tired right down to her bones, there was no chance of getting any sleep. She'd go downstairs, maybe sit in the library for a while. It was calm in there, with its dark walls and shelves stuffed with books old and new. Pulling her cardigan over her arms she stepped out into the hall, where all was silent, and made her way down the stairs. Startled to find Dante in the library, sat at an old bureau scribbling down some notes, she almost turned around to leave but he glanced over his shoulder before she could slip away.

'Avoiding me?' he asked, that direct, unnerving gaze of his rooting her to the spot like she was a rabbit in headlights.

'I can't sleep, that's all,' she replied. 'I thought the library would be calming.'

Dante turned his chair right around and studied her. 'If you're worried what they all think of you, don't,' Dante said. 'Worry and embarrassment are both pointless emotions.'

'Doesn't stop them hurting though,' she said, plonking herself down on the leather sofa. What was the point in going anywhere else? At least talking would be a distraction, even if the conversation was with Dante. 'Everyone here thinks I'm losing the plot,' she said.

Dante's eyes bored into her. 'What's your definition of "losing the plot"?'

'I don't want to get into some intellectual debate. You know what I mean.'

'I do,' he said, the corners of his eyes crinkling with amusement, 'and I know what your game is. "Bestselling author has nervous breakdown at writing retreat." That might sell a few more copies, resurrect a bit of interest. That's what you need, isn't it, now that you can't write another book.'

A chill spread through her body and the seconds ticked by. The crinkles of mirth disappeared, and Dante's eyes were dark, glinting at her meanly.

'Of course that's not my plan,' she said in disgust. 'Please don't pretend you can see what's going on inside my head. You don't know me.'

'Except I do.' He got up from the desk chair to sit beside her on the sofa. 'I know you have a secret.'

Every hair on her body stood on end, but she forced herself to stay calm. Dante was making wild guesses, that was all. He put all the writers on the retreat under the microscope when he got the chance, though admittedly none with the same zeal he applied to her.

'Can you really not remember what happened last night?' he continued, when she didn't respond. 'The things you said to me?'

'You know what, I think I'll go up to bed. I feel tired all of a sudden,' she said, struggling to her feet. *Ignore him. I can't trust a word he says. He's just winding me up on purpose, playing mind games, amusing himself.* She wouldn't fall for his nonsense. God knows what the man was putting in this self-help book of his, but if he was teaching people to be anything like him, she hoped it didn't sell many copies.

'Stop trying to pretend, Stacey Cockle, author of *Two Lost Souls*.'

Freezing to the spot once more, she turned to face him. Sprawled out on the sofa, he was as casual as anything, grinning like a Cheshire cat at how marvellously clever he thought he was being. But sheer panic was beginning to build inside her, the grin on his face becoming monstrous as she looked into the eyes of the man who had the power to ruin her life.

'It's you,' she said quietly, stepping backwards towards the fireplace. 'You're the one who…'

Dante frowned, but then he began to ridicule her again. 'The one who… ? The one who *what*? The one who can read you like the book you're not able to write? Come on, Stacey. You told me how you feel like a fake. Like your secret is burning a hole inside you.'

On a table near the fireplace was a glass paperweight, and she closed her fingers around it while Dante got to his feet, turning his back on her to retrieve his work from the writing desk. 'You should just unburden yourself,' he said. 'Tell everyone the truth. Set yourself free.'

'You're Kirkbride,' she breathed.

'Seriously, Stacey, you should look at getting help,' he said, as he finished collecting his papers and gave her a scornful look. 'Pretending to be crazy, trying to get everyone to feel sorry for you. Well, *I* don't feel sorry for you. Fame, fortune, a huge house and a wonderful, supportive family. I'll get out the violins, shall I?'

'Please,' she said, 'please, all I want to do is talk about this sensibly. I want to make things right, I really do. But my life isn't as perfect as you say; my husband is under so much pressure at the moment, and I need to think about how I'm going to manage things, you know, to limit how much damage it's going to cause if – when – I confess to what I've done…'

Dante began to laugh. 'I don't give a fuck about your husband, or any of what you're saying. But go on, Stacey, say the words out loud. Tell me what you did. You can say it to *me*, can't you—'

Tick tock, Stacey. Post a confession video by the end of the retreat, or I will make your life a living hell.

I don't care about the money. I care about the truth.

Tick tock.

Tick tock

Try ignoring me now.

'Just leave. Me. Alone!' she yelled, as she lifted her hand and, in a blind panic, threw the paperweight straight at Dante's face.

Chapter 12

The hot, sunny spell had broken by the morning and cloud hung low in the sky. It must have rained heavily in the night, because the lawn was littered with petals from the rose garden, the blooms having taken a battering in the downpour. Everyone was subdued at breakfast. There was no happy chatter or people on the terrace sitting in the sun, instead the writers were eating mostly in silence, and Tom and Charlotte left not long after she entered the room.

What the hell happened to Dante? She'd fled as the man swore and cursed at her, holding his hand up to his right eye. She'd darted up the stairs to her own room where she threw herself into bed, pulled the covers right over her head, and waited. There was silence for a while, then some low, distant voices that she thought might be their hosts. Eventually, his footsteps came back upstairs again, and his door closed on the top floor.

He'll be okay, she'd whispered repeatedly to herself in the dark. He probably went to ask Erik and Janice for something cold to put on his face, and with that done, he'd gone up to bed. Eventually, she'd drifted into a fitful sleep.

I didn't mean to do it. The thought kept going through her mind as she forced her feet over to the breakfast buffet, though she had no appetite whatsoever. *I was just so frightened. It was as though my world was falling apart in front of my eyes.* And it was the way Dante had apparently found the whole thing amusing; laughing at her, taunting her, looking at her like she was something on the bottom of his shoe. She'd just lost control. *But I did steal from him. How do I expect him to treat me? And now I've thrown a paperweight at his face!* She'd assaulted him, for God's sake! He could go to the police if he wanted to.

Trying unsuccessfully to shake away her worries, Stacey filled a bowl with yoghurt and strawberries before sitting down at a vacant table, trying as hard as she could to appear calm and unruffled, though her heart was beating so fast that she was giddy. *Will Dante tell everyone I attacked him? Will* he tell the police? If he was going to, he would have called them last night, surely, not waited until the morning. Closing her eyes for a second, she counted slowly to five. If he did go to the police, she'd say she was having a nervous breakdown and didn't know what she was doing. *It's hardly as if anyone here would contradict that,* she thought grimly, but then another thought struck her. *Will he tell everyone I stole his book?* Perhaps he wouldn't bother waiting for her to confess, now. He'd just expose her for the liar and the fake that she was. *Let's face it, it's what I deserve.*

'That's the last of the sun, then,' June said, as she joined Stacey at her table, wrapping her tassled pink cardigan closer around her. Stacey huddled into her hoodie, while Chandice and Heidi sat down either side of her and the weather chat continued. Apparently, nobody knew anything had taken place the previous night, and everyone was making an exaggerated effort to be kind to her, as if they did all truly believe she was unwell.

At least I might have got him to leave me alone, she thought to herself. *Perhaps it's over. Perhaps it's really over.* Her conscience needled her painfully. *She* was the one in the wrong! Was she *glad* that she might have hurt the man she'd stolen from badly enough that she'd scared him into letting her get away with publishing his work? Was that who she was now?

Her pulse spiked as Dante entered the room, sporting a black eye and trying to avoid anyone's gaze, quietly walking over to the breakfast buffet without so much as a word.

'What the…' Chandice started, but Stacey quickly got to her feet and met Dante beside the bowl of fresh fruit before she could finish her sentence.

'Dante, can I speak to you for a second?' she asked quietly.

'I'd rather not,' he said, his eyes darting around as if he didn't know where to look.

'I just need to know…' she lowered her voice still further, 'have you told anyone…'

'No,' he hissed at her. 'I haven't told anyone that you're fucking crazy and threw a paperweight at my head. I'd rather forget about the whole thing. Just leave me alone.'

'But… can we talk about this sensibly?' she pushed him. 'About *Two Lost Souls*? I'm so sorry for what I did all those years ago, and… and last night. It was unforgiveable, lashing out like that when this is all my fault in the first place. I'm not that kind of person, Dante… I mean… Kirkbride.'

'Listen, I'm not sure who you think I am,' he said, 'but you need to get some serious help. You could have had my eye out, for God's sake! Just stay away from me.'

Back in her room, Stacey sat down at her writing desk, where Tom had placed the pages from *Two Lost Souls*. Though every nerve in her body screamed at her not to do it, her hand reached towards the pile, and she started shuffling through the pages. Eventually she settled to reading the words; words that she had originally loved; that she'd practically convinced herself were hers, but had now begun to hate. They were alien things, scenes from Kirkbride – Dante's – world, and nothing to do with her. She shuddered. No, it was far worse than that. These pages had enslaved her. These sentences were a ticking time bomb, these paragraphs had sealed her fate as a cheat. The book was her prison, that was the truth. It was a relief when her phone screen lit up and she could tear herself away from the grisly fascination the stolen book now held for her.

The message brought anything but comfort.

Confess that you stole Two Lost Souls by the end of today, or I post this all over the internet.

Her finger hovered over the video, but a stab of pain shot through her as she took in the thumbnail image. The footage was of her and Dante the previous night, and after she pressed play, she watched the argument in horror; watched the moment she'd grabbed the paperweight, her fingers closing around the glass orb as if she was possessed. *Why did I do it? Why? What's happening to me?* Then came the final, and worst, part of the video; the split second when she'd snapped and thrown the paperweight straight at a defenceless Dante's face.

Chapter 13

Staring at her reflection in the mirror above the basin, Stacey blinked a few times and finally put down the bar of floral scented soap that she had been scrubbing and scrubbing at her skin with for who knew how long. She itched to pick it back up again but forced herself not to.

I have to get a grip. But how could she? The video was damning. If everyone saw that; they would see her true colours; because she could see them herself now. She'd always thought she was good – hoped that she was the sun in people's lives; bright and happy, her one mistake just a single grey cloud in the distance. Now she knew the truth. She wasn't the sun; she *was* the dark cloud. Dropping to her knees on the fluffy bathmat, tears spilt from her eyes.

Kirkbride isn't Dante. It was clear her tormentor had been standing in the hallway, filming her and Dante discreetly around the door that had been ajar. It couldn't have been set up by Dante hiding a camera in the room – the video was shaky, and even had a thumb in it at the start.

Please, she typed back, *just meet with me. It doesn't have to come to this.*

Leaving the bathroom, she sat down cross-legged on the bed, staring helplessly at the gentle rain falling outside her window. *I already told you I'll give you the money I make from Two Lost Souls going forward,* she typed, when they didn't reply. *And I can start paying you back the money I've made from it in the past, if you give me time.*

After a tense few minutes, a reply came through. *I told you I don't want money. You've got until 10 p.m. tonight to either post a video admitting what you did, or the world sees you attacking Dante.*

A knock on the door made her jump. 'What?' she called out. 'Who is it?'

'Grant.'

Grant? His voice caused a riot of emotions to burst inside her. Relief – after all, Grant made her feel safe – but why was he here? Did he already know she'd attacked Dante? Or had their hosts at the retreat contacted her husband, fearing for her safety after the way she had been behaving?

'Stacey, let me in. I'm worried about you, and when I arrived and said who I was, some of the people here, they… it doesn't matter. Just let me in and we can talk. I know things aren't right.'

Giving herself a shake, Stacey finally got off the bed and went to unlock the door. 'How did you know I needed you?' she asked him.

A tear escaped and rolled down her cheek, and Grant brushed it away. 'I just knew, Stacey. Me and you, we know each other, don't we?'

At these words, she had to bite down on her tongue to stop herself breaking down completely. 'Take me home,' she choked out, as Grant's searching eyes met hers. 'I hate it here. Please, just take me home.'

…

'What happened?' Morwenna asked anxiously as she stepped inside to envelop Stacey in a hug. 'Grant told me he came to get you from the retreat. He said you were really unhappy there. I'm so sorry…'

'Why are you sorry?' Stacey asked as she closed the door behind her friend. Morwenna was kicking off a pair of scuffed trainers, which she wore paired with a dress in a ditsy floral print. She looked summery and elegant, while Stacey was in the faded leggings and baggy t-shirt she'd pulled on upon her arrival back at her house, and catching sight of herself in the hall mirror revealed the dark circles under her eyes.

'It was me that suggested going on a writing retreat,' Morwenna said, cutting through Stacey's thoughts. 'That's why I'm sorry. I shouldn't have pushed you into it.'

'You hardly pushed me,' Stacey said. 'And besides, you were only trying to help. It's not your fault it didn't work out. It's mine.'

Almost breaking down once again at this ridiculous understatement, she quickly made her way across the hall and Morwenna followed her into the kitchen. Grabbing a couple of wine glasses, she filled her own almost to the brim and passed the second – filled to a more sensible level – to Morwenna.

'Where's Grant?' Morwenna asked.

'He's taken the kids out for burgers. I just needed a bit of time alone to clear my head.'

Morwenna nodded and sipped at her wine, before saying, 'You are more than just the person who wrote *Two Lost Souls*, you know that, don't you? People love you and care about you because of who *you* are, not because of a book.'

Finding this statement too painful to respond to, Stacey let the conversation lapse into silence, gazing instead across the kitchen to the fruit bowl where green apples were lined up neatly. A bizarre urge to seize the fruits and throw them around the room gripped her, and she could almost have laughed. Nobody had any idea of the devastation on the horizon. It was like a tornado was coming and they were all sitting around in its path, none of them any the wiser – apart from Stacey, who was powerless to do anything to save herself, let alone anybody else. She was damned either way; whether she confessed to the plagiarism or whether she stayed quiet and Kirkbride posted their video, either way everyone would find out who she really was, and perhaps then they'd decide they didn't love and care about her, certainly not the way they once did. How would Grant and Morwenna feel, knowing she'd kept such a huge lie hidden all these years? Would they ever be able to trust her again? Could she really expect them to?

'I can tell you about my awful date, if you like,' Morwenna said at length.

Stacey nodded, but as Morwenna began to talk, she could barely focus. The sound floated in and out, and only the odd few words and sentences registered with her. One of them was "condescending". Another was "he didn't seem to have a neck", which showed Morwenna's desperation to cheer her up, as she was never usually one to criticise people for their appearance.

'Stacey?' Morwenna said, placing a hand on her back. 'Stacey, are you okay?'

Raising her head, Stacey realised she had slumped forward onto the kitchen island, burying her face in her hands. She blinked at Morwenna in confusion. 'I think I need to lay down.'

'Okay,' Morwenna said, just as there was the sound of a car door outside. 'Perhaps I should leave you to rest. It sounds like Grant is back, anyway. I'll call you tomorrow, I'm sure you'll be feeling better after a good night's sleep.'

The second Morwenna had left, Stacey ran upstairs to the bedroom, slamming the door behind her just as Grant and the children came inside.

I can't face them. I can't look my husband in the eye, I can't hug Teddy and Ava, not like this!

It felt as though her whole body was filthy; as if the lies were scrawled all over her skin in paint that would never wash off. Feeling as though she would start screaming, she then stopped and stood very still. Kirkbride. There was something about this whole thing that didn't add up. Why were they bothering with these elaborate games to get her to confess? If they'd written *The Darkest of Paths,* there should be evidence. Old drafts, plans, even the email they sent with the manuscript attached when they had agreed to critique each other's work. Why go to so much effort – following her to the writing retreat, trying to scare and humiliate her, when surely they could prove her theft anyway?

Sitting down heavily on the bed, her mind became crystal clear. The explanation was obvious. Kirkbride couldn't prove it. For some reason – a reason she couldn't fathom – Kirkbride could not show that they had written *The Darkest of Paths.* The original work must have been lost, and the email too.

The realisation was so startling that she almost laughed out loud in sheer relief. They couldn't prove it! And if they couldn't prove it, well, she'd call their bluff. It was an awful thing to do, of course it was, but it wouldn't be for ever. She needed time. She would still put things right eventually; not in a dramatic public confession, but she'd find some way to make peace with Kirkbride and atone for what she'd done. Just not yet.

PART THREE

Chapter 14

Stacey woke drenched in sweat and got out of bed to open the window. Though it was early December the room was impossibly hot and stuffy.

'Whass going on?' Grant said thickly.

'I'm too hot. It doesn't matter. Go back to sleep.'

Slipping out of the bedroom onto the cool landing as Grant dozed off again, she made her way down to the kitchen. Moonlight drifting in through the bifold doors gave the room an eerie glow, and despite being hot while trying to sleep, a chill now spread through her as she sat down on a stool at the kitchen island.

Kirkbride. They were all she could think about tonight. It had been months since the retreat, and she'd not had any further contact. Not, that was, until earlier in the day.

She squinted blearily at her phone screen, willing the message to have been a figment of her imagination, but no. From the same number they'd used at the retreat, had arrived the words: *This isn't over.*

Well, if it wasn't over, why hadn't they posted that video of her attacking Dante? God knows she was glad they hadn't, but her relief had always been tinged with unease. *If they can't prove the plagiarism, then that's that,* she would reassure herself. *Kirkbride has given up.* If she hadn't convinced herself that was true, she wouldn't have made it through the months since the retreat – Grant was still constantly stressed about his building project, and sometimes the tension at home even put Teddy and Ava on edge. The family couldn't take a big drama, not right now. But this new message had thrown her mind into chaos once more.

'What's going on with you at the moment?'

She drew in a sharp breath at Grant's voice and quickly closed the message. 'I thought you'd gone back to sleep,' she said.

'I woke up again.' He came over and began to rub her shoulders. 'You've been so down, ever since you got back from the writing retreat.'

'I was down before that.'

'I know, but this is different. I'm worried about you. I wish you would open up to me.'

She squirmed away from his shoulder rub, and he sat down beside her. 'Even Morwenna is worried about you. She messaged me earlier and asked if you were okay. She said you don't seem to want to see her.'

'She's got a new boyfriend she wants to tell me about. I'm pleased for her, don't get me wrong, but going out, meeting her, I can't… I feel all wrong inside. All screwed up.'

'She's your friend, though. I know you're hurting, and it's not easy if she's happy and you're not, but she's hardly going to rub it in your face. Don't avoid her, spending time with her might make you feel better.'

…

'She's invited us to what?' Stacey said.

'Pre-Christmas drinks, at her house. Her new partner will be there.'

'Why did she ask you and not me?' Stacey said as she gathered up some stray toys and books from the kitchen. Why could Teddy and Ava not go anywhere without leaving a trail of stuff in their wake?

'Because you're ignoring her.'

Stacey took out her phone and felt a pang. Morwenna had messaged her a few times the previous day, but she hadn't been able to face reading any of it.

'If you keep pushing her away, you're going to lose her,' he said. 'There's only so much people can take.'

She turned to him. Was he still talking about Morwenna? 'Grant, I'm sorry,' she said. 'And yes, of course I'll go to her party. I just feel wobbly, that's all.'

'I know,' he said, putting his arms around her and kissing her hair. 'I'll be right there by your side, you know that.'

'Mumeeee!' Came a high-pitched voice from upstairs.

'And Stacey,' he said, as she pulled away from him to go and see what Ava needed.

'What is it?'

'I'm proud of you.'

'What for?'

'For carrying on, even though you're struggling. You've been writing a little, haven't you? And I know I've been a bit distant. This is just a difficult patch, that's all. We'll get Christmas out of the way, I'll finish the flats eventually and sell them, and then things will go back to normal. That's what we all need, I think.'

'Mummy, mummy, mummy, mummy,' Ava's voice rang out.

'I'd better…' Stacey said, her stomach churning. *Things will go back to normal.* His statement couldn't be further from the truth. How could things ever be normal again?

…

Stacey blinked in surprise as she stepped into Morwenna's house, the Victorian mid-terrace having been transformed with tasteful Christmas sparkle, along with a delicious, spicy scent that wrapped around her like a cosy blanket.

'You look beautiful,' Grant said, admiring her sequined dress as she shrugged off her coat. The garment was immediately whisked away, along with Grant's jacket, by a flustered Morwenna. He gave Stacey's arm a squeeze. 'If you find it overwhelming, just tell me,' he said. 'We can always slip away early if it's too much. But I'm sure you'll be okay.'

Nodding gratefully, she gave Grant a shaky smile, a rush of love for him making a lump form in her throat. *I don't want him to ever look at me differently.*

'Morwenna looks happy,' Grant said as the beaming woman – radiant in a spotty figure-hugging dress – emerged from down the hall and started back towards them. 'She's gone to a lot of effort.'

Appearing in front of them having squirreled the coats away, Morwenna swept Stacey up into a hug before stepping back to look at her with a mixture of happiness and concern. 'I'm so pleased you could come,' she said. 'I've missed you. And your dress is stunning.'

Stacey glanced down at herself. The low cut, attention-grabbing dress had seemed like a good idea at home, when she'd thought the cheery sequins would lift her mood. But now, despite the admiration, Stacey felt self-conscious, as if the truth about her was radiating out from every inch of bare flesh.

'I know it's been a while,' Stacey said, spotting that the dots on Morwenna's dress were actually tiny robins. 'It's been…' she struggled to find words to explain, but Morwenna was distracted, glancing towards the living room door, from which a buzz of conversation and laughter drifted.

'Here he is,' she said as a man emerged, grinning widely, his shirt complementing Morwenna's dress with its pattern of miniature Christmas puddings. 'Stacey, Grant, this is Joel.'

Chapter 15

Stacey's head filled with white noise. The second she'd set eyes on him she'd known exactly who he was. She placed her hand against the wall to stop her knees from buckling, forcing herself to keep her composure. 'I'm so glad to meet you at last, Stacey,' Joel Shakespeare said, sounding entirely innocent and sincere, though his eyes glinted knowingly. 'Morwenna is always talking about you. I've never met a famous author before.'

The silence as Stacey stared at him was so long that Grant butted in, making some comment about how pretty the house looked, while Stacey's mind felt like a sheet of paper being screwed up in a ball. This couldn't be happening. This was impossible. She blinked a few times, but it made no difference. Unless he had a twin, the man standing in front of her was unquestionably the same Joel Shakespeare that had been at the retreat. *No.* Not just Joel from the retreat. His appearance here, the look he'd had in his eye when he'd said he was glad to meet her, the fact he'd omitted to say that he already knew her – it was no coincidence. Joel had followed her here, back to her day-to-day life, just as he'd followed her to the retreat. *Kirkbride.* Her lips mouthed the word silently, and she could have sworn the side of Joel's mouth twitched in a satisfied smile as his eyes met hers once more.

'I… sorry, I just need to…' Stacey said as she pushed past them down the hall and into the downstairs toilet. Closing the door firmly she leant her back against it, taking deep breaths and trying to stop herself from screaming. The way he'd looked at her. He'd been so triumphant. He thought he was so clever! He was dating her friend just to get at her, he had to be; playing games with Morwenna's feelings, when the poor woman had already been messed around plenty enough in the past and didn't deserve for it to happen again. It was too awful. It was unthinkable that through that split second decision Stacey had made over a decade ago, her friend would now get her heart broken. She let out a low moan, and there was a knock on the door.

'Stacey? Are you okay?' Morwenna's voice reached her and horror swept through her again. *What the hell am I supposed to say to her?* How could she begin to explain? Sorry, but your wonderful new boyfriend is just using you to get to me? She couldn't say that. She just couldn't.

'Yes, I'm fine,' she said, her voice strained. She took another breath. 'Just give me a minute.'

She'd have to come out soon. Her behaviour was already odd enough, but she could explain it away by claiming to feel faint. Locking herself in the downstairs toilet half the night – that wouldn't be so easy to justify.

Just try to calm down. Focus on something else.

But everything in the tiny room was assaulting her senses. The bottle of soap was gingerbread scented, and the hand towel had snowflakes on it. It couldn't be any clearer how much Morwenna was enjoying this cosy new life she had with her boyfriend. *She loves him.* It had been clear as day; written all over her face.

But her boyfriend is Joel. Her boyfriend is Kirkbride!

After taking many more deep breaths and checking her reflection in the mirror, Stacey curled her fingers around the door handle. She would make an excuse and leave early, but she'd have to get through an hour or so, or her behaviour would seem downright rude. She could do an hour, couldn't she? An hour of pretending and plastering on a smile? But the second she stepped out of the room she almost went to pieces when her eyes fell on him again. He had his arm around Morwenna's waist, and Grant was laughing at something the couple had said.

'Oh, Stacey,' Morwenna said, 'come and get a drink and sit down for a minute if you're lightheaded. There are some nibbles too – you should eat something.'

Stacey allowed herself to be guided towards the kitchen, while Grant and Joel were already getting on like a house on fire. *What the hell is happening?* It was as if she'd slipped into a parallel universe. This simply couldn't be real, could it?

Morwenna was enthusing about how glad she was to finally introduce her to Joel, and Stacey glanced around at her excited friend. She was intending to say something light-hearted, something to break the tension inside her while she figured out what to do, but her brain didn't seem connected to her mouth. 'You shouldn't trust him,' she blurted out.

Chapter 16

'Are you feeling better now?' Morwenna asked gently when she joined Stacey in the relatively quiet kitchen. 'I think everyone is here now, so I can catch my breath for a minute.'

'You've invited a lot of people,' Stacey said as Morwenna stirred a gently steaming pan on the hob, from which an enticing smell filled the whole room. How did Morwenna know this many people? Had she always been so popular?

'It's just some friends, and people from Tiny Town,' Morwenna said, referring to the children's role play cafe that she managed. Stacey shuddered at the thought of working in the place. Much as Morwenna seemed to enjoy her job, the idea of clearing up the carnage wrought by kids in a building full of pretend cafes, building sites, hairdressers and supermarkets had always put Stacey on the verge of panic. But right now, she'd clear up a hundred play cafes if it could undo seeing Joel in her friend's house.

'I think this is done,' Morwenna said, placing down her wooden spoon. 'Would you like some? It's mulled wine.'

'Thanks,' Stacey said, as Morwenna placed a mug down in front of her and she folded her hands around it gratefully. Her friend's small kitchen had always been a comforting space; homely with wooden worktops, a table that was almost too big for the room, and a shelf heaving with recipe books. Something tasty nearly always seemed to be cooking whenever Stacey came round.

Just take a moment to think, she told herself as her palms began to sweat with the thought of being in the same house as Kirkbride. *I have to tread carefully.*

'When did you meet Joel?' she asked at length. *Let's not catastrophise. Perhaps it really is a coincidence.* It was far-fetched, but it was *possible* it was just a random chance, surely.

'Oh, it was not that long after you got back from the writing retreat,' she said, and Stacey's desperate hopes were immediately dashed. That was too much coincidence. 'I'm sure I told you at the time.'

Morwenna was beaming as she sat down opposite Stacey at the table, and she struggled to meet her friend's eye. It was no accident – of course it wasn't. Just one look at Joel's face when they'd met in the hall had shown her beyond any doubt that he'd targeted Morwenna deliberately.

I have to warn her. But how? She couldn't say she knew him – how would she explain where from and why she hadn't acknowledged him, without giving herself away? She needed to go home and process it all, figure out a way forward that was calm and rational and would cause the least amount of damage.

'Stacey,' Morwenna said softly, 'don't try and pretend you didn't say what you did. You told me I shouldn't trust him. You've obviously got some issue with him, so tell me what it is.'

'I'm not feeling great, that's all. I've probably caught something from Teddy or Ava. My head feels like it's full of fog.' Catching sight of a birthday card on the windowsill, Stacey frowned. Morwenna's birthday was ages ago.

'It was Joel's birthday yesterday,' Morwenna said, as she noticed Stacey's gaze. 'I cooked dinner for him here last night.'

'That's nice,' she said vaguely, her mind racing. How could this be happening? Another thought struck her. 'Has he moved in, then?' *Please say no.* The deeper Morwenna was into this relationship, the worse it would be when it all came crashing down.

'No, he has his own place,' Morwenna said, her eyes bright with excitement. 'Oh, you should see it…' she trailed off awkwardly and began fussing with a plate of mini mince pies on the table.

'He has a nice house?' Stacey forced herself to ask. No wonder he wasn't interested in money. Morwenna's new *boyfriend* was clearly loaded as well. Anger at Joel suddenly overwhelmed her. How *dare* he deceive someone as sweet and kind as Morwenna? Her friend had never hurt anyone in her life. Joel's – Kirkbride's – grievance was with Stacey, not the innocent people she cared about. It was a twisted and cruel way of getting what he wanted.

What I stole was words. He's stealing Morwenna's happiness. He would leave her devastated when his fake relationship with her was revealed. When Stacey had stolen *The Darkest of Paths* it had felt victimless. It was still wrong, of course, and she bitterly regretted it, but she'd thought, really *believed*, that Kirkbride was gone. That they'd never find out. That nobody would ever be hurt by what she'd done.

'Yes, it's a nice place,' Morwenna continued, jolting Stacey out of her dark thoughts, 'but never mind about that. I'm more interested in talking about you right now. How are you really, Stacey? I've barely seen you for months now.'

'And you're sure about Joel's... intentions?' Stacey said, ignoring her friend's questions as her panic threatened to overwhelm her. *This is a nightmare.* 'It seems like this has all happened very fast.'

'His… intentions?' Morwenna said, laughing. 'This is the twenty-first century, Stacey. Are you going to ask me next if we have a chaperone when we go out together?'

'I… I just mean—'

'No, I shouldn't have laughed,' Morwenna said, as Stacey gulped back some mulled wine. 'I'm sorry. I appreciate you looking out for me. I know in the past people haven't been that understanding about the situation with my dad and everything, but Joel has been fantastic. In fact, he's been really helpful; he did loads of work tidying dad's back garden so that he could sit out there again, and he's done all sorts of jobs in his house as well. To be honest I don't know what I would have done without him. My dad couldn't afford to pay somebody to do all that work, but Joel did it all without even being asked.'

For a moment they were silent, until Joel himself burst in with a few guests in tow, and Morwenna helped him get everybody a drink while Stacey looked on in silence. The couple took every possible opportunity to touch each other, their public displays of affection making the bile rise in Stacey's stomach. He was a good actor, she'd say that much for him. She winced as every affectionate gesture he made turned to the opposite in Stacey's mind, as if the gentle caresses were like physical blows against her friend. He would break Morwenna's heart.

Once the small crowd had left, Morwenna sat opposite her again and fixed her with a look. 'Please talk to me. What's so bad that you can't tell me?'

'He's nearly ten years younger than you,' Stacey said, though she regretted it at the look on Morwenna's face. What point had she been trying to make with that statement? Her thoughts were fraying and chaotic.

'Yes, Joel's around eight years younger than me,' Morwenna said, her voice clipped. 'What does that have to do with anything?'

'I just… look, it doesn't add up, that's all. Why would he want to spend all this time helping your dad and—'

'Why wouldn't he?' Morwenna asked, her voice rising as Stacey dug her hole deeper and deeper. 'We're together, and he's helping my dad because he cares. I don't understand what you're getting at. And to be completely honest, you're being quite hurtful.'

Flustered, Stacey drank some more mulled wine and was so distracted she almost swallowed a star anise. If he was only thirty-one now, he'd written the book when he was, what, eighteen? Well, it was surprising, but possible. The book was about teenagers, after all.

'I just…' Stacey stammered, 'I'm getting weird vibes from him. I don't want you to get hurt.'

'So, you think Joel is out to make a fool of me, what, because he's a little younger than I am?' Morwenna said, pain creeping into her voice. 'Do you know how that sounds?'

Morwenna stood up, and guilt bloomed in Stacey's stomach at the hurt in her friend's eyes.

'I'm sorry,' she said, 'this is coming out all wrong. I only mean that you shouldn't rush into it. Just take a breath.'

Pointing a finger at her, Morwenna's voice rose again. 'Joel loves me, and I love him. And I'm not rushing into anything; we've been together for months. We know how we feel. We're serious about each other, it's not just some silly fling.'

Leaving in a swish of robin-covered skirts, heels tip-tapping on the floor, Stacey stared after her friend as she disappeared down the hall. They'd known each other for years and Stacey could count on one hand the times she'd heard Morwenna raise her voice to anybody, let alone her.

Joel had got well and truly under her skin.

Chapter 17

About to go and find Grant, Stacey stopped in her tracks as Joel stepped into the kitchen and closed the door behind him.

'Stacey.'

'Joel,' she choked out, after a moment of paralysis.

I stole his book. I stole from him, and now he's here.

For a moment her vision greyed as if she was about to faint.

'Recovered from your time at the writing retreat, then?' he asked, his voice casual, but his eyes glinted with malice. Suddenly, she wasn't afraid; she was angry. He was so cocky, standing there in his novelty Christmas shirt, so incredibly pleased with himself for infiltrating her life like this. Going after her was one thing, but Morwenna? Was nothing sacred to him? 'I don't know what your game is, coming here and dating Morwenna,' she hissed at him, 'but pressuring me like this isn't going to help. If you could prove any of your *allegations* about my book, you wouldn't be sneaking around playing silly little games.'

That knocked the smile from his face. Her hunch had been spot on. He couldn't prove it.

'I told you to give me time,' she continued. 'I've told you I'm sorry, and that I want to make things right.' Fury at his treatment of Morwenna overwhelmed her and her cheeks grew hot. 'But you… you came here and got my best friend to fall in love with you! What the hell were you thinking? And you're claiming to have the moral high ground!'

She tried to push past him, unable to bear another second in the same room as him, but he caught her arm before she could leave. 'I might not be able to prove what you did with *The Darkest of Paths*, but I have proof of something else, don't I?'

'Get off me.'

'Dante wasn't exactly the nicest of people, but no matter what kind of man he was, that doesn't change the fact that you—' he raised his voice, 'tried to kill him.'

'For God's sake keep your voice down!' Stacey cried. 'I wasn't trying to *kill* him. I lost control, it was… it was an accident.'

'An *accident*? Was stealing the book an *accident* as well, then? Very clumsy, aren't you?'

'Please — I can't talk about this right now!' she said, his presence suffocating her. 'I need a minute.'

'You had some front, ignoring my threat about posting the video of you attacking Dante,' he said, more quietly. 'But you really should have listened to me. I've got nothing to lose, Stacey. But *you* do. I don't believe that you'll confess if I "give you time". I think you're hoping I'll give up and go away. But I'm not going to stop at showing the world how you attacked an innocent man. I'm going to destroy your whole life. Your marriage, your family, your friendships; all of it. I'm going to take everything away from you. Or,' he added brightly, 'you can confess, and this all goes away.'

…

The living room was packed with happy, smiling people, drinks in hand, while Christmas piano music played subtly in the background and the lights on the tree glittered prettily. Morwenna was avoiding her like the plague, offering plates of mince pies and canapes to her guests, while Joel charmed everyone he met, and nobody paid any attention to her. She looked at the time on her phone, but they'd only been there for forty-five minutes. Could she convince Grant to leave so soon? He was currently deep in conversation with a man she didn't know, and then Joel joined him. Fresh anger surged through her as she watched Joel talking animatedly. Of course he would focus on her husband. Of course he would. Unable to bear it any longer, she strode up to them and stood next to Grant.

'Your mum just called,' she said to him, ignoring Joel pointedly. 'Teddy isn't feeling good. I think I'd better go.'

'What's wrong with him?' Grant asked. 'I'll come too—'

'No, it's okay,' she said, not wanting her lie to be exposed. 'He's got a bit of a temperature, that's all. I'll go and check on him. You stay here if you want to.'

'Okay,' he said uncertainly. 'If you're sure.'

'I am.'

'Let me get your coat,' Joel said, following her out into the hall, where she quickly rounded on him, tears pricking her eyes at the desperate situation he'd placed her in. 'If I confess,' she said, 'Morwenna will find out your relationship with her is fake.'

'That's your problem. You started all this, not me. You could have done the right thing months ago and none of this would ever have happened.'

'Do you really not care at all? she said, before quickly lowering her voice. 'You've made it impossible for me to ever confess, because as soon as I do and Morwenna realises who you are, she'll know that none of it was ever real between you. I cannot… I *will not* do that to her.' She took a shaky breath. 'So, if my confession is what you want, you're never going to get it, not now. You need to end it with Morwenna, in the kindest way you can, and then you need to leave.'

'Oh, I don't think so,' he said. 'I'm only just getting started. And I like it here. I'm not going anywhere.'

Chapter 18

You've made it impossible for me to ever confess. Joel was reeling from her words, and once she'd left, he couldn't face rejoining the party straight away and instead slipped upstairs. Morwenna's second bedroom was a cosy study, and he took her copy of *Two Lost Souls* from the bookcase, before sinking down on the squashy armchair in the corner of the room.

It wasn't a helpful thing to do, but ever since he'd discovered what Stacey had done, he couldn't stop himself picking up *Two Lost Souls*, flipping through to whatever page it fell open on, and reading. Initially, he couldn't truly believe it was the same as the manuscript for *The Darkest of Paths* – the one, final copy that he had in his possession. And every time he was reminded yet again that yes – bar the editing that had obviously occurred during the publishing process – they were one and the same story. Lately, he read it to remind himself why he was doing what he was doing, because truthfully, he hated the subterfuge. The sneaking around, the pretending, the distress he was causing. *She deserves it,* he insisted to himself. *She could make it stop any time by just doing the right thing.* But no matter how much he hated her he hadn't been able to bring himself to post the video of her attacking Dante online; if nothing else because it would appear that she was having a nervous breakdown and people might not believe her confession if her mental health was in question.

He stopped flicking through *Two Lost Souls* – landing on page 53 – and lowered his eyes, beginning to read as the hubbub of the party continued on downstairs.

Carl stuffed his hands into the pockets of his hoodie as he strode out towards the barn, breath misting in the cold morning air. Speeding up at the sound of a commotion, he found his dad, Howard, inside, red faced and cursing.

'Why aren't you at school?' the man barked as soon as Carl stepped through the door.

Ignoring this question, Carl said instead, 'What's happened?' since something clearly had.

Remarkably, given the former fuss, the bemused man didn't seem immediately sure what his son was talking about, but then he said, 'Door's being a twat again.'

'It's swelled up,' Carl told him. 'You need to shave some of the wood off of it, then it'll open properly.'

'You don't need to tell me that.'

'Why don't you do it then?'

Carl sighed as his dad ambled to the back wall of the barn, where the old farm machinery was lined up. 'I don't have time for that. We need to get all of these sorted out to open the rural life museum.'

'A rural life museum,' Carl echoed. What strange new scheme had his dad cooked up now?

'Yes. I've mentioned it before.'

He hadn't, but Carl let that slide. Resting his hand on an old seed drill, he considered how to talk his dad out of this latest white elephant.

'People want an experience,' Howard said, gesturing expansively across the barn. 'They want to see what used to go on here.'

Carl turned away to roll his eyes. The machinery had come with the estate, which had been farmed for hundreds of years. Many of the fields had been sold off by Howard's parents as they tried to get the estate's finances in order ahead of their blundering son inheriting. Carl had long suspected his dad's main love at Hillcroft Manor was the old farm machinery, since he didn't give much time or effort to maintaining the house itself. It was completely typical of him to be obsessed with some tiny detail of a much bigger thing. Like he obsessed from time to time about the tiny detail of whether or not Carl went to school.

'This stuff is not an experience,' Carl told him firmly.

'Not now, but it will be. You can help me since you don't do much else.'

'I do plenty.' It was true. Once he'd checked on the chickens and the small vegetable patch outside the kitchen, his days were filled by wandering through the estate, watching every intimate detail of life unfolding. A mushroom that wasn't there the day before, frogspawn in the pond, an egg broken on the ground that had fallen from a bird's nest. Every day something new happened, and if he didn't understand what he saw he'd look it up in Hillcroft's library, which

was a treasure trove of old reference books. Carl's head was an encyclopaedia of the grounds of his home. What else did he need?

'We can really make something of this place,' his dad said, warming to his theme. He had his hand on an old petrol-powered sheep shearing contraption now, the sight of which Carl had always found unsettling. 'All it takes is a bit of elbow grease.'

Carl cast his eyes over the barn. The ploughs, turf cutting spades and swath turner; the bull tether, cake crushers and barley beards remover; the seed sower, handcart and root choppers. Plus a whole lot more besides. All of it in a terrible state of repair.

'You could have the grease from every part of my body, but it still wouldn't work,' he said patiently. 'You have to be realistic—'

His dad laughed, jowls wobbling in a most unflattering manner, but then his face softened. 'And what would you suggest?'

Carl shrugged. 'Sort the gardens out. Open a cafe. People like to eat cake, don't they? We could sell the eggs from the chickens, too, and maybe vegetables if we started using the big kitchen garden near the river and growing as much as we used to. We've got the holiday cottages already and the people staying there would come and get food from us and go in the café.'

There was a silence as Howard considered this. 'Perhaps you're right,' he said. 'Though God knows how you know anything about what people like.' Howard regarded his son levelly. 'You know I only go on at you about school because I keep getting phone calls about it. Bloody busybodies with nothing better to do. You're fine as you are, I know that, lad, but getting these idiots to understand…' His dad sighed. 'Just go in a couple of times a week. Keep them off my back.'

'I'll go tomorrow,' Carl said, his heart heavy. School was stupid. He didn't need it. But at least he didn't have to worry about it until the next day. He'd go down to the stream for a bit. There'd be something good to see today, he just had a feeling.

Joel closed the book sharply and thrust it back into the bookcase. It was stupid to torture himself about it. He knew what Stacey had done; he didn't need to prove it over and over. He sat back thoughtfully, allowing his moment of anger to dissipate. He needed to stay sharp. Stacey – and the world, of course – didn't know that at least half the book was true. Sure, his name had been changed, and his childhood home had not been called Hillcroft, but being raised by a dilapidated garden and a library stuffed with old books had given him an edge. He was independent. Uninhibited. It didn't matter what anyone else thought, as long as he was true to what he believed. As long as he had integrity. Stacey had no integrity. She was a woman made of mirror, reflecting what people wanted to see.

And mirrors could be smashed.

Chapter 19

'Stacey? Did you hear what I said?'

Trying to force her face into a neutral expression she pushed her half-eaten bowl of muesli away. 'I heard. You said Joel used to work for a property management company.'

'Yes, and he had some good ideas about the warehouse conversion. He even… well, he probably wasn't serious.' Grant said, turning his back on her as he went over to pour himself a second cup of coffee. 'Do you want one?' he asked.

'No, thanks. What wasn't he serious about?'

There was a long pause that set Stacey's teeth on edge. Why all the suspense? Her nerves were frayed as it was, she couldn't take much more. 'Please, just tell me.'

'Well, he said he was interested in getting into property developing. He's between jobs at the moment and has some money to invest. I said maybe he could meet with me soon to talk about it properly, but I'm not sure if he was that keen or not. To be honest though, I don't know how it will get finished without a cash injection from somewhere.'

Under the table, Stacey curled her hand into a tight fist. Wasn't sure if he was that keen or not? Joel was playing hard to get, more like, not wanting to seem suspiciously eager when of course this must have been his intention all along! Just like he'd gone to the retreat to try and get into her head, now he was going bigger. The audacity of it took her breath away. Was this seriously what he was going to do? Slip insidiously into every area of her life? Getting her husband and her best friend on side so that he could carry on putting pressure on her, squeezing her until she burst and spilled her secret – when she'd said she was sorry and wanted to work with him to put things right, if he'd only give her time?

Did I really mean that, though? Would I ever really have tried to fix anything – especially as he can't prove what I did?

She shook that unsettling thought aside. Of course, she would have found a way to make peace with Kirkbride. She was a good person. She *was.* She had only tried to delay to protect Grant at a time he was under so much pressure.

Protect Grant, or protect myself?

'Where did he get all this money he wants to invest?' Stacey asked, struggling to keep her voice light. Money for investing on top of having a fancy house? What was he, a millionaire?

'I don't know. I was hardly going to ask him that, was I?'

'Sounds pretty sketchy to me,' Stacey commented, dipping her spoon morosely back into her bowl of muesli.

What can I do? What the hell can I do?

Confessing would break Morwenna's heart and ruin her life, but if she didn't confess, well, she'd be at Joel's mercy. God only knew how far he'd be prepared to go.

Grant sat down opposite her at the table and gave her a searching look. 'Morwenna said you had a falling out over Joel.'

At the reminder of their argument, yet another wave of despair washed over her. 'Nearly everything I said came out wrong,' she explained. 'I really didn't mean to offend her, I was only trying to find out more about Joel,' she sighed. What a mess she was making of everything. 'In her shoes I would be furious with me too, with what she thought I was implying. Was she still upset after I left? Did I spoil her party?'

'No, if anything she was worried about having upset *you.* She said she overreacted, and you were only trying to be a good friend.'

Breathing a huge sigh of relief, Stacey managed a shaky smile.

'Stacey, I know you made up that phone call from my mum, saying Teddy was ill. He's absolutely fine.'

'It was all too much,' she said, not untruthfully. 'I didn't want to keep upsetting everyone. Every time I open my mouth I put my foot in it.'

Teddy and Ava chose that moment to sprint into the kitchen, faces red with trivial outrage.

'Teddy won't let me have a go!' Ava burst out.

'You played it literally *all day* yesterday,' Teddy cried, his statement being out by twenty-three, since Ava had in fact only spent one hour the previous day playing Minecraft.

'For goodness' sake,' Stacey said, staring at the two children. Ava was a mini version of herself – with a pointed chin and straight, black hair, while Teddy didn't look much like either of his parents; instead inheriting the ginger hair that ran through Grant's family, though had skipped her husband himself. The pair now stood watching her, Teddy's cheeks still rosy, while Ava had quickly regained her quiet dignity and awaited her response with surprising patience. 'Why don't you both put your trainers on, and we'll go out for a bike ride?' Stacey suggested finally.

'That's a nice idea,' Grant said. 'I think we all need to get some fresh air. And the sun's coming out, too.'

...

'I'm glad you suggested this,' Grant told her as they stopped for a break at a playground. Though it wasn't a large park, it was one of Stacey's favourites as it was high up and had views stretching down to the canal which flowed through Wrexton. Many years ago, the town had been a hive of industrial activity with a bustling network of canals, but now the majority of the large, red brick warehouses lining the water's edge were either empty or gradually being turned into luxury flats like those Grant was creating. Trendy restaurants and bars lined the canal not far from his building project, and, in the summer, holidaymakers in narrowboats chugged along.

Teddy and Ava had abandoned their bikes to sprint over to the swings, while Stacey and Grant sat on a bench, watching the children playing together, their animosity from earlier that morning having been entirely forgotten.

'We haven't spent much quality time like this together recently,' Grant was continuing. 'We should do it more often.'

'Yes, we should,' Stacey said. 'I'd like that.'

After lapsing into silence for a few moments, she said, 'Was it true what you were telling me earlier, that you might not be able to finish the warehouse without some extra money? Wasn't selling some of your other properties enough?'

Grant shook his head, and Stacey looked at him properly for the first time that day. He was visibly exhausted. His eyes didn't twinkle like they used to. In fact, he looked haunted.

'Grant,' she said softly, placing her hand on his thigh, 'I do love you.'

'I love you too,' he said, looking at her curiously. 'Why did you say it like that? Did you think I was starting to doubt it?'

'I… I just mean that I know I've been a bit distant. A bit… difficult.' Joel's face flashed through her mind, and she winced.

'Are you still upset that the retreat didn't work out?' he asked her.

The kids were screaming and laughing about something or other, and, straining to make out their hysterical conversation, Stacey eventually gathered that Ava had got covered in a spider's web that was draped around the frame of the swings.

'What happened there, anyway?' Grant asked, when she didn't reply to him. 'Surely you can face talking about it now, after all this time. Why did you hate it so much?'

'I don't know,' she lied. 'I guess I didn't feel like I fitted in.'

Grant took a deep breath. 'Look, I know for some reason you didn't take to Joel, but I think I need to try and get him on board with the warehouse flats. I've been mulling it over this morning, wondering if he was genuine and if I should chase him up about investing, and I think I have to. I could really use his help right now, and besides, I like him. It's nice to see Morwenna so happy.'

Stacey curled her toes over inside her trainers to stop herself from saying something she'd regret. *I like him.* Of course he did. Grant liked him and Morwenna *loved* him, and Stacey didn't have a single clue what to do about it.

'I'm hungry,' Teddy yelled, running back towards them, and immediately Ava chimed in, 'So am I.'

'We'd best carry on then,' Grant said. 'We'll go to that bakery down by the canal. You know the one I mean, Stacey.'

'Currant Affairs.'

'That's it. The one that does those huge doughnuts with sprinkles on.'

This caused an eruption of excitement, and Stacey got to her feet with a sigh. Currant Affairs was a stone's throw from his warehouse. Even having said he was enjoying family time, in Grant's head he was still at work.

...

'I can't believe this,' Grant was saying, as Stacey stopped beside him and got off her bike.

'What's up?' she asked, but as she followed Grant's gaze it became obvious what the problem was. Although the building site was deserted with it being a Sunday morning, the metal fencing around it had been wrenched open. Somebody had broken in.

'This is… this is just…' he muttered darkly to himself, before taking out his phone to call his builder. Stacey stood in silence as Grant stepped through the fence to see what had happened, while Teddy and Ava cycled up and down the pavement. Moments later he burst back out in a fury, ranting into his phone about all the ground floor windows being smashed. Her brows knitted together. The large, arched industrial windows had cost an arm and a leg.

Grant was waving his free hand about angrily as he continued his heated phone conversation and she stood helplessly, only one word in her head: Joel.

Chapter 20

'So, what will you do?' Stacey asked as he finished his phone call and she walked over to him.

'Desh is going to drive over, and we'll take a look together. I don't have the keys with me, and we need to check inside the building.' He heaved a huge sigh, while Stacey's eyes widened as she spotted Joel coming towards them down the path.

'I don't believe this,' she muttered under her breath at his cheery hello.

'Joel!' Grant said, turning around to greet him with what could best be described as desperation, like a man scrambling towards a life raft. 'What are you doing down here?'

'After talking to you last night about the flats I thought I'd come and have a look,' Joel said. 'Just being nosy, I guess.' He paused as he took in the mood of the group and let his eyes slip over to the fence. 'Has something happened?'

'We're out for a family bike ride,' Stacey said. 'We're about to get coffee and doughnuts.'

'I can't do that *now*,' Grant said. 'I need to stay here and wait for Desh. I can't… I can't fucking believe this!' he kicked out at the fence while Teddy and Ava were out of earshot, playing further down the path.

'Why don't *you* go and get a coffee with Joel?' Grant said suddenly, with a meaningful look at her. He wanted her to try to butter him up! Her insides squirmed. *I could really use his help right now,* Grant had said that not half an hour ago, and with his expensive windows smashed, it was truer than ever.

'I'm sure Joel has better things to do than hang around with me and the kids,' she said, pretending to miss Grant's hint as she glanced quickly down at the children who were now peering into the canal. 'Don't you and Morwenna have any plans today?' she asked Joel.

'Morwenna's having a lie in, and I'm in no rush. That's if you don't mind me joining,' he said, as she struggled to contain her emotions. He knew full well she couldn't object in front of Grant, so she was forced to nod her agreement.

'Great,' he said, 'the coffee is on me.'

...

Leaving their bikes with Grant, Stacey gathered up Teddy and Ava before following Joel into Currant Affairs. Usually, the place had a soothing effect on her; with the scent of warm bread and pastries and all the loaves stacked up on rustic wooden shelves, but today it was heaving with people, and alongside the usual offerings the counter was stuffed with mince pies and gingerbread. Stacey's head felt like it was about to explode. The absolute last thing she needed right now was Christmas. She'd had Bea on the phone last week, talking about the festive celebrations. Why on earth had Stacey agreed for the Cockle clan to come to her and Grant? It might technically be her turn to host, but she could have explained it was a bad time. However, when Bea had started saying that she was happy for everyone to go to her house if Stacey needed to "watch the pennies," her pride had been pricked, and she'd promised them all a lavish feast.

Why can't I think before I open my mouth? Why do I always say the first thing that comes into my head?

Joel had his phone out as he joined the queue, and, peering over his arm, she spotted that he was reading a message from Morwenna. A message that ended with a heart emoji.

This is more than I can bear. Grant and Morwenna were sleep-walking into a disaster, and she had no idea how to make it stop. She was damned if she did confess, and damned if she didn't, and Joel apparently couldn't care less who got hurt in the fallout.

'Enjoy the rest of the party, did you?' she said to Joel, pleased that her voice was composed and betrayed no sign of the turmoil inside. Would Joel *actually* invest money in Grant's business? That was exactly what her husband needed, but Joel's words from the previous night echoed in her head. *I'm going to destroy your whole life. Your marriage, your family, your friendships; all of it.* Perhaps he would invest, but there would be some sting in the tail, that was for sure.

'I did, as it happens,' he replied, sliding his phone back into his pocket. 'Though your argument soured things a bit for Wenna. After all the effort she went to, as well.'

'I really am sorry about upsetting her,' she said. 'But *you're* the one who's really going to hurt her, unless you stop these games before things get completely out of hand.'

Before Joel could reply, a drama erupted between Teddy and Ava, who, oblivious to the conversation between Stacey and Joel, had simultaneously spotted a pound coin on the floor and begun a debate about who would get to keep it.

'I saw it first,' Ava declared, and Teddy was about to argue when Joel said, 'What have you found?' and Teddy opened his fist to reveal the disputed treasure.

'Why don't we do a swap,' Joel said, fishing around in his jeans pocket. 'I think I have... yes, I do.' He produced some loose change, and though it was obvious to Stacey, and the children, that there were two fifty pence coins in his hand, it took him an unusually long time to figure out which coins he was after. Stacey frowned, was he hungover or something?

Or tired out from his exertions throwing bricks through windows. For a moment she wanted to shout at him, scream that he had to stop making Grant and Morwenna pawns in his game.

But he's here because of me. This is my fault. Why hadn't she owned up at the retreat? Or even better, when he'd first emailed her? She should have swallowed her pride and done as Kirkbride had asked. Then he would never have come to Wrexton; never met Morwenna or Grant, and the only person to be hurt by her confession would have been her – the person who actually deserved it.

Teddy and Ava were eyeing each other suspiciously, wondering whether fifty pence each really was fair, before Teddy eventually nodded agreement. Once the transaction was complete – Joel placing the pound coin in a charity collection box – Teddy said, 'Who are you?'

'I'm your mum's friend's boyfriend,'

'He means Morwenna,' Stacey said stiffly. 'He's Morwenna's boyfriend.'

Teddy and Ava eyed Joel curiously. They both loved Morwenna and wouldn't accept just anyone to be the other half of someone they liked so much.

'What are you having, Stacey?' Joel asked as they reached the counter.

'A skinny latte, please,' she said, directing her answer to the young woman behind the counter rather than Joel. 'And two of the big doughnuts.'

'That's a nasty cut,' Stacey said, nodding at the plaster on Joel's wrist, revealed as his sleeve pulled up when he paid for their order.

'A glass broke when I helped clear up from the party last night,' he said. It was clearly a lie, and it was just as clear he was enjoying the fact that she knew he'd smashed the windows. He smiled at her smugly, before turning to Teddy and Ava, who were looking at all the cakes on display. 'We should probably get one to take away for your dad,' he said to them. 'Why don't you choose one?' Glancing back at Stacey, he added, 'It'll cheer him up, after the difficult morning he's had.'

...

Grant burst back into the house not long after Stacey had finished putting Teddy and Ava to bed, grinning widely, his eyes having regained their twinkle. He swept her up into an embrace and kissed her on the lips, and she couldn't help but laugh at his exuberance, until she realised what must have caused his happiness.

'He's going to help!' Grant said, as if he could barely believe his luck. 'He can invest all the money I'm short of right now, plus more on top if needed.'

'That's great,' Stacey said flatly. 'You've been celebrating, then?' Somehow or other, the day had turned into Grant and Joel heading to the pub to discuss business – a task that had taken the rest of the day – while she had cycled home with Teddy and Ava and fretted the hours away until he returned.

'It's going to be okay!' Grant was saying over and over. She wouldn't have been surprised if he started literally dancing for joy, such was his elation and drunkenness.

His stress over the warehouse finally lessened, Grant's hands were soon all over her. She tried to put her racing thoughts to one side and enjoy the moment, but Joel's face danced around in her mind, and she found herself pushing her husband away. He blinked in confusion and stepped back a couple of paces from her. 'Grant, I—' she started, but he cut her off.

'Is this because it's Joel?'

She nodded silently.

'Then I don't want to hear it,' Grant said. 'I'm not letting you bring me down. Not tonight.'

He made for the stairs and Stacey grabbed his arm, emotion overwhelming her. 'Please, for the love of God, don't go into business with him. I…' the desire to spill the truth nearly overwhelmed her.

I don't care if Grant knows about the book, not anymore. I'll take his disappointment, his hurt over so many years of lies.

If it protected him, it was well worth the pain and discomfort that confessing would bring for her. But the words died on her lips. Morwenna *couldn't* find out why Joel was with her. It would destroy her. And how would Grant feel once he realised Joel was neither his friend, nor had any real interest in his business? He was the happiest she'd seen him in months, maybe even a year. Her mind felt like it was tearing into pieces. What was she supposed to do?

Grant was ignoring her, concentrating instead on shaking his arm free, which in his drunken state caused him to stumble against the bottom stair and he said, 'Fuck's sake,' at nothing in particular.

'Please,' Stacey cried, hoping by sheer force of emotion she could get through to him.

'Give me one good reason why not,' Grant said.

Staring at him, the confession began to bubble up again, but she swallowed it back down. Grant was drunk, he was in no state to have a rational conversation, and besides, she needed to think. She needed to speak to Joel and try to understand what he was planning.

At her silence, Grant nodded. 'You can't, can you?'

Chapter 21

'It's a brilliant thing you're doing,' Morwenna said softly. Her head was on his chest, one of her legs thrown casually over his. As her naked body pressed against him the urge to roll her over onto her back and get on top of her again was overwhelming, but he tried to focus on what she was talking about.

'I'm not just doing it for Grant,' he said. 'It makes sense for me, as well. I need a project to keep me busy, and there's not much left to sort out at your dad's place now.'

'Even so, Grant was in a real mess. He must think he's won the lottery finding you. *And* you've got the experience with rental properties. That'll come in handy for him.'

He smiled uneasily. He might have told Grant that he'd worked for a property management company to make himself sound more appealing, but in fact most of his adult life he'd had no stable employment at all; helping on farms when he was younger, followed by working on building sites and doing whatever odd jobs he could find. He'd managed a good stint for a landscape gardener at one point, tackling the heavier work. He'd enjoyed that and would have happily carried on, until the man unexpectedly died and left Joel jobless once again.

Why didn't I just tell Grant the truth? A day's work was a day's work after all, but he'd needed to sound as appealing as possible. A sketchy work history and no formal qualifications might make Grant fear he was unreliable.

'I think it's good that Grant cares so much about giving people nice places to live,' he said. 'He's not only out to make money. You should see some of the dives I ended up in when I left home with barely two pennies to rub together.'

'Before you inherited all the money from your dad?'

'Yes,' he said awkwardly. It wasn't precisely true that he inherited from his father and in any case, it sickened him to think about the money. He'd gone years without touching any of it. Even when he'd been jobless and virtually homeless, he hadn't given in. That was until he discovered what Stacey had done and the lengths he would have to go to get justice. Getting close to her husband, and even Morwenna, without any money would have been a hundred times harder.

'I need to get some sleep,' Morwenna said. 'I'm still tired from the party and that argument with Stacey, and we have a toddler's birthday first thing at Tiny Town in the morning.' She went to brush her teeth, while he stared up at the ceiling of her bedroom. Stacey's words from the party swirled in his head. *You've made it impossible for me to ever confess, because as soon as I do and Morwenna realises who you are, she'll know that none of it was ever real between you.*

He shook the thoughts away as Morwenna returned. 'Were you awake in the night after the party?' she asked. 'I woke up at one point and you weren't here.'

Joel couldn't meet her eye. His clandestine window breaking trip – he'd hoped Morwenna would be too deeply asleep to notice him leaving. He'd covered his tracks as best he could, though. When he'd got back to her house, he smashed one of her glasses deliberately in case she questioned the cut on his wrist.

'Oh, I just… it was quite intense, that's all. Meeting all those people, my mind was buzzing. I went out for a walk and then I tidied up the house.'

Morwenna kissed him. 'You didn't have to clear everything up for me.'

'It wasn't any trouble.'

She snuggled up against him again and he held her close. 'Everyone loved you,' she said.

'Except Stacey.'

'Forget about Stacey. I don't know what's going on with her. She blanks *me* half the time since getting back from that retreat she went on. And some of the stuff she came out with at the party!' She took a breath. 'She's obviously going through some things, and I shouldn't have let it get to me. I think she was trying to look out for me, in some bizarre way, but she really hurt me. She practically said that I was too old for you to be genuinely interested in me. It was as if she thought it was impossible somebody would love me for *me*, and that you must be after something.'

Joel gave her a squeeze, though inside he felt sick.

'You know, I think the person she really dislikes right now is herself,' Morwenna continued quietly. 'I'm just not sure why, or what's changed. Oh,' she said, reaching across to her bedside table. 'This is for you. It's probably not your sort of thing, it's a tragic kind of romance, but you could read it, if you're interested. Though I can't say it gives me any insight into how Stacey's mind works.'

Joel's eyes fell to her hand, though he knew what he'd see.

'Did you know her back when this got published?' he asked innocently.

'No, it wasn't until a while after, when Teddy was a toddler and she'd come to Tiny Town at least twice a week. I think she was lonely – she didn't have a lot of friends, and she hadn't really gelled with any other new mums. I felt a bit sorry for her, really. She didn't find adjusting to being a parent very easy – actually, neither of them did, Grant struggled too – and her family were hopeless about it. She said how all her sisters, and sisters-in-law, too, had textbook pregnancies, perfect births and told her they took to being mums like ducks to water. I said they were almost certainly lying, or at least exaggerating, but she lets stuff like that really get to her – always comparing herself to people and thinking she comes up short, even after how well *Two Lost Souls* did. I can sort of understand why she is the way she is, though.'

His ears pricked up. 'Can you?'

'She was hurt by how little anyone believed in her when she said she wanted to be an author. She's scared of failing. Always wanting to prove herself. Anyway, take a look at her book if you want to. See if you can find some insight that I can't.'

He took the book from her and flicked through the pages. This was the last place to look for an insight into *Stacey*, that was for sure, but he'd show willing.

…

Carl stomped through the grounds, a scowl on his face. That boy, Harry bloody Stubbins, had called him a retard. Yet somehow Carl was the one who had been suspended for giving the little prick a shove. He hadn't even meant to knock him right over, though it had been satisfying to see Harry fall on his arse, a comically surprised look on his face. Not that Carl gave a shit about being suspended from a place he didn't even want to go, but why should he put up with people talking to him like that? Not that he really knew what Harry was getting at – he often didn't when it came to the conversations of the other teenagers – but it was clear it was an insult of some sort or another, as a quick check in the dictionary once he arrived home had confirmed.

He was startled out of his dark thoughts as he left the trees and blundered into something in the long grass, almost tripping over. The "something" cried out in protest and Carl stared down at a girl maybe two or three years his senior, smoothing down her pastel blue t-shirt and raising a delicate eyebrow.

'I… I'm sorry. Are you hurt?'

'I'm okay,' she said, her voice soft, friendly. 'What are you doing here?' she asked, after she'd got to her feet and her eyes had flicked over him.

'Walking.'

'Well, technically you're trespassing,' she said, a hint of a smile in her eyes. The early summer breeze was whipping her hair about and she reached up and gathered it all into her hand, holding it out of her face until the air stilled.

'Usually no one's here to notice. And besides, the boundary is in the wrong place, that's what my dad says.'

The girl reached down and picked up the book she had been reading, which had sunk down into the tall grass. 'You live next door, then?'

It was an odd phrase to use. Was there really a "next door" when your house was in the middle of acres of land? If she was saying she lived at Ash Farm it would take a full fifteen minutes to walk from his front door to hers. Not that the farmhouse was anything like as big as Hillcroft Manor, but it was still a generous sized home, surrounded by fields and meadows; the exact boundaries of which were hotly disputed between his dad and Frank Draper, whose relative this girl must be.

'I'm Carl,' he said.

'Marigold. Although people usually called me Mari. M-A-R-I,' she spelt out slowly, 'but said like Marie.'

'My mum used to grow lots of marigolds,' he said. 'They keep the whitefly away from tomatoes in the greenhouse.' He paused. 'That was a weird thing to say. Sorry.'

She shrugged and his eyes fell onto the scooped neckline of her t-shirt. Realising what he was doing he looked away from her cleavage as fast as he could, but her hazel eyes glowed knowingly. 'Why haven't I seen you before?' he asked quickly.

'I don't live here. Well, now I do, I guess. I came here with my mum after she split up with my dad. Frank's my uncle, and there's loads of room in his house. He said he gets fed up of rattling about the place on his own.' She glanced over her shoulder in the direction of the farmhouse, as if thinking she should head back, and then looked back at Carl, eyes searching his face. 'You mentioned your mum,' she said. 'I heard about her; that she died when you were only a child.'

He nodded, and she reached out and touched his arm lightly. 'I'm sorry. I can't imagine what that must have been like. My uncle said it came out of the blue.'

'Yes,' he said, though it wasn't true. People called it sudden and unexpected, but it wasn't. His mum had always known she was going to die young. Her dad and one of her aunties went the same way, along with one of her three brothers once he hit forty. In every single case there was a common factor, one which his mum had taken into her heart as part of a deep family mythology. They all had blackouts. Dizziness, fainting. And then they died. And so it had been with her. She fainted when she was homeschooling Carl one perfectly normal afternoon, and a few months later she went to bed one night and never woke up.

If you faint, you die. *Those words were inscribed on his heart, written through him like a stick of rock. He knew he had it too, whatever it was. He'd not fainted, but his brain didn't work like other people's. He was different to them – too different. His parents had always told him different was good, but was it good when it meant Harry Stubbins called you names? Was it good when it meant you couldn't do what other people could do? Once, his dad had had a letter from the school saying something about assessing him. He'd thought that sounded helpful – but his dad had snatched it away before he could even finish reading it, with much of his usual ranting about busybodies, do-gooders, and people who wanted to "put everyone in a neat box", whatever the heck that* *meant. Carl planned to spend as long as he could living his life before he ended up in a box like his mum – though technically his mum had been buried in an ecologically friendly hemp shroud, not a coffin, and then laid to rest in a woodland burial site that Howard took him to visit from time to time.*

'I should probably…' Marigold was saying, watching him with her head cocked slightly to one side.

'Yeah,' he said quickly. Shit, he'd gone silent for a moment too long, and she thought he was weird. He didn't want her to think he was weird.

'I'll see you again sometime, though,' she said, and his heart lifted.

She began making her way through the field towards her uncle's house and his eyes followed her retreating back, but then she turned to look at him and he quickly scurried away, embarrassed. There were girls at school, of course, but they weren't like **this** *girl.*

Chapter 22

It was clear something had happened the second Morwenna opened the door. Her face was wreathed in smiles. She was practically glowing. Already Stacey regretted offering her a lift to yoga – witnessing how loved-up her friend was sent a physical pain through her body – but when Morwenna held out her hand she had to stop herself recoiling in horror at the sight of her friend's newly bejewelled finger. 'He didn't?' she said, trying to keep her voice light.

How could he? How *dare* he? But she had to recover herself quickly. The last thing she wanted was to offend Morwenna the way she had at the party, and besides, the more she aggravated her, the closer she would get to Joel instead. She needed to keep Morwenna close, and make sure she was there for her when it all came crashing down.

'He did!' Morwenna said delightedly in answer to her question. 'We're going to start looking at wedding venues this week. And I'm moving in with him soon, as well.'

Desperate to scream to Morwenna that none of it was real, instead she forced out her congratulations, and if it sounded half-hearted Morwenna was apparently too excited to notice.

Finally, after having to pretend to be calm and relaxed for an excruciating hour of twisting her body into various poses, followed by listening to Morwenna gushing about her wedding plans over lunch, Stacey was given a moment to breathe when Morwenna went to the toilet. The second her friend's back was turned, Stacey snatched up Morwenna's phone from the table before it locked. Joel thought he was being so clever, but let's see how he'd explain himself when she challenged him face to face over this farcical engagement. She quickly sent Joel's new contact details to herself – the number he'd used to contact her at the retreat no longer seemed to work – and replaced Morwenna's phone carefully in the exact spot she'd picked it up from.

'Joel is so excited to join Grant's business,' Morwenna said as she sat down again. 'He said he's signing some papers soon and making it all official.'

Stacey blinked. 'He did?' It was the first she'd heard of it. Or was it? A dim memory of Grant talking about paperwork at breakfast surfaced, but she'd been rushing around getting the kids fed and ready for school, and she'd zoned out when Grant had started talking about Joel to stop herself losing her mind.

Suddenly, the cafe was unbearably noisy; the cry of a baby; the bursts of laughter; the scraping of chairs, all grated painfully on her nerves. She glanced beyond her friend to the street outside the window, trying to imagine the cold air on her flustered face, but the sight of people rushing around doing their Christmas shopping made her feel worse, if anything.

'He's lucky Grant didn't mind him lying about his previous job,' Morwenna said, and Stacey frowned in confusion.

'He did what?'

Morwenna rolled her eyes. 'He made up that he'd worked for a property management company to make himself sound more appealing to Grant. Well, I believed him too, but he felt really guilty and told me he'd made it up. It was a silly thing to do, and I told him as much. He doesn't need to pretend to get people to like him.'

Stacey almost spat out her mouthful of coffee. Didn't need to pretend to get people to like him? Pretending was *all* he did. His life was more fake than hers was, for God's sake!

'Where did he really work, then?' she asked, keeping her voice neutral. 'Why would he lie?'

'His education was really patchy,' Morwenna explained. 'He's always struggled to find work, and the money he's investing with Grant came from a very large inheritance when his father died.'

'He shouldn't have lied.'

'I know that, and he knows that. He's genuinely sorry, it was out of his mouth before he had a chance to think it through.' Morwenna suddenly laughed. 'His background is uncannily like that character in your book – you know, Carl. That boy in the big country house,' she continued, as if Stacey could possibly not have known who she meant.

'Anyway, isn't it nice?' Morwenna said. 'My fiancé working with your husband?'

Nice? It was horrifying. Unbearable. Stacey's mind was racing, but then her thoughts cleared. *Enough is enough.* She needed information, as much as she could get. The more she knew, the better she could tackle the havoc Joel was creating. 'How much money is he investing?' she asked, her voice seeming to echo back at her from a great distance as she forced herself to focus on Morwenna. She'd start with figuring out if all the talk of him investing was backed up by reality.

'I don't know the exact figures,' Morwenna said, a little startled by the directness of Stacey's question. 'I guess you'd have to ask Grant.'

Stacey finished her latte. She'd do better than that. She'd ask Joel. And she'd tell him exactly what she thought of his engagement to Morwenna while she was at it.

...

Of course he kept her waiting. No reply to her message asking to meet – though she could see he'd read it – and he left her standing around in the spitting rain. Why had she said to meet him in a park, for goodness' sake? Well, she knew why. She didn't want to meet him at a place where there was a slim chance they might be spotted. A "chance" encounter in a park was innocent enough, and what she had to say hopefully wouldn't take long.

'Stacey,' he said, all smiles as he walked up to her. Wearing a pair of dark, well-fitting jeans and a grey jacket, a tasteful checked scarf around his neck, he looked calm and collected, while she felt like a nervous wreck. 'You've heard the news I take it?'

'You mean your fake engagement to Morwenna?' she said, falling into step with him and snuggling into her own oversized black scarf. It was too cold and damp to sit down; they'd have to saunter around like a couple taking a winter stroll. Probably the kind of thing he did with Morwenna; she could just imagine the pair of them on romantic walks, candlelit dinners, cosy nights in, and all of it a lie. Pain stabbed at her again at the thought of how he was treating Morwenna, and abruptly she stopped and grabbed his arm. 'How dare you?' she said. 'Using my friend like this? My husband? So that, what, you can eventually turn them against me? Or threaten to hurt them just to get at me? Morwenna *loves* you, Joel! She's showing off her engagement ring, making wedding plans, and you—' her voice rose to a cry. 'You're just using her! You're going to break her heart and for what? To make some point? Do the right thing and end it now. Let her down gently. I don't want her to find out this has all been a vendetta against me – she should at least be able to look back on her time with you without feeling like every part of it was a lie.'

Words failed her as she ran out of steam and glared at him, but he couldn't keep eye contact with her. In fact, he was visibly rattled by what she'd said, and they carried on walking in silence as the rain misted on her face and hair, chilling her through to the core. What was he thinking about? Why the silence? Why had he looked so chastened?

'I know you don't have a lot of respect for me,' she continued, 'and I don't expect you to after what I did. But no matter what you think of *me*, I do care about Grant and Morwenna, and if you think I'll sit back and let you hurt them…' All at once she stopped in her tracks as a realisation hit her. She knew exactly why he looked so disturbed by her words! 'You love her back,' she said. 'Don't you, Joel?'

Chapter 23

'You love her, and you don't want to lose her. I'm right, aren't I?' she pressed him. Could it really be true? 'And Grant?' she continued. 'You genuinely like him as well, don't you? You don't want to upset either of them.'

'Of course I don't *want* to upset them!' he said, emotion forcing him to finally break his silence. 'Wenna didn't steal the book. Neither did Grant.'

'How much money have you said you'll invest in the warehouse flats?'

'It doesn't matter.'

'Why? Because you don't have the money? That tale you fed Morwenna, making yourself sound like Carl just to freak me out, and this talk of a huge inheritance – it'll all fall apart when you have to put your money where your mouth is. Think of what it will do to Grant when he discovers you can't really bail him out, on top of how you already lied to him about your previous job. You've built yourself a house of cards. One push and it will all come tumbling down.' In fact, if the circumstances were different, she could almost have felt sorry for him. He was clearly in way over his head – his deception snowballing just the way hers had when she stole *The Darkest of Paths*. Could he not see the parallel? She wanted to take him by the shoulders and give him a good shake.

Joel looked at her as if he really didn't know what she was talking about, while the droplets of rain in his hair sparkled in rays of wintery sunlight making it through the clouds. 'I do have the cash,' he said. 'And I am just like Carl.'

For a second the desire to scream at him was so strong she could barely stop herself giving in to it. What was wrong with him? Could he not open his mouth without lying? Quickly moving to one side to dodge a toddler splashing excitedly in a muddy puddle, she fussed with her scarf to hide her confusion, words failing her.

'It's not a "tale",' he said finally.

'What are you talking about?'

'Well, I *am* Carl. I just didn't want my real name in the book.'

'I don't believe you,' she snapped. Her skin was prickling with unease, her temples beginning to ache. 'You're not Carl,' she said uncertainly. 'You're just trying to mess with my head.'

'Vineworth Manor it was called, my old home. Hillcroft Manor you know it better as, I guess.'

'No,' she said, though a swirling feeling had started inside her body. 'You're lying.'

The toddler Stacey had had to dodge was beside them again, splashing in a succession of small puddles along the pavement with obvious delight. The antics were making Joel smile, which only increased Stacey's confusion. Who was this man? For someone so consumed with a desire for revenge, he was apparently also quick to notice, and share in, joy around him.

'You thought it was all fiction,' he said.

Stacey started to shake her head. No. This couldn't be happening. *The Darkest of Paths* wasn't *true*. The country house; that eccentric, dominating father; Carl and the girl, Marigold. No, it was impossible. Both of the teenagers died at the end of *The Darkest of Paths*. That was the whole point of the story. It was like a reimagining of Romeo and Juliet, the two teenagers dying as a result of their family's ridiculous dispute over the boundaries of their estates. It was supposed to be slightly ludicrous, absurd. It made those unnecessary deaths all the more poignant. Joel was many things, but he certainly wasn't a ghost.

'*Inspired* by true events, I guess you could say,' Joel continued, and she took the time to really look at him properly. She'd looked at him plenty of times before, of course. She'd seen the surface, the beguiling man who'd tempted Charlotte at the retreat and had now won the heart of her best friend, but she'd missed something. Something important that was etched through his face. This wasn't a man who was hellbent on hurting her for the sake of it, who was manipulating her husband and Morwenna without a thought for their feelings. He'd said himself he didn't want to hurt anybody. This man in front of her wasn't cruel. He was something far simpler than that, yet it made the whole thing so much more complicated. He was sad. Lost, even. The way he'd smiled at that toddler hadn't been pure amusement, as she'd assumed. No, it had been wistful. It had been as though he set himself apart, lived his life as a spectator. But why?

'Joel,' she said gently as they reached the far end of the park, where a holly bush stood, festooned with red berries. 'Let's talk about this rationally. We've established that you love Morwenna.'

He nodded.

'And Grant – you are genuinely going to save his building project?'

'I am.'

'Then let's just leave everything how it is. You know I can't confess without the two of them realising who you are and that you started out using them to get at me. They might forgive you, but there's no guarantee. You can be with Morwenna and help my husband, with my blessing. Why ruin it all because of a book?'

His eyes flashed. 'I don't want, or need, your blessing, and that book is my history. It's the only thing I have left of Marigold.'

Despite the rain, Stacey couldn't help collapsing onto a damp bench beside the holly bush. 'Marigold – she really is gone?'

'Yes, she's dead,' he said harshly, his mood having changed entirely at the thought of his first love. 'Wake up and look at what you're doing. Trampling on a young girl's memory. Profiting out of her misery. Morwenna told me your family never believed in you, but that's not my fault. Stealing someone else's words: there's no excuse for that. Take responsibility and own up.'

She was about to protest that Grant and Morwenna would still be hurt by her confession and by his deception, but he held up his hand to stop her. 'Morwenna and Grant don't need to know that I had anything to do with the book. We *can* carry on exactly as we are. All I want is for you to post a video where you admit that *Two Lost Souls* was written by J. M. Kirkbride. No one needs to know exactly who that is.' He pointed his finger at her. 'They just need to know that it is *not* you.'

Chapter 24

She stared at him in astonishment as he sat down beside her. Could it really be that simple? Morwenna would get her wedding, a marriage to a man she loved; and Grant would get his business back on track, and neither of them would be any the wiser about why Joel had started the whole thing?

All it takes is coming clean. All it took was destroying her reputation and the respect and admiration people had for her. Destroying her career, in other words – if it could even be called that when the book was never hers in the first place.

'What happens if I don't?' she asked him breathlessly. What was he prepared to do, if he didn't get what he wanted from her?

'If you don't? Well, I told you already. You took something of mine – of mine and Marigold's – so if you don't confess, I'll take away *everything* of yours. Your marriage, your friendship with Morwenna. And that's just the start. The plan was never to threaten Wenna and Grant to get you to confess. The plan is to take them away from *you*. To leave *you* with nothing, the way I was left with nothing.'

She frowned down into her lap. Did he really think he could do that? Break up a friendship and a marriage that went back *years* when he had only been in their lives for mere months? But what difference did that make, anyway? Her mind was already made up the lie had gone on long enough and it was time for it to end.

Joel watched as she took out her phone and opened one of her social media profiles.

'What exactly do you want me to say?' she asked him.

'The truth.'

Her finger hovered in front of the screen. She could live stream her confession – just get it done and out there and over with, no faffing about. If she was going to do it, she needed to get on and do it. The fallout she'd deal with later.

Just rip the plaster off. It's now or never. Joel was right here beside her; he'd see she was doing as he asked, and apart from the toddler and his mother, who were making their way towards a gate out onto the road, the park was empty. The timing couldn't be more perfect, if perfect was the word for what she was about to do.

'What are you waiting for?' Joel asked, as he stood to make sure he was out of view when she started filming.

Fingers shaking, she willed herself to start the live stream, but her body wouldn't obey. Instead, her eyes were drawn to her number of followers – thousands upon thousands of people. Not just people, fans. She'd been sent so many messages over the years; readers saying how her book had touched them, inspired them, got them through hard times or kept them up all night reading. People liked hearing from her; about her life, about Queenie, about whatever was on her mind. *They don't want to hear from a nobody.* They wanted to hear from her because they believed she'd written *Two Lost Souls.* That was who she was.

Charlotte's face flashed through her mind, telling Stacey at the retreat that *Two Lost Souls* was her all-time favourite book. She'd fetched the copy she'd brought with her, and Stacey had signed it, just as she had signed countless other copies, countless other times in the past.

'Stacey?' Joel said.

More thoughts came flooding in. TV interviews she'd done. So many conversations she'd had with so many people all about the book. *Her* book – even though it wasn't – yet it defined her. Those bloody pages, they were what she was to the world. *And have I committed fraud?* She'd signed contracts. She'd said she had the rights to publish that manuscript. How much trouble would she be in? Beginning to shake violently, her phone almost slipped from her hand and her eyes stung with tears. Everyone would know. Everybody. Even people at her children's school – Teddy and Ava's teachers, their schoolfriends, other parents. How would she ever be able to show her face again? My God, she'd given signed copies of her books as prizes in PTA raffles. She'd judged short story competitions; she'd done talks at libraries and been a guest at book club meetings. Her head started to buzz. She'd have to hide away, forever.

Before she knew it, she leapt up from the bench and shoved her phone in her pocket. 'No,' she said, pushing past Joel blindly. 'I can't. I can't.'

Fleeing from the park, she drew in great gasps of air as she made it out onto the street, dashing away before Joel could catch up with her.

Chapter 25

Stacey jumped out of her skin when she arrived back home from the park – after a detour to pick Teddy and Ava up from school – and walked into the kitchen to find Joel stood by the kettle, bold as brass, making himself a mug of tea.

Having ushered the kids out of the room, she swallowed down her panic. 'What are you doing in my house?'

Joel finished stirring his tea – he'd used her favourite mug, the one with gilt pineapples on it – and smiled at her as if their conversation in the park hadn't happened at all. 'I'm helping Grant.'

'Helping Grant with what?'

He inclined his head towards the other side of the room, where a new shower tray was propped against the wall. 'Grant said you keep nagging him to sort out the shower before your family come for Christmas or get someone in to do it. He said you don't seem to understand that now your money from *Two Lost Souls* is drying up you can't afford to get people in to do things any more, and that he doesn't have time because he's working seven days a week to try and finish the flats.'

'He said that, did he?' Stacey asked, hurt blooming inside her as Joel casually sipped his tea.

He's trying to wind me up. Don't rise to it.

'Do you want one?' he asked her.

'No,' she said. Her nerves were shredded, and she swayed on her feet, grabbing at the kitchen island to steady herself.

I can't have him here in my house. I can't. I can't!

'Perhaps you should sit down for a minute. You seem upset.'

'Where is Grant?' she asked, her voice a croak.

'He had to go back to the plumbing supply place. I said I'd stay and get started.'

'Mummy!' Teddy yelled as he burst back into the kitchen with Ava in tow. 'Snacks.'

'Just a minute,' she said, shakily letting go of the kitchen island and hoping her legs would hold her weight.

The two children paused as they took in the sight of Joel. 'I work with your daddy now,' he explained, while Stacey had to clench her hands into tight fists to stop herself from screaming. 'I'm just helping him with something in the house.'

'I want a snack,' Teddy said to her again.

Absentmindedly opening the nearest cupboard, Stacey extracted two packets of crisps which Teddy and Ava leapt on immediately.

'It's careers week at school soon,' Ava said, 'you *have* to come and talk about being an author! Teddy said everyone loved it last year. You'll do it, won't you?'

After she had murmured something non-committal, the children ran out of the room, and she turned to Joel.

'I get dragged into these things,' she protested weakly. 'I'm not trying to show off – the school needs parents to go in and talk. It's to inspire children,' she added, beginning to babble as her eyes stung with tears. 'It's not for me. It's not to massage my own ego…'

Joel sipped his tea, looking at her over the rim of the mug. She expected him to reply, even if it was to have yet another go at her, but he stayed silent, which was almost worse.

…

Trying her best to stay out of the way while Joel and Grant were busy with the shower, she curled up with Ava to listen to her read, before encouraging a reluctant Teddy to practice his list of spellings for the week.

I'll take away everything of yours.

No. Don't think about it. He wouldn't be able to do it, of course he wouldn't! She'd tried to confess; she'd tried to do what he wanted. Surely, he could understand what a mess it would make of her life. She'd been physically shaking when she held the phone up, if she hadn't fled she would have been sick.

'Grant said to tell you we need to turn the water off for a bit,' Joel said, popping his head around the door to the living room.

'Okay, fine.'

'And he asked if I'd stay for dinner. I told him I didn't want to intrude, but he kind of insisted, so…'

Leaping to her feet as Joel walked off, she caught his arm in the hall. 'I am *not* having you sitting down in my house for a meal with my family,' she said, with a glance to the living room where Teddy and Ava were now absorbed in watching TV. 'It's too much. You can't expect me to do that.'

'Okay, well, you can explain your feelings to Grant,' he said, before adding sarcastically, 'I'm sure he'll understand.'

…

'I've got to say, he does work hard,' Grant remarked once Joel had left after dinner. 'We'll easily be able to finish sorting that shower tomorrow morning. We could have done it today if I'd remembered to get everything we needed.'

'He's coming here *again* tomorrow?'

'Why not? You want it finished, don't you?' he paused for a moment. 'He was great with the kids at dinner – Teddy and Ava couldn't stop talking to him.'

Stacey carried on shoving plates into the dishwasher. Joel had been insufferable. He'd listened to Teddy and Ava's chatter with great interest, asking lots of questions and making them laugh with daft jokes. Even the *cat* liked him! Usually, Queenie had little interest in their visitors, but she'd been more than happy to get attention from Joel, who had made a point of remarking what a beautiful cat she was.

'I told you I can do the dishwasher,' Grant said, glancing round at her from where he sat at the dining table catching up with emails on his laptop.

'I don't mind,' she said. In truth, having a simple task to focus on was the only thing stopping her mind coming apart at the seams. She paused for a moment. 'Did you tell Joel we're short of money because I haven't managed to finish another book?'

Grant's forehead creased. 'I don't think that's exactly how I phrased it.'

'However you phrased it, he knew, and he brought it up.'

'Well, I'm sorry about that. But I'm sure he wasn't trying to upset you – why would he want to? He was probably just making conversation. He knows full well that you don't like him. I wish you wouldn't make it so obvious. It's embarrassing, frankly.'

'So, you think it's okay, do you?' she said, her frayed emotions from the day catching up with her as her voice rose. Joel's constant presence made her feel like she was inside a pressure cooker; if she had to come face to face with him again the next day she would literally burst – she was sure of it.

I have to get rid of him.

She paused, staring down at the plate she was holding and trying to push that thought aside. No, *she* was still the one in the wrong. *But two wrongs don't make a right.* Joel shouldn't be threatening to tear apart her family and her friendship. And she had children – was he seriously suggesting he'd break up her marriage and disrupt Teddy and Ava's lives over *Two Lost Souls?* He might want to protect his precious memories of Marigold, but *she* needed to protect what was in the here and now.

Grant was still watching her, his face weary. 'Do I think *what's* okay?' he asked her. 'For him to talk to you?'

'No, for him to talk to me like *that*,' she said, a vague idea beginning to form. 'He's overfamiliar and I don't like it. And besides, have neither you nor Morwenna thought to question where he's suddenly sprung from? Why's he moved to Wrexton? He doesn't know anyone here; he doesn't have a job here, so why? How does he explain that?'

Now Grant was exasperated. 'Just stop! He's a nice, genuine guy, who has done absolutely nothing to you. He moved here because he was looking for a new start, and as for whatever he did or didn't say to you earlier—'

Stacey was struggling to fit the final plate into the dishwasher, and at these words from Grant she gave up and placed it slowly and carefully down on the worktop. Yes, she had an idea, all right.

'Grant, I need you to listen to me. I'm telling *you,* my *husband,* that a man is making me feel uncomfortable in my own home. Please don't tell me I'm imagining it.'

That, finally, got through to him and he got up from the table to come and put his arm around her. 'Okay,' he said. 'I will have a word with him. He shouldn't be making you feel that way.'

'Thank you,' she said, feeling victorious and guilty, in equal measure.

Chapter 26

Initially it seemed her talk with Grant had done the trick. Joel came to help finish the shower, but Grant kept him out of her way, and for a whole week she heard little mention of him from her husband or from Morwenna.

Could it really be that easy? Grant had said he'd have a word with Joel, but it must have been one hell of a word to stop the man dead in his tracks. But if she'd thought her troubles might be over, she was brought back down to earth with a bump when Morwenna asked if she'd join her wedding dress shopping after their yoga class.

'I don't know…' she started, 'isn't it still a bit early? You haven't set a date yet, have you? And it's Christmas next week, I've got heaps to do and I'm already going out later with some of the school mums for drinks—'

'We *have* set a date!' Morwenna said, eyes glowing with happiness as she ignored half of what Stacey said. 'It's in the spring next year. Please, Stacey, I've got an appointment at the bridal shop, and I don't want to go on my own.'

The afternoon was excruciating, Stacey forcing herself to smile so often that it made her face ache. Morwenna looked stunning in every dress she tried, while Stacey's insides tied themselves in as many knots as there were tiny pearl beads on the gown Morwenna tried on last.

'This is the one,' she said as she emerged from the changing room in a swish of skirts. 'What do you think, Stacey?'

Gazing at her friend as she twirled slowly on the spot, Stacey had to agree that yes, this ivory dress with its dramatic low neckline and spray of pretty pearls was indeed the one. But no sooner had the words left her lips than her phone vibrated, and she found a message from Joel.

Please stop sending me emails, it read. *I don't feel that way about you Stacey and if you carry on I'll have no choice but to tell Grant and Morwenna.*

What on earth was the man going on about? She'd only ever emailed him as Kirkbride, she didn't know any other email address for him, though presumably he had one that used his actual name. Trying to shake off her unease as Morwenna disappeared behind the voluminous satin curtain of the changing room, Stacey opened her sent emails and drew in her breath with a gasp.

...

'Are you *sure* you're okay?' one of the school mums asked her for the umpteenth time as they spilled out from the bar onto the street. 'I don't want to just leave you.'

'I told you, Grant's coming to get me,' she lied as she wobbled on the uneven pavement. She'd tried to cancel going out that night, but the other mums wouldn't take no for an answer, and in the end she'd decided a few drinks might be exactly what she needed. A wave of nausea washed over her. How many glasses of wine had she put away? Far more than the others, that was for sure. Pretending she could see Grant's car arriving, she was relieved once they had all left so she could start making her way down the street towards Joel's house – the address of which she'd found on some papers Grant had left lying around in the kitchen.

I'll tell him what I think of his disgusting emails.

Clearly, he'd managed to get hold of the password for her email account one of the times he had been in the house – probably when he was there for dinner. Grant's laptop had been out on the side; Joel had been using it, in fact, Grant had been showing him something to do with the warehouse flats. But it was a laptop that she also used, and which had her passwords saved on it. She'd been busy cooking and Grant hadn't been by Joel's side continuously; he could have found her password and then been free to send himself emails posing as her to his hearts content. Which was, it would seem, exactly what he *had* been doing for the past seven days.

The walk took longer than she'd anticipated, though the cold air did nothing to clear her head.

I'll show him what I think of his sick little game.

Some of the emails had been disgusting. The idea of putting her mouth, hands, or any other bits of herself anywhere near the intimate parts of him made her want to scrub herself from head to toe. His street swam before her eyes, and she stumbled her way down to number 57, before pausing at the sight of Joel's home. It wasn't quite as big as her house, but it was striking. A modern, glassy sort of box – slightly at odds with its suburban surroundings – it nevertheless was impressive.

I have to get rid of him. Those words were her mantra now; no longer the positive affirmations she used to recite each day when she was still trying to write. She'd never write, she knew that now. All she could hope for was to get Joel away from her life and her family. And make sure he would never come back.

Picking her way up the path beside the drive, her coat sleeve caught on a rose bush, and she fought for a few seconds to free herself, nearly losing her footing in the process. Had Joel really bought this house just so he could move here and put his schemes in motion?

'Joel!' she yelled as she hammered on his front door. She opened the letterbox and called through it. 'Come down here and face me.' She had to grab onto the wall as she straightened up, and as her gaze swept over the neat drive, she spotted something that she'd completely missed when she arrived. Morwenna's car. Morwenna was here with him.

Her resolve weakened briefly, but then she raised her hand to pound on the door once again.

'What the hell are you doing?' Joel hissed at her when he opened the door. His hair was messy, and his clothes rumpled. Behind him, Morwenna appeared, in a similar state of dishevelment.

'Oh, I see,' Stacey said, raising her voice to start drunkenly singing, 'Joel and Morwenna, sitting in a tree, F U C K I N '

'Oh my God,' Morwenna said, rushing forward, her face all concern. 'Stacey, come on, come inside. Let's sober you up a bit.'

Instead of an answer, she leant forward and abruptly threw up all over the front of Morwenna's hastily flung on dress, her vomit dripping down and making a small pool on Joel's polished concrete floor.

For a second there was a shocked silence, until Morwenna recovered from her moment of horror and spoke softly. 'Come on. Let's get cleaned up.'

'I'm sorry,' Stacey said, wiping her mouth on her coat sleeve as tears pricked her eyes. 'I'm so sorry, Wenna, your dress—'

'Don't worry about my dress,' Morwenna said kindly as she tried to usher Stacey inside. 'It's old, anyway. I'll bung it in the wash, it'll be fine. But what are you doing here? Has something happened?'

'Yes, something's happened!' Stacey cried, remembering why she had come now her shock at throwing up on Morwenna had subsided. 'And if you want to know what, you should ask *him*!' she waved her arm vaguely at Joel, who shrugged at Morwenna's questioning gaze.

'How did you find my address?' Joel asked her.

'Never mind about that,' Stacey said, trying to force her drunken mind to function properly.

There has to be a way of getting Wenna to understand. 'You should know a few things,' she said to her friend. 'Joel isn't who he says he is. This is all about me. *Me!*'

'Morwenna, I'm sorry,' Joel said. 'I should have mentioned it before. Stacey has been… hassling me. I didn't want to say anything—'

'You liar!' Stacey burst out. 'You're the one hassling *me!* You're sick; sending those emails to *yourself* so you can pretend I did it!'

Instead of answering, Joel took his phone from his pocket, and after a couple of taps on the screen handed it to Morwenna, whose eyes widened.

'There you go, you see,' Stacey said. '*He* hacked into my account and sent these to make it look like I'm harassing him!'

'You should be with me, not Morwenna,' her friend read out, voice strained. 'I want you Joel, and I know you want me too. I want you inside me.'

'See?' Stacey said, though from Morwenna's expression she could see her friend had now reached some of the dirtier emails.

'How could you do this?' Morwenna asked her quietly. 'How could you?'

Stacey blinked. What was happening? Why was Morwenna pretending she didn't get it? It was obvious what was going on, surely? 'No, *Joel* did it,' she repeated. 'And who knows, maybe he enjoyed sending them.'

'Is this all some sort of joke to you?' Morwenna shouted, forcing her to look at Joel's phone. 'You've sent him hundreds! Hundreds of disgusting messages. And now you have the audacity to deny it?'

'Of course I didn't send them,' she said, fear seeping through her.

She has to believe me. She has to! 'Why won't you listen to me? Joel got into my account…' But Morwenna wasn't paying attention to her protests, and raising her eyes to meet Joel's smug expression, Stacey flew at him. '*You* did this! Admit it!'

'Get off him,' Morwenna grabbed her. 'Leave him alone. Leave us *both* alone.'

'He set me up,' she said. 'Why won't you listen to me?'

'Because you're not making any sense! Why would Joel do that? I can't…' Morwenna's voice broke, 'this is why you were so reluctant to help me look at dresses earlier, isn't it?'

'Yes!' Stacey seized on these words, confused as her fuzzy brain struggled to keep up with the conversation, 'because I don't want you to marry him!' Realising too late that she'd made it worse, she reached out helplessly towards Morwenna, who pushed her away.

'And there it is,' Morwenna said. 'You admit it. *You* want Joel yourself! You've been jealous right from the start.'

'Jealous?' Stacey cried. 'Of that lying, two-faced—'

'Stop!' Morwenna's voice was almost a screech. 'I can't listen to you another second. Just go away. Get out of my sight! Go. Away. Now!'

'Wenna, no, listen to me…'

The words died on her lips as the colour drained from Joel's face and he fell backwards, only Morwenna's quick reactions stopping him from smacking his head on the concrete floor. 'Joel?' her friend cried out, shaking him, 'Joel?'

...

'It's all right,' Grant whispered to her softly as she opened her eyes to the dimly lit bedroom. 'I've brought you some water. Nobody is angry with you.'

'What… why would they be?' she croaked. Grant held out the glass and she took it, gulping the water gratefully.

'Don't you remember? You went round Joel's house last night.'

Letting out a sigh, Stacey closed her eyes as fragmented images drifted through her mind. Why had she let herself get so drunk yet again? What had she said?

'Look, Stacey, we can all see you've been struggling for a while now, and that you've been odd around Joel, but drinking like this, and starting arguments with people…'

'Joel makes me uncomfortable,' she said, 'I *told* you that.'

At the memory of his cruel trick with the emails a flash of anger shot through her, but before she could speak, Grant said, 'You don't remember what happened, do you?'

Stacey leaned across to put the empty glass down on the bedside table. What on earth *had* gone on the previous night? Grant was being so odd. She squinted at her husband. 'How did I get home?'

'Morwenna called me to come and get you. That was, once Joel had woken up.'

'Woken up?'

'For God's sake!' Grant said. 'You turned up drunk at his house, yelling at him. Morwenna was nearly hysterical when she phoned me, saying you'd upset him so much that he fainted.'

At this, Stacey frowned heavily. Dim images swirled around, though they wouldn't solidify. 'He *fainted*? Because I shouted at him?'

She lay back down with a groan. *What on earth have I gone and done now?* 'I thought you said no one is angry with me,' she said. 'If you're angry with anyone, it should be him. Have you seen what he's been up to with the emails?'

Sitting down beside her, Grant drummed his fingers on his leg, and she prodded him gently in the back. 'I said have you seen what he's done?'

'Have you really got nothing to say for yourself?'

'Not you as well!' she said, sitting up despite her exhaustion and the headache that was spreading around her skull. '*He* did it Grant. Please, *please* believe me!'

'But why? Why would he?'

Clutching desperately for a response to this that wouldn't incriminate herself, she said instead, 'Well, why would *I?* I don't fancy him! And even if I did, I wouldn't email him stuff like that! I told you how uncomfortable he made me last week when he came to help with the shower. He...' she seized on a sudden burst of inspiration. '*He's* harassing *me.* It wasn't just what he said about my writing that day, and the money, he... he touched me as well. He said some stuff; disgusting things about what he wanted to do to me. I was so shocked, I...' she swallowed hard, and a couple of convenient tears overflowed from her eyes. 'But we needed his money, so I thought I'd just put up with it. I don't want your business to fail...'

'Where did he touch you?' Grant asked.

'The kitchen, I just told you—'

'I mean, where on your body?'

'I...' she tried to focus.

Just say something! 'He squeezed my bum,' she said, and a wave of guilt washed over her, but it was swiftly followed by anger. How did Joel expect her to act after what he'd done? Having her friend and husband believe she'd written those emails was unbearable.

'I'm scared of him,' she said, doubling down on her accusations. 'The things he said... I don't want to ever be on my own with him. I don't even want to be in the same room as him.'

I have to get Grant on my side. I have to. 'He's making it look like I've got some obsession with him to cover his tracks,' she continued, when Grant made no response.

I have to get rid of Joel. The words started to repeat over and over. *I have to get rid of him. It doesn't matter what it takes.* And if Grant wasn't swayed yet, she'd have to take things up another notch. 'He's going to attack me one day, I know he is,' she said, beginning to shake in desperation. 'He's making it so he can get away with it.'

'I'm going to stop you there,' Grant said. 'And please, just listen before you say anything.'

She fell silent. *He'll believe me now.*

'Wenna and Joel showed me the messages, sent from you to him.'

'No, I told you,' she cried, 'I just explained about that!'

'Please, just wait,' he said, holding up a hand. 'And as for what you said about him touching you, I got back just a minute or so after you came home with the kids last week. I could see you'd found Joel in the kitchen, so instead of coming straight inside I watched the two of you talking through the window.'

'You *spied* on me?'

'I could see the conversation was tense and that you were upset. But I never saw him touch you. He didn't touch you, Stacey.'

'You're saying I'm lying?' she breathed.

'The only reason I'm not furious with you about how you treated Joel and Morwenna last night is because I think you're unwell,' he said. 'The way you're behaving towards Joel, and how you keep drinking and shutting me out, it's scaring me.' His voice cracked. '*Do* you have feelings for him? Is that what this is? Or do you truly believe what you're saying to me? Do you think he's behind all of this?'

'He *is* behind all of this!'

Grant's face crumpled, and a yawning horror began to spread through Stacey's body.

He really thinks I'm ill.

'You believe what you want,' she said, words tumbling out as tears blinded her. 'You go and have fun with your new best mate.

If the word of your own wife isn't good enough, then fine. Invite him to the house. Invite him for dinner. Why don't you invite him right now, if you care so little about what I feel? Just do what you want. I don't even care any more.'

Grant's face was white, his eyes edging towards the door.

'He's here right now, isn't he?'

'Stacey, stop,' Grant said as she leapt out of bed. 'He just came to sign some papers. Stay in here and rest, he'll be gone in a minute…' He took hold of her by the shoulders, but she shook him away and tore down the stairs.

Joel was on his feet as soon as she burst into the room, holding his hands out in front of him as if he feared she would physically attack him. Shoving him out of the way, she made for the table, where papers were spread out. She grabbed them and started to tear them in half, and Joel made no move to stop her. Eventually she burnt herself out and stared down at the wreckage, before something caught her eye. It was the page of the contract that Joel had signed, and she stared at the writing. Apart from the zigzag that formed Joel's signature, his name and address were written by her husband. Grant tried to take her arm and she shook him away roughly. An image of the handwritten message on a page of *Two Lost Souls* – when she'd found the book torn apart in her room at the retreat – flashed through her mind: TELL THE TRUTH, the words said, though it had been hard to read the letters. Back then she'd assumed it was an attempt by Kirkbride to conceal their identity, in case she witnessed their usual handwriting, but now a startling idea began to nag at her, strengthened as she looked up and met Joel's eyes.

'Stacey…' he started.

'You can't write,' she said in amazement. Could it really be true? But there was no doubt in her mind; the look on his face said it all.

Chapter 27

'Are you still thinking about it?' Morwenna asked. They'd walked down to the cliffs not far from her dad's cottage, enjoying a stroll to work off all the food they'd eaten the previous day. Joel turned and smiled at her. It was the first Christmas in years that he'd not spent alone, and as he looked at Morwenna, wrapped up in a winter coat, her earrings shaped like Christmas trees blowing about in the breeze, he felt such a rush of love that he put his arm around her and squeezed her close.

What on earth am I doing? Who am I trying to fool? He loved Morwenna. He liked Grant. He enjoyed his new life. At Stacey's revelation he'd been relieved. He didn't want to hide any more than he had to from the people he cared about. He wished he didn't have to hide anything at all.

'Thinking about what?' he asked, though he knew full well.

'About Stacey. I know you're trying to play it down, but the way she attacked you over your dysgraphia, it was horrendous. She upset you so much that you collapsed *again*. I'm… I'm absolutely furious with her for how she's treating you! She's making you ill! I don't know what the hell is going on in her head.'

If you faint, you die. He shoved the thought aside, his skin prickling uncomfortably. Stacey had gone berserk, screaming at him that he couldn't possibly have written a book, while Grant had watched her performance in astonishment, with no idea what she was talking about.

'I wish you'd told me about the dysgraphia,' Morwenna continued. 'And Grant as well. I don't know how I didn't realise.'

'Well, handwriting is virtually obsolete,' he said. There had never been a time he'd needed to do it in front of her. He also avoided any kind of typing when she would see him doing it. He *could* type, a little, but the letters would often come out in the wrong order, and it took him a long time. The notes he'd left for Stacey at the retreat had been typed and printed out at home in advance, ready to take with him. He could use speech-to-text to message people – and usually did – but for situations where he couldn't, predicative text, AI and spellcheckers were a godsend. Longer writing tasks were a challenge. It had been draining to churn out the harassing emails he used to set Stacey up. But as for writing a book, well, that felt entirely out of reach. Getting his ideas out of his head and into written words – eighty thousand written words, since that was the length of *The Darkest of Paths* – was a completely overwhelming prospect. But then, he'd never told Stacey that *he* had written *The Darkest of Paths*. He'd said J. M. Kirkbride had written it, and that was true. He was half of J. M. Kirkbride, but not the writing half. The inspiration half.

He sighed. Stacey had called and messaged him many times since she'd realised the truth, but he'd ignored her. Let her stew in her own juices, at least for the moment. Besides, it had thrown him, now she'd realised he hadn't written it. It had put him on the back foot because no matter how much he turned it over in his mind, he simply couldn't understand how Stacey had got hold of the manuscript in the first place.

'I just told Grant my handwriting was too untidy for me to fill in any important forms,' he said to Morwenna. 'It's not untrue. That's what I usually say, not that it comes up often nowadays.'

'Well, you don't need to hide anything,' Morwenna said. 'Not from me, or Grant.' She shook her head, her face clouding again. 'I don't know if I can ever get past what Stacey has done. She won't back down, and the stuff she says doesn't even make sense. It's ridiculous.'

Joel focussed on watching the waves, unable to meet her eye as a tight ball of discomfort formed inside him.

I hate doing this stuff. I hate lying to Morwenna. He was still hiding nearly everything from her. He longed to spill it out, to tell her the truth about all of it, but he couldn't. It wasn't just about him. It was about what was right. It was about getting justice. Surely it wouldn't take much more for Stacey to crack and post a confession online to make him stop. Her friendship with Morwenna was already damaged, possibly beyond repair, and though Grant was standing by Stacey, convinced she was unwell, he might feel differently if he saw the video of her chucking a paperweight at Dante's head. He wouldn't share that yet, though. He'd keep the video to himself for the time being, leave the threat of it hanging over her.

Morwenna rested her head on his shoulder and brought him back to the present. 'We should probably get back to Dad,' she said.

'And carry on working through all the strange bottles in the drinks cabinet?' he suggested.

'*And* the old board games,' Morwenna said. 'Need to make the most of it – I've got to be back at Tiny Town in a couple of days.'

The last light was fading as they made it back to the cottage, and as soon as they stepped inside it was somehow different. Morwenna called out a cheery greeting but received no reply, and when Joel followed her into the living room, they found that her dad had died peacefully on his recliner in front of the merrily crackling fire, looking for all the world as if he had just fallen asleep.

Chapter 28

Marigold looked around the dilapidated vegetable garden and turned back to him, slightly bewildered. 'You really used to grow all of your family's fruit and veg here?'

'Well, not me by myself,' he said. 'I helped my mum with it, and dad too, though he mostly worked on the holiday cottages the other side of the river so we could start renting them out. We still have chickens and a few vegetables, but it's up near the house now. I don't think my dad can face coming down here.'

In fact, it was a part of the garden Carl tended to avoid as well. Initially, knowing how much his mum had loved it, he'd tried to look after it himself with the help of books about growing produce, and memories of jobs he'd done with his mum. But it had been an impossible task for a boy not even ten years old. Gradually weeds had taken hold, and the garden had run wild. The greenhouse which used to be full of tomatoes, peppers, chillies and basil had lain empty for years, and the shed where the tools were kept was sad and weather beaten. He felt like he'd failed. Not just the garden, but his mum, because she'd be so sad to see it in such a state. If he hadn't had Marigold by his side he would have turned and fled, but she was holding his hand tight, and he forced himself to stay. 'My parents used the cycle of the moon to know when to plant and sow things,' he said.

'They did what?'

He turned to her, though he wasn't surprised she didn't know what he was talking about. He'd learnt the hard way – especially from the times he had ventured into school – that his upbringing was so far removed from other people's that half the time they didn't know what he was going on about.

'You must really miss her,' Marigold said, before quickly adding. 'That was a daft thing to say. Of course you do.'

'I miss her most when I'm here in this veg garden,' he said. 'This is where it's most obvious she's gone. But in the rest of the garden I'm not so bad. She liked everywhere to be pretty wild, so when I walk around it's like she could be

just around the corner. I think she's still here, in some ways. I don't think she entirely left.'

'Well, I don't want to leave you, either,' she said, her voice strong. 'I don't want to go to uni. I want to stay here with you.'

Carl was quiet for a time. 'Can we talk somewhere else?' he said finally. 'I don't want to be here anymore.'

She nodded and they quickly slipped away, skirting a huge bramble bush that tried to grab at their legs with its thorny stems—

His phone pealed, breaking him away from the pages of *Two Lost Souls,* and he glanced at the screen to see Stacey's name. He quickly rejected her call, but before he could pick the book back up, Morwenna padded into the living room, snuggling up beside him on the sofa. Joel loved having Morwenna in his home with him all the time now. She'd moved in after Christmas, and though she'd struggled since her dad's death, she'd distracted herself by making the place look more homely; a huge, boldly patterned rug now graced the polished concrete floor, and many of the ornaments from her father's house now occupied various surfaces, especially the brightly coloured ceramics her mum had loved.

'Couldn't sleep?' he said as he kissed her forehead. She'd gone to bed early, while he'd stayed on the sofa in front of the gradually dwindling fire in the log burner, dipping in and out of reading *Two Lost Souls.*

'I'm going for a dress fitting tomorrow,' she said, 'but I feel weird about it.' She fixed her eyes on him. 'I keep wondering if we should postpone. Dad's funeral was only a couple of weeks ago and my head is still a mess half the time, can we really get married in just four months?'

'We don't have to,' he told her softly. 'We can do whatever you want to do.'

Morwenna sat up abruptly. 'That's just it,' she said. 'That's the problem! I don't *want* to decide. I want somebody to tell me what to do.' She put her head in her hands and Joel watched her for a moment. 'I… look, your dad wanted you to be happy. You know he kept talking about the wedding, and I truly believe he would want us to go ahead.'

'You do?'

'But,' he added, 'he also would want you to enjoy it, and if you feel like it will be too soon for you to do that, it's okay. There's no rush, is there?'

Morwenna gestured at the book beside him on the sofa. 'That's the other thing,' she said. 'I asked Stacey if she'd come to the dress fitting with me. It was supposed to be an olive branch, though God knows she's the one who should be making the first move after how she's behaved, but she's being so weird with me. Right when I could really do with some support from her. She's so…' she made a noise of irritation. 'I don't know what it is. Self-obsessed? Selfish? Or she just plain doesn't care. She doesn't seem sorry for anything she's done. Grant thinks she's having a mental health crisis, but…'

'You don't think so?'

'Oh, I don't know,' she said wearily. 'Perhaps she *is* having real problems, in which case I should be doing more for her than inviting her to dress fittings. But how am I supposed to know what's going on in her head? All I know is that she's hurt me. A lot.'

'I don't know what Stacey was like before,' he said quickly, keen to reassure Morwenna, 'so I can't make a comparison, but it seems to me like she's been caught out and now she's trying to get Grant's sympathy any way she can.'

'Exactly!' Morwenna said. 'That's how it seems to me.' She breathed a sigh. 'I don't *want* her to be ill, of course I don't, but at the same time, at least that would mean she was still the person I thought I knew. Otherwise, who is she? Was she ever really my friend? To treat *you* the way she has and then barely say two words to me after my dad dying, it's not right – she can't have ever really liked me. I'm angry for letting myself get so wound up by her! If she doesn't give a damn, why should I be up at night worrying about *her?*'

'You shouldn't. You've been too forgiving already,' he said, with a flash of triumph. Stacey didn't deserve to have such a loyal friend.

Morwenna gazed at him intently, eyes reflecting the soft glow of the remaining flames. 'I don't know what I'd do without you,' she said.

...

After they'd made love, Morwenna fell deeply asleep with her head in his lap, and he pulled a blanket over her. After a few moments he picked up *Two Lost Souls* and flicked to a different section.

'What the hell did you think you were doing, boy?' his dad's face was an alarming shade, and Carl reached up to his lip, where pain had exploded.

He stared in horror at the blood on his fingers. His dad had hit him hard enough to make him bleed!

Howard stepped back from them, shock at what he had done clear to see on his face, which was becoming less puce by the second. Marigold was hastily smoothing down the skirt that had been pushed up around her waist, before grabbing her t-shirt from where it was discarded on the grass and pulling it over her head. Carl quickly stepped between her and his father. His dad could say what he wanted to him, but he wouldn't let him upset Mari.

'I love her,' he told Howard, his voice strong.

'Love?' Howard said, as if he'd never heard the word before. He pulled Carl towards him. 'That's not love. That's just fucking.'

Marigold stood beside him, and she took his hand.

'No son of mine is having anything to do with the niece of that bloody maniac next door!' Howard said. 'You know full well—'

'About the boundary,' Carl said. 'Yes, I know.' His lip hurt like hell, and he felt sick. He couldn't believe his dad had seen him on top of Marigold; his bare backside, Marigold's legs wrapped around him.

'I'm going to build a fence,' his dad said, 'and you and her are staying on separate sides of it. You are not seeing this girl again.'

Joel sighed and put the book down. It was no use burying himself in his past when the present was such a mess. Usually, he deleted messages from Stacey unopened, but tonight he decided he would listen to the voicemail she had left. As her loud, high-pitched voice filled his ear he sat bolt upright, making Morwenna stir and moan in her sleep. 'Shit,' he said under his breath as he quickly deleted her message. 'Shit, shit, shit.' He stared down at Morwenna, but Stacey's words still filled his head.

You're dying, aren't you Joel? The fainting – you've got what your mum had, just like in the book. And you need to tell Morwenna, or I will.

Chapter 29

'Do I really have to go?' Stacey asked, as she stood in front of the mirror doing her makeup.

'Yes!' Grant's voice reached her from the bedroom. 'My mum's already agreed to take the kids for the day. And anyway, how will it look if you're not there?'

He came to join her in the ensuite, running his hand around her waist, and she tried not to stiffen as he kissed her neck. He and Joel had decided to hold a swanky event to launch their show flat and try to get some interest from buyers. He was expecting it to be busy, and despite her protests, he was keen for her to be there. She breathed a sigh of relief when Grant went back into the bedroom to finish getting dressed. The effort of trying to hide her true feelings about anything involving Joel was exhausting. Her heart sank as he continued talking. 'Joel is bringing Morwenna, so you and her can finally clear the air.'

Stacey accidentally stabbed herself in the eye with the mascara wand and swore.

'What did you say?'

'I said, "great",' she lied.

'Look, I know you don't want to see Joel,' he said as he appeared in the doorway, doing up his shirt, 'but this project is as much his as it is mine. He deserves to be there to see it all coming to fruition. It wouldn't surprise me if most of the flats get reserved today, there's been so much interest. And anyway, you've not mentioned him for weeks now. Whatever was upsetting you around Christmas, you're past that now, aren't you?' A pleading tone entered his voice, anxiety creasing his forehead. He was so worried about her, so desperate for her to be okay, and it tore at her heart. It also trapped her in an impossible position – anything negative she said about Joel simply made him think she was having a relapse, but keeping silent meant Joel could continue with his schemes unchecked.

Stacey gritted her teeth to stop herself arguing with him. It was disgusting, the way Joel was ignoring her, and even more disgusting was the way he was treating Morwenna. Letting her friend think she was going to get a happy-ever-after when she was really going to end up a widow. And that was if he even made it to the wedding at all. The man was nothing but a selfish liar, yet he had the audacity to bang on about how important the truth was. He hadn't written the book – he'd clearly paid some unacknowledged ghostwriter to do it for him – and he wasn't being honest with his own fiancée. He could hardly claim to have the moral high ground. Worst of all, now he'd turned Morwenna against her, Stacey would struggle to get her friend to believe her about Joel's illness. But she had to try. She couldn't let her walk blindly into getting her heart broken.

Grant disappeared off downstairs and Stacey leaned close to the mirror to apply a coat of lip gloss. *You're not getting away with this, Joel,* she whispered, but then she paused, staring at her reflection. The "M" in J. M. Kirkbride. He hadn't used a ghostwriter – *Marigold* had written it. *That* was why Joel would never quit. This fixation he had was because she'd stolen the life's work of somebody who could never fight back. Joel had loved Marigold. He'd loved her enough to start this vendetta, and he wouldn't stop until he'd got what he wanted. Of course he'd do anything to make her confess, or he would – probably really would, in fact – die trying.

Stacey smoothed back a couple of stray hairs with shaking hands. It made no difference to what she was going to do. Marigold was gone and soon Joel would be – no matter how tragic it was, it couldn't be changed. She just had to make sure that she warned Morwenna exactly what kind of future – or lack of it – she could expect with her husband-to-be.

...

The show apartment was impressive. Being on the top floor gave it beautiful views, and the generously sized living space had lovely old beams and an exposed brick wall. The remaining décor was a cool white and a few elegant palms in pots complemented the neutral furniture. The kitchen had granite worktops with shiny new appliances and was clearly to be the focal point of the gathering; champagne glasses were laid out, and Joel was placing down a pile of forms and pens.

'I know Marigold wrote the book,' Stacey said quietly.

He stiffened in surprise, but then just said, 'Then you know why it's so important to me.'

'Where's Morwenna?'

'She's gone to get some orange juice. For the people who don't want to drink,' he added unnecessarily.

'She'll be back soon, then.'

'Look, I don't want any trouble. Not today. And I suggest that you leave Wenna alone. She's been upset enough by things you've done.'

Stacey glanced round at him as she straightened up the rows of glasses. 'Oh, there'll be trouble,' she said. 'As soon as this open day is over, I'm telling Morwenna you're ill, and there's nothing you can do to stop me.'

'Stacey?' Suddenly Grant was beside her, hovering nervously, so she gave him an innocent smile. 'I was just saying what a great job you've done. It's beautiful in here.'

Satisfied that she wasn't about to have a meltdown over his business partner, Grant dashed off to carry on with last minute preparations and Stacey stepped closer to Joel. 'I'm telling Wenna what's going to happen to you,' she said. 'She needs to know.'

...

The next couple of hours were too busy for Stacey – tasked with doling out drinks – to catch her breath, let alone say anything further to Joel or to Morwenna, but as the stream of potential buyers petered out, Stacey poured herself a glass of champagne and sat on a stool at the breakfast bar to sip it and steady her nerves for the awful task that lay ahead. Morwenna was laughing happily as she chatted with Grant and Joel, blissful in her ignorance. *If I tell her the truth about his illness I'm going to crush her.* She rubbed at her temples. *It's not my fault.* Joel should have told her the truth weeks, *months* ago. He should never have let things go so far.

Slipping down from the bar stool, Stacey drew in a deep lungful of air. The group had stopped laughing now, and instead Grant and Morwenna were looking at something on their phones. She let her breath out slowly. It was now or never.

'Wenna?' she said, as she made her way towards the group. 'Could I talk to you for a moment?'

But instead of Morwenna it was Grant who turned to her, holding his phone out and saying, 'What on earth is this?'

Stacey was about to bat his hand away, when the social media post on his screen registered with her. Dante had posted it to her author page; a photo of the black eye she'd given him back at the retreat, alongside a photo of her in her room when it had been full of the torn book pages. Horror engulfed her as her eyes fell on the photo of his bruises. *I did that to him. I could have killed him, for God's sake!* She scanned through what he'd written – which was essentially an exposé of how she'd behaved at the retreat. How she'd been "out of control" and "attention seeking". *It's all true though. It's exactly what happened!* It became clear as she read on why he had written it now, even though so many months had passed, as he mentioned the title of his new book a few times. But she soon reached the most damning part of his post, where he had outlined her meltdown in the library in lurid detail.

'Is it true?' Grant was asking her as she read the words. 'Did you really throw a paperweight at this man's head?'

Instead of her husband she looked up at Joel, and in his eyes was a dull glint of satisfaction.

Chapter 30

'Why would Dante say it if it wasn't true?' Grant pressed her, as Joel and Morwenna quietly got on with clearing up the show flat to give them a bit of space to talk.

'Because he's trying to sell his book!' she said in a panic. 'He's using my name to get himself some attention, that's all it is.' Fresh guilt bloomed inside her at the lies spilling from her lips. She'd denied everything, but what else was she to do? How could she explain why she'd attacked Dante? Would Grant really buy it if she said it was part of the breakdown he believed she was having – and did she really want him to think she was that unstable?

Her reasoning did, at least, make Grant pause, while she deleted the post Dante had made on her profile. Unfortunately, it had already been up for a few hours, so a lot of people had seen what he said. And there was nothing she could do about what he'd posted on his own social media – though thankfully he had far fewer followers than she did. Her cheeks were burning with shame, and fear spread through her in jittery waves. *I assaulted him. Will people believe him?* Would Joel share the video he had of her attacking Dante? No. If he was going to do that, he'd have done it, surely? People would dismiss Dante's claims as nothing more than bizarre self-promotion. It would be okay. It would.

'But there's a photo of his bruising,' Grant said at length. 'And you are *in* that photo with your book torn to pieces, you can't deny that happened.' His face was full of pain. 'Just tell me the truth. What went on at the retreat? You never explained why you were so upset there.'

Spotting out of the corner of her eye that Morwenna and Joel were about to leave, Stacey dashed over to them. 'Morwenna,' she said desperately, as her friend pulled on her jacket. 'You have to listen to me about Joel.'

'Oh, will you just stop about Joel?' Morwenna cried, taking Stacey aback at the emotion in her voice. 'I can't do it, Stacey. I can't. Please… just leave me alone.'

'Come on,' Joel said, taking Morwenna's arm. 'Let's go home.'

'No, you don't,' Stacey said. 'You don't get to walk away. Was this you? Did you *tell* Dante to write this to stop me talking to Morwenna?'

'Me?' he said wide-eyed, taking a step backwards. 'What are you—'

'Stacey, please,' Grant said, 'let's go home and talk about this calmly.'

'Oh, I'm calm,' she said, taking out her phone, 'I'll be very *calm* when I show you that Joel was *at* that retreat!'

Jabbing at her phone screen she opened up the profile of the writing retreat and scrolled back through months of social media posts, while Joel, Morwenna and Grant looked on helplessly. 'Here!' she said triumphantly as she found what she was looking for. 'This is us…' her words trailed off as she stared at the screen. There were various photos of them all; writing in their notebooks in the garden, mostly, but none of Joel.

'Joel isn't in any of these photos,' Grant said.

Her mind raced. 'They asked us,' she said slowly. 'They checked if we minded our photos being put on their social media. Joel must have told them not to! He must have… I'll look on the other writer's profiles. Someone will have pictures from the retreat. I'll message them all right now; they'll tell you that Joel was there.'

Typing furiously, she ignored Grant saying to Joel and Morwenna they should go home and not to worry. They'd all feel differently when she proved Joel had been at the retreat. Never mind the fact he'd try and explain why he'd been there – they'd be so horrified by his lies that perhaps they wouldn't even listen to him going on about *Two Lost Souls.* Besides, this had gone way beyond the book, now. He was playing with people's lives, with their futures and their happiness.

I have to get rid of him. I have to make this end!

'Stacey, stop!' Grant said, grabbing her arm just as she pressed Send. 'Did you attack Dante? Yes or no. I'm not angry, I only want to understand. I know you wouldn't throw something at him for no reason—' his eyes suddenly filled with emotion as an idea occurred to him. 'Did he… did he do something to you? This… Dante – is that why you attacked him, because he hurt you? Is that why you've been so down?'

'I'm down because of him!' she said, stabbing her finger towards Joel, who had his arm around Morwenna as the pair hovered in the doorway. 'But what's the point in telling you the truth about anything? I *told* you Joel sent those emails to himself. I'm telling you he was at the retreat—'

'He can't fucking write!' Grant exploded, before turning to his friend and muttering, 'sorry, Joel.' Then his eyes were back on her, filled with desperation. 'Please, will you listen to reason? He has said himself that he finds it difficult to write even a sentence or two. He couldn't have written that quantity of emails. And why on earth would he go to a *writing* retreat? The stuff you're saying is insane, Stacey. It's insane.'

'Don't be so naïve. There's all sorts of ways he could have got those emails written!'

A silence met this statement, making it clear they weren't interested in a word she said, and she saw red. 'Forget it,' she shouted. 'I told you how much he scares me, and you don't listen to me about that, so why would you listen to me about anything else? Joel was at the retreat, I'm telling the truth. He was torturing me, Grant, he still is – making me look crazy, and you're letting him win!' Her mind was racing, and she wobbled on her feet, clutching at her chest as she gasped for air.

I have to get rid of him. I have to. I have to!

'Stacey?' Grant said, 'Stacey, are you okay?'

'I think she's having a panic attack,' Morwenna said, stepping back inside the flat, her voice suddenly all concern. 'Come on, Stacey, let's get you sat down…'

Pushing Morwenna away as her phone chimed, she quickly looked at it, expecting to finally be able to prove that Joel had been at the retreat. Sure enough, Charlotte had seen her message and replied. 'Here, you see…' she choked out to Grant and Morwenna, but her words trailed off in a sob as she read the message, and the phone dropped from her hand.

Please don't contact me. None of us want to speak to you.

…

'I don't understand,' she said. 'I asked them if Joel Shakespeare was at the retreat. All they have to do is say "yes"!'

She'd not received a single other reply. Grant placed a bowl of chicken soup down in front of her and she shoved it away, a little of the liquid slopping over the edge onto the dining table. 'I don't need soup,' she said. 'I'm not ill.'

'Well…' he started, as he sat down opposite her, 'you clearly weren't feeling okay about things when you tore your book up at the retreat. And Stacey, you had a panic attack after reading Dante's post earlier. I was so scared. I've never seen you like that.'

'I had a panic attack because nobody will listen to me about Joel!' she threw at him, trying to forget the awful moments back at the show flat. Grant had almost been in tears trying to calm her down, but Morwenna had taken charge, kneeling in front of her when Stacey's knees had buckled, holding her hands and getting her to breathe slowly in and out, until her desperate gasps for air had turned into hopeless sobs.

He reached out for her hand. 'Stacey, I know to take what Dante said with a pinch of salt. It didn't take more than a few minutes of reading the kind of crap that man posts online to realise what he says is nonsense at best and, well, dangerous nonsense at worst, but that stuff with the book pages happened. And saying that Joel was at the writing retreat… it makes me think that you're—'

'What? Psychotic? Delusional?' Panic was engulfing her again. Morwenna would never believe her about Joel's illness – not until the moment he dropped dead, anyway. She had no chance of protecting her friend, if Morwenna even was still her friend, and Grant thought she'd lost touch with reality entirely.

I'll confess, she thought suddenly. *I'll do it. But I won't keep his name out of it, I'll tell everyone he's half of J. M. Kirkbride! I'll expose him for the liar he is, even if I have to drag myself down to do it.* Yes, she'd destroy her own reputation, but she'd destroy Joel's too. Grant and Morwenna would be disgusted with how he had deceived them both. But the second the idea popped into her mind it immediately died again.

I can't confess. I can never confess.

Grant shook his head. 'Just tell me you know none of this has anything to do with Joel. *Please.* You know it doesn't. Joel is just Morwenna's fiancé and my business partner. That's it. He's not messing with you; he's not trying to upset you or hurt you – he's not interested in you at all!'

At that moment they both jumped at the sound of the doorbell. 'I'll deal with it,' he told her. 'You stay here and try to eat. It'll do you good, you'll see.'

Stacey pulled the bowl of soup back towards her, but Grant's voice drifted to her from the hall. 'You can't be here,' he said, making it obvious who was outside. She leapt to her feet.

'What did you do?' Stacey yelled at Joel as she burst into the hall. 'Why won't they speak to me?'

'Who?' he asked innocently.

'The writers! Have you *told* them not to talk to me? Did you guess I'd try and contact them after you told Dante he should post all that stuff about me?'

'Uh… I should go,' Joel said. 'I just came to give you the reservation forms from earlier, Grant. I thought you might need them. And Stacey, Wenna isn't angry with you any more – she could see how hard you were finding things earlier, and she just wants you to be okay. We're both here for you, you know that—'

At his cloying, insincere words, Stacey let out a scream and ran into the kitchen. Before she knew what she was doing she'd seized a knife from the magnetic rack on the wall. Her head filled with buzzing and back in the hall she pointed the knife at Joel. 'Admit what you're doing to me,' she said. 'Admit it now!'

Joel put his hands up and backed away from her. 'Stacey, I'm sorry I've upset you so much.'

'Tell the truth! Tell Grant that you know me and that you're trying to ruin my life.'

His eyes fixed on hers. 'But, why Stacey? *Why* would I want to ruin your life? It doesn't make any sense.' His words dripped with meaning. *Confess.* She could practically hear him willing her to do it. To come clean and make it all go away. But she wouldn't confess. Not now, not ever.

'Get out of my life!' she screeched, taking a swipe at him with the blade. Grant stepped in front of her, and to her horror it caught his arm, making a slash through his skin from which blood started to seep. She opened her fingers and let the knife clatter to the floor. 'No,' she said. 'No, Grant, I didn't mean to do that. I didn't mean to…'

He was ushering Joel out of the house, and, seemingly oblivious to his wound, he put his arms around her.

'Your arm,' she said, 'you're bleeding.'

'I'll be okay. And *you'll* be okay, Stacey. You're not well right now, that's all. But we're here for you. All of us are. Let me look after you.'

Chapter 31

Stacey woke groggily from a nap to the sound of voices in the hall. 'Thank you for picking the kids up and keeping them entertained,' Grant was saying. 'I really appreciate it.'

'It was no problem at all.' Morwenna replied. 'We took them to the park, played some football—'

'Joel is so fun!' Ava interrupted excitedly. 'Can we see him again tomorrow?'

'I'm glad you enjoyed yourselves,' Grant said quickly, clearly fearing Stacey could overhear the conversation. As if she didn't realise how much the kids loved Joel. Since her "crisis" as Grant insisted on calling it, Morwenna and Joel had managed to become an indispensable source of help for Grant while his mum was away on a holiday-of-a-lifetime cruise for weeks. Technically, of course, Stacey had little else occupying her time and could easily ferry Teddy and Ava about herself, but for the past couple of months she'd barely been able to bring herself to do anything, as hopelessness engulfed her and sapped every ounce of energy.

'Your meds will kick in soon and you'll feel a lot better,' Grant had told her just the previous night. She'd nodded, though no pills were going to make any difference to the nagging, clawing feeling of guilt inside her, and she turned over and over in her mind how she could end the whole thing once and for all.

Why don't I just post a bloody confession video like Joel wants me to? The question haunted her. *Make this whole, horrible thing come to an end. Can it really be worse than carrying on as things are?*

But it was too late. If she'd confessed that day in the park – the day she'd been on the verge of doing so – it would have been okay. Well, not *okay,* but far better than it would be now. Now, everything was beyond awful. Now, her life was a shadow of what it had once been, and the knowledge that Joel would die and leave Morwenna bereft – yet there wasn't a single thing she could do to warn her – broke her heart. No matter how she'd wronged him by stealing the book, what Joel was doing was wrong, too. Already he and Grant were planning ahead to their next project together, while the day Morwenna would marry him grew disturbingly close, and he carried on pretending everything was fine. *He's a coward!* Why wouldn't he admit to anybody that he was ill? Why wouldn't he take some responsibility for what he was doing?

'I don't suppose Stacey's about?' Morwenna's words cut through her dark musings. 'I'd love to see her. I'm not angry with her about anything that's happened with Joel, if that's what she's concerned about. I know none of this is her fault.'

'Stacey?' Grant called.

Instead of replying, Stacey pulled her fluffy blanket right up over her head and squeezed her eyes tight shut.

...

'So, you've really done it then?' Stacey said. 'You're completely finished?'

'We are.'

Stacey tried to smile and be happy for him. After Grant had shown her and the children the completed warehouse flats – the building looking particularly smart now that small bushes and neat parking spaces filled the ground that had been muddy building site for what felt like forever – they'd gone out for a meal in a nearby restaurant to celebrate his achievement. With the promise of the sales soon completing and money flooding in, Grant was fizzing with excitement, while she was struggling to swallow a single mouthful of her salad. Since Grant was oblivious to her distress, Stacey focused on wiping pizza sauce from Ava's chin, while Teddy eagerly perused the options for dessert on the children's menu.

'There's something else to celebrate as well,' Grant said.

'Oh?' she looked up at him. It was as if she had a sixth sense for the word "Joel", and knew it was coming before he even spoke.

'Joel asked me to be his best man at the wedding.'

Stacey's fork clattered down against her plate and at that moment she felt her phone vibrate. A message from the number Joel had used all those long months ago to contact her at the retreat – the phone that had apparently been off ever since.

Meet me by Currant Affairs in 5 minutes.

…

'I've got nothing to say to you,' she told him, her voice shaking. She'd managed to contain her emotions long enough to make it around the corner to the – thankfully deserted – street outside Currant Affairs; the bakery all closed up and quiet for the night, but now coming face to face with him, any composure she had crumbled.

I can't take any more of this. I can't take another day. He'd tied her up in knots, trapped her in a nightmare where whatever she did the outcome would be a disaster.

'Well, I've got plenty to say to *you,* he replied, as he pulled her down an alleyway to the side of the building, forcing her to skirt around a pile of bin bags with a disconcerting puddle beneath it. Lit only by the small amount of streetlight making it through, the alleyway was dank and narrow, buildings either side looming over their heads.

'Get off me!' she said, shaking her arm loose. 'If you touch me again, I'll scream.'

'Yes, of course you will, because it's always about you, isn't it?' he said. 'Grant told me earlier how you'd all be out tonight, celebrating. You know Wenna is beside herself because of you? Distraught that you wouldn't speak to her when she dropped the kids back at yours. I tell her not to waste her time on you, but she's too kind for her own good. You are worrying Grant and Wenna half to death with your so-called breakdown and seemingly loving every minute of it—'

'I am not loving any minute of anything!' she cried. 'I hate my life. I'm in a living hell, and it's all your fault!'

'My fault? You've had chance after chance after chance to confess. I told you how bad things would get if you didn't, and you *chose* to stay silent. That is not my fault, Stacey. And you say you're in hell, but I don't believe that. If you were in hell, you'd confess you stole the book, and you seem in no rush to do that. Instead, you're content to have everyone running around after you, keeping things going, while you sit and wallow.'

Sagging against the wall, Stacey accidentally put her foot in the puddle around the bin bags but could barely bring herself to care. To her surprise, Joel's face softened. 'I don't enjoy any of this, you know. I don't like making people suffer, not even you.'

'Then don't do it any more!' Stacey said, surging forward and grabbing hold of him by his jacket. 'Please, Joel. Forget about the book and focus on Morwenna. Tell her about your health! Knowing she's going to have her heart broken cuts me up inside – and knowing she'll have no warning what's coming…'

Joel stepped back from her, extricating his jacket from her clutches. 'Perhaps it's kinder if she doesn't know.'

'You're not serious.'

Rubbing his face with his hands, his eyes grew harsher again, as if the reminder of his own mortality strengthened his resolve to get "justice". 'I'm giving you one last chance,' he said.

Stacey watched him silently. His face was drawn, hair untidy like he'd been pulling his hands through it. His obsession was destroying him. It was destroying them both. Why wouldn't he give up? Why wouldn't he drop it, for God's sake, instead of tearing her world apart over a book?

'Where does Morwenna think you are?' she asked, instead of answering his threat.

'She's on a spa evening with a friend.'

'Did you know you had your mother's illness when you started seeing her?' she pressed him.

He switched his weight from one foot to the other and didn't answer her directly. 'If you're thinking that waiting for me to die means no one will ever find out what you did, you're mistaken. If I die before you confess, Morwenna and Grant will get a recording from me explaining how you stole *Two Lost Souls* from Marigold. Not as good as the public confession I've asked you for, but it will do, if it comes to that. Like I said, it's your last chance. Everything is in place now. In a matter of weeks, I can take it all. Everything you care about.'

She closed her eyes for a second. It had already occurred to her that his death would get her off the hook, but with her friend caught up in it all she certainly hadn't hoped for it or looked forward to it happening.

Would I wish him dead, though, if it wasn't for Morwenna? Would I hope for him to be gone for good? She shook that thought away before it could take hold. She might wish to be rid of him, but not like *that.* Of course she didn't wish for his death, did she? She was a good person – a good person who had made one horrible mistake a long time ago. Wasn't she already paying the price for it? Hadn't she already been tortured enough? Joel apparently considered the conversation to be over, as he started to make his way past her towards the street.

She darted past the bin bags to catch up with him. 'What do you mean?' she asked him. 'What will you do?'

He was silent for a moment, the rain that had begun to fall settling in beads on his hair as he considered whether to answer her. Down the street, a sudden burst of laughter from a couple walking hand in hand startled her.

When did I last laugh? The way things were going, she'd likely never feel happy again.

'I can access the account that the cash from the flat sales will be paid into,' Joel said at length.

She froze.

'I know what a state Grant was in before I came,' he continued. 'He even remortgaged your home. If you don't confess, well, the money is going to disappear. That account will be emptied, and your husband will lose everything, even your house.'

She shook her head slowly, a deep pain starting inside her. 'You won't. You'll be caught.'

'I won't take the money *myself,'* he said. 'But there are plenty of scammers about pretending to be banks, getting people to do transfers. It would be *such* a shame if I fell victim to something like that.'

She gaped at him. 'You're crazy. You'd give all of Grant's money to *criminals*—'

Pulling in his breath through his teeth, he shook his head at her as if she was a naughty child. 'So, you *do* think stealing is wrong.'

'No!' she cried, as emotion overwhelmed her. 'You can't make me confess, Joel. I've told you what things are like for me! Confessing will tip me over the edge. I can't do it. My family need me, my *kids* need me, I can't carry on as a nervous wreck…' her words all caught in her throat, and she shook from head to toe, but if she expected any sympathy, she would soon be disappointed.

'That reminds me,' he continued, 'Teddy and Ava often say how worried they are about you. That you rarely do anything with them, and how you're always so tired and emotional.' He paused. 'Ava said she didn't want to go home after we took her and Teddy to the park this afternoon. She said she wanted to stay with me and Wenna. Not that big a leap for someone to get a bit concerned, is it? Maybe question how well you can care for those children? I mean, if they don't even want to go home *now*, what will it be like once everyone has seen the video of you attacking Dante, and Grant loses all his money? A violent mother and a household on the brink of bankruptcy, that's not a safe environment to bring up children, is it?'

With that, he walked away, leaving her staring after him with her heart hammering in her ears.

Chapter 32

Stacey shook her head and placed the book back down. The kids were in bed, while Grant was doing something with spreadsheets on the laptop downstairs, no doubt relishing the prospect of his columns and rows being in the black soon.

If that money disappears, it'll ruin him.

Had Joel been serious when he'd said that? Would he really destroy Grant's business when they were such good friends? When he'd asked him to be best man at his wedding? And as for what he'd said about Teddy and Ava…

Inspired by true events. Those words had been whirling around in her head – the words he'd said to her when she'd confronted him in the park before Christmas. Some of the book was real, like his mum's illness, but what else was true, and what was fiction? Marigold had died, that much was clear, but how? In the book, Hillcroft Manor had burned down, and the two teenagers lost their lives in the blaze. There *could* really have been a fire, but if so, Marigold must have lived long enough to write the book, though not long enough to reply to Stacey's emails about *The Darkest of Paths.*

She let out a long groan of frustration, picked up *Two Lost Souls* again, before quickly discarding it. There were no clues in those pages. If there were, she would have seen them by now. She sat bolt upright as more of his words from the day in the park flashed through her mind.

All I want is for you to post a video where you admit that Two Lost Souls was written by J. M. Kirkbride. No one needs to know who exactly that is. They just need to know that it is not you.

No one needs to know who that is. That sentiment had made sense when she'd believed the book was Joel's own work. *He* didn't want the drama. *He* liked his new life and didn't want to rock the boat. But why didn't he want people to know that J. M. Kirkbride was *Marigold*? Shouldn't he *want* that – for her to be acknowledged for the book she clearly wanted published? Why keep her name out of it? He'd still be able to avoid the drama either way, so why stop her getting the credit she was due?

Her phone rang, startling her. For a moment she was convinced it would be Joel, but Morwenna's voice filled her ear. 'Stacey, look, I know you haven't been feeling great, but it's been so long since I've seen you. Let's put everything behind us. I miss you.'

Stacey put the call on loudspeaker and lay back on her bed. Her mind was buzzing. She was on to something, she was sure of it.

'Stacey?' Morwenna pushed her.

'Yes, sorry, I heard you,' Stacey said. Joel's threats had made her mind more lucid than it had been in weeks, bolstered by a last, desperate need to save herself. She had to seize this moment of clarity. She needed to think about everything differently, go through all her conversations with Joel and piece together why the book held such power over him.

'Okay, well, would you and Grant like to come round for dinner one night?'

'Yeah,' Stacey said, seizing on the opportunity. Things about Joel's past didn't add up and this would be the perfect chance to ask him. She had to get answers, as soon as she could. 'How about tomorrow?'

...

'I'll help,' Stacey quickly volunteered as Joel started to clear the plates from the table. She followed him into the kitchen while Morwenna and Grant were discussing plans she had to completely redesign the bland back garden behind Joel's house. *Not just Joel's house. Her* house. Every reminder of how entwined her friend's life had become with Joel's was another stab in the heart. The web Joel had woven spread everywhere, consumed everything.

'Why don't you want anyone to know Marigold wrote the book?' Stacey said quietly as she placed the empty salad bowl down next to the plates by the sink. 'Why do you want me to say it was J. M. Kirkbride and leave it at that?' Grant and Morwenna were talking loudly in the dining room down the hall, but she didn't want to take any chances on them overhearing, so she kept her voice low.

Joel's head whipped around, but he simply said, 'I told you before I just want everyone to know it wasn't you.'

'Yes, I know what you said, but I don't think it's as simple as that.' She leaned close to him. 'You don't want anyone to know she wrote it because you're worried that it's going to tarnish her memory, and I want you to tell me why.'

Joel turned away from her and opened the oven, from which the scent of an apple pie drifted. 'It'll be a few more minutes,' he said.

She grabbed his arm to force him to look at her, but he couldn't meet her eye.

'Everything okay in here?' Morwenna stood in the doorway and Stacey turned to her guiltily, quickly releasing Joel's arm.

'Stacey was just grilling me about the wedding plans.'

'I see,' Morwenna said, smiling. 'Well, it's not long to wait now.' She opened the fridge to get a fresh bottle of wine and Stacey stared down at her glittering engagement ring. *You're going to be a widow.* The words hovered at the back of her throat.

'You'll come to my final dress fitting, won't you?' Morwenna asked. 'I'd really like you to be there.'

'Uh… yeah,' Stacey said, digging her nails into her palm to keep her voice steady. 'Yes, I will.'

Morwenna left them and Stacey rounded on Joel. 'What happened back then between you and Marigold? I mean the truth, not whatever version of it ended up in the book. I can't deal with the lies any more – you need to tell me exactly what went on, right now, or believe me, I'll find out some other way.'

Joel began to rinse off their dinner plates before slotting them into the dishwasher, acting as if she hadn't spoken.

'Joel!' Stacey insisted. Was he seriously going to ignore her?

Now it was Grant's turn to interrupt them, calling from the hall, 'We're just going outside for a second,' before the door closed behind him.

Her eyes slipped to the window, where Grant and Morwenna soon came into view, striding across to the back corner of the garden. Her friend started gesturing around as she explained her grand vision – occasionally flipping through an A4 notebook she'd carried out with her and pointing at the pages, where she must have written down her ideas.

'She's settling in well, then,' Stacey said, the words like acid in her mouth.

'It's her home as much as mine.'

Finishing the dishwasher, Joel opened the oven and started faffing about with the pie and Stacey exploded, 'Then focus on *her*. I know there's no point in me trying to tell Wenna that you're ill because no one believes a word I say about you, but I *will* keep on digging up dirt on your past. I'll work out exactly what went on, because I don't think you want anyone to discover the truth, do you?'

'I'm not listening to this.' He tried to step past her, swaying a little on his feet, but she moved into his path to continue firing questions at him, fuelled by desperation. 'What are you scared of? Why don't you want Marigold's name linked to the book? What are you so worried everyone will discover? How did she die, Joel? What happened to her? Was it your fault? And what did your mum die from, anyway? The book never says. Do you even *know*?' It seemed impossible he couldn't know, but then, he had such a na ivety about him sometimes, as if he had no idea how the real world worked at all.

Before she could press him any further, the colour drained from his face, and he crumpled before her eyes. She tried to grab him, but his head made a sick thud as it hit the oven door, and he slumped to the ground.

'Joel?' she said, crouching down beside him. She shook him, but he didn't open his eyes, and blood began to trickle from the back of his head.

Chapter 33

Joel's eyes opened and he looked around him woozily. Where on earth was he? At a small sound beside him he turned and began to reach out his hand for Morwenna but quickly withdrew it when Stacey's face filled his vision.

'Where's Wenna?' he asked, his voice hoarse. What the hell was going on?

Stacey picked up a water jug from the table and poured him a cup, which he drank gratefully. 'Gone to get something to eat, probably,' she replied. 'I doubt she had any breakfast this morning. She's been by your bed all night.'

'I'm in hospital,' he said vaguely, as the surroundings finally began to make sense. He peered at Stacey closely, trying to piece it all together. He'd been in the kitchen, clearing up after dinner and arguing with her. But now a strange expression clouded her face, and it unsettled him. 'How did you get in here?' he asked her uneasily. 'I don't want you here.'

'No one was about.'

Joel finished the water and tried to sit up, but a blinding pain in his head had him slumping back down again.

Stacey stretched her legs out, watching him silently, as if she was waiting for something. His mind became fuzzy, untethered, like it was fabric flapping in a strange breeze. Fractured thoughts and images confused him as he began to lose consciousness. Was he talking to Morwenna? 'Wenna, I'm sorry,' he said.

'It's okay,' a feminine voice soothed him. 'Why don't you admit the truth? Tell me about Marigold. Because I've done some digging, and I know who she is. I understand why you want to keep her name out of it. And yours, too, for that matter. Because if everyone finds out Marigold wrote the book, people might realise that you are Carl. And you don't want that, do you?'

'I didn't mean to deceive you, Wenna,' he said vaguely, 'but Stacey… Stacey has to pay.'

'Oh, I understand,' the voice soothed him sweetly. 'You can be honest now. Tell me everything, there's no need to be afraid.'

'I didn't mean to get Marigold pregnant,' he said. 'When the baby died, it broke her heart.'

Awful images started to assault his brain, and his statement was met with silence. Shocked silence, probably. Wenna would be disgusted when she realised how many lies he'd told. He let out a moan as pictures whirled behind his eyes like some dreadful merry-go-round. Marigold's body; cold and lifeless. His dad's voice. 'She is your sister,' he'd yelled, his face beetroot red. 'Your *sister*.'

'No,' Joel croaked at the vision of his father, his words just as they had been back then, not that they'd done much to appease his dad, or Marigold's mum. 'She's my *step*sister.'

And with that, darkness enveloped him.

15 years ago

He put down the pages and gazed at Marigold, who was laying on her back staring up at the ceiling of her bedroom. He liked her room – at the front of the house it was bright and sunny, filled with colourful things; decorative throws, cushions, clothes strewn everywhere in all the colours of the rainbow. A pile of jewellery lay heaped on top of a chest of drawers, winking in the sunlight. The house had been so drab before she came and now it had life again. Like when his mum had been alive. No. He wouldn't start thinking about that.

'A boundary dispute?' he said to Marigold.

'In the book I'm writing about us. I'll change the name of the house, and I'm not going to write in the book that we're… you know.'

'Stepsiblings.'

Her cheeks turned pink. She hated him bringing it up. Not that he was wild about it either but burying their heads in the sand was no help. Besides, it wasn't as if they'd known each other as children, Marigold and her mum had only moved into the house that summer. 'People might not have so much sympathy for us,' she said. 'If I'm in a different house and I make the dispute about a strip of land, it has this kind of… delicious absurdity,' she continued. 'We're not really doing anything wrong. We're not *related* related, but I think I should keep it out of the book, even so.'

Joel shrugged. Marigold knew what she was talking about better than he did. 'Well, my dad *is* having a boundary dispute with a neighbour,' he said. 'That man down the road, Bill. I think he might be even crazier than my dad, which is saying something.'

'Exactly,' Marigold said. 'A bit of truth, a bit of fiction.'

'Nobody would believe my dad could ever find anyone willing to marry him, anyway. I don't know what your mum sees in him.'

At the bang of the front door, Marigold leapt to her feet, pushing him off her bed. 'Go,' she said, 'go now! You can't be seen in here!'

He shuffled off reluctantly. Marigold had included his dad's undignified discovery of their relationship in her book, which had happened much as she described, and his dad really had hit him. But in the book Marigold hadn't added in Howard yelling about her being his "sister".

Back in his room he flung himself down on the bed and listened to the footsteps making their way straight upstairs and creaking along the landing, no doubt to check that he and Marigold weren't in bed together. He sighed.

Then the footsteps grew louder and louder, and noises assaulted his ears that made no sense. Voices from a distance, beeping, doors opening and closing, a curtain being pulled back and then a voice right beside him.

'Oh, you're awake!' Morwenna said, wrenching him out of his memory as she clasped his hand in hers.

'Was Stacey here?' he asked in confusion. Had she been? He thought he could recall her sitting in the chair by his bedside. What had they been talking about?

'Stacey? No, I wouldn't have thought so…' she stroked his face. 'I was so afraid. I thought… I thought I might lose you. Stacey said you fainted in the kitchen while you were talking to her.' She must have noticed his confusion because she said, 'You hit your head when you fell, and we couldn't wake you up. That's why you are in hospital. I thought you were going… I thought…' her words trailed off. 'I should have made you go to the doctor when you first started collapsing. I shouldn't have let you tell me it was just stress; I should have—' she dissolved into tears and laid her head on his chest.

'I'm sorry.'

'No. No, don't be sorry! You're going to be all right. They've done a scan, and they'll run tests to try and find out what's making you faint. Look, I'd better tell them you've woken—'

He grabbed her arm with as much strength as he could. 'They're doing what? I don't want tests, Wenna! I just want to go home.'

'It's okay,' she soothed him. 'Don't get upset, just rest. Please, rest. Let them help you.'

His eyelids drooped. Maybe it would be okay for her to find out. Maybe she *should* find out. 'I'm dying,' he said dreamily.

'You don't know what you're saying,' she told him, her voice cracking. 'You're not going anywhere.' She paused and then made her voice artificially bright. 'We're about to get married. We've got so much to look forward to. I want… I want to start a family with you.'

Dread settled in his stomach, but he couldn't make himself speak. A family. A baby.

The family curse. The words whirled around and around. *The family curse.* He'd started to believe it had missed him, despite the fate of his and Marigold's baby. When he was young, he'd thought the things that had made it so difficult for him at school were part of the curse, but years had gone by and he'd never fainted, so he thought he'd be okay. He'd never known what his baby had died from, it could be anything – nothing to do with the curse at all. He'd convinced himself of that. Until, that was, he began his campaign against Stacey and he'd started passing out. *Written through me like a stick of rock.* Written through his whole body. Written in his DNA.

Chapter 34

15 years ago

'Did you hear what I said?' Marigold asked him.

He turned to face her, though his head was spinning. It couldn't be real, could it? They'd tried to stay away from each other the past couple of weeks, to make Howard, and Marigold's mum Theresa, think they'd split up so they could have a bit more freedom and not have their respective parents watching their every move.

'I think I'm five weeks along,' Marigold said. 'Maybe a little more.'

He stared at her. A baby?

'Say something!' she said, panicked now.

He put his arms around her. 'Don't worry,' he said, without a second thought. 'It'll be okay.' He kissed her hair. 'I love you and I'll look after you. Both of you.'

She looked up at him and the warm September sun spilled over her face. They sat near a horse chestnut tree, the ground littered with conkers and their spiky cases.

She was gazing at him with eyes clouded with worry, but he didn't feel at all concerned. Having babies was a natural thing, and they'd manage. He was a bit confused, though. He knew that people had babies after having sex and he also knew people had sex for fun, but those were surely two separate processes. Had they done something different one time to change the purpose of the thing? Wouldn't he have realised? 'How did it happen?' he asked.

'I… I'm sorry, Joel, I should have told you I'd stopped taking the pill, but I was scared you'd talk me out of it. Getting pregnant was the best way I could see to make sure we stayed together. My mum and your dad are so determined to keep us apart and they would have found a way.'

A yawning feeling opened up inside him, the way it always did when one of his peers talked about something he didn't understand but knew he should. She'd said she was taking some pill or other, but he thought she meant it was for an illness. What did it have to do with her pregnancy?

'You don't know what I'm talking about, do you?' Marigold said gently. It wasn't the first time they'd ended up in a conversation like this, though never about anything so serious. He sat quietly, feeling ridiculous, as she explained the whole thing to him.

'I guess your dad never talked about this with you,' she said.

'No.'

'And you weren't ever in school for sex education?'

'No.'

She nodded. 'No books about it in the library here, then?'

He shook his head. The books were all old and didn't cover stuff like contraception – a term he had never even heard until Marigold had used it in her explanation. Marigold put her arms around him. 'Joel, I… I hadn't really thought any further ahead. Your dad's going to kill you. I – I'm worried he might *actually* kill you. He was so angry when he found us together.'

'I'm not scared of him,' he said, as he absent-mindedly kicked at some of the spiny conker cases near his feet. 'We'll have to go away. We'll live somewhere else, and when my dad dies we'll come back and live here. You've seen the state of him. He can't have many years left.'

'Joel, that's not a solution.'

'We'll figure it out,' he said. 'You'll be nineteen at Christmas, I'm seventeen next year. We can leave here and start a new life together.' His voice was strong and confident. He'd find some kind of job. Maybe Marigold could even go to university like she'd been planning before she'd met him. Joel could look after the baby while she was studying. People would think it was a bit weird, maybe, or tell him he couldn't do it, but he didn't care what people thought. He could do whatever he set his mind to.

'Joel… we'll have to go soon. By the end of this week. It's too risky to stay any longer, I'm sure my mum is already suspicious about what's going on with me.'

'Then that's what we'll do,' he said. 'We'll leave. It'll be fine, Mari, you don't need to worry.'

She snuggled against him. 'So… you do want it then?'

'Want what?' he asked.

'The baby! Especially after what happened to your mum; my mum said something about it perhaps being genetic. That could mean you have it, couldn't it? And the baby, too.'

He hugged her tight. *The family curse.* 'It'll be okay,' he reassured her with false confidence, though his insides squirmed with fear. 'You don't need to worry about that.'

…

'What is it you want to talk to me about?' he asked Morwenna, as they sat back after finishing their meal.

She gave him a strange, faraway look. 'Do you really not know? Come on, Joel, we need to be honest with each other now.'

He closed his eyes for a moment. It was hardly as if he hadn't known this was coming.

'I didn't want to upset you while you were recovering, but you wouldn't let me stay in the room at hospital while they talked to you about the scans. You refused to have any tests to investigate the fainting—'

'It's not necessary.'

Morwenna was silent for a long while. 'Please,' she said finally. 'I'm begging you now. Tell me what's wrong. Tell me why you made me leave the room when they were talking to you.'

A cold feeling settled around him, but before he could say anything she spoke again. 'Show me your ring finger,' she said.

She knows. He rubbed his palms against his jeans as they began to sweat.

Of course she would have seen it. How could I possibly have thought she wouldn't notice?

'Wenna…' he started.

'Tell me your phone number.'

'Look, I—'

She pointed at the clock on the wall behind him, tears in her eyes now. 'Tell me what time it is,' she said.

'Stop!' he said. 'Please, just stop.'

A tear trickled down her cheek and he reached across for her hand, but she snatched it away. 'You have a brain tumour, don't you? That's why you find it difficult to do these things.' She swiped at the tear, but more followed, one dripping onto the table.

He stared at her. 'No,' he said in astonishment. 'No, I don't.'

'Don't lie to me!'

His pulse was racing. Morwenna had put her hands over her face and her shoulders were shaking. Some of the other diners in the cosy country pub were turning around at the sound of her tears. He went over to sit on the empty chair beside her and stroked her back. 'I *don't* have a brain tumour,' he said softly. 'I don't.'

'You really don't?' she asked, raising her head with a touch of hope in her voice.

'I really don't.'

'Then… what *is* going on with you? When we went to choose our wedding rings, I saw that you weren't sure which finger was your ring finger. Those board games we did at my dad's at Christmas, you were trying to hide it, but I could see how challenging you found some of them, especially if you had to do anything with numbers. I know you, Joel. I can see it! All of it. I didn't want to make you feel uncomfortable or embarrassed if you weren't ready to talk to me, but it's getting ridiculous now. I'm sorry for what I did just then, but I didn't know how else to get you to open up apart from… shocking you into it, I guess.'

He sighed.

'It's so much more than the dysgraphia, though, isn't it?'

'It is.'

She clutched his hand. 'Tell me. Please. Just tell me.'

Chapter 35

15 years ago

Joel paused on his way down the stairs. Marigold had gone to bed exhausted – she said the pregnancy was making her tired, and he'd said she should get as much rest as she could now that they were planning to leave in only a few short days – but his mind was buzzing as he tried to figure out where they should go and what they should do. Voices drifted up to him from the living room, where the door was ajar, so he tiptoed down and sat on the bottom step to listen. It would be something to do with him, or him and Marigold. It always was.

'I said I am not discussing this with you!' his dad's voice thundered, his footsteps loud as he crossed the room. Joel leapt to his feet again, sure Howard would imminently burst out into the hall, but Theresa's voice was desperate, and he paused. 'Let's have a reasonable conversation about it. I'm not trying to have a go at you—'

'No? By saying I don't know how to bring up my own son properly?'

Sinking back down onto the stairs, Joel leaned forward, straining to hear as the voices lowered a little.

'Just read it!'

'I will not.'

Joel couldn't stop himself from smiling at this childish response from his dad. Howard's face would be all red and flustered and he could just imagine Theresa's normally calm demeanour beginning to slip. She'd be twisting her long, beaded necklace around her fingers, trying to "count slowly to ten" like she told Marigold to do on occasions of high emotion.

'Fine. Gerstmann's syndrome,' Theresa continued. 'I was reading about it earlier. Difficulties with writing, maths, recognising fingers…'

'So, you've slapped some label on him,' Howard said. 'Put him in a neat box.'

Joel frowned. His dad had said something like that before. Years ago, when the school sent a letter about assessing him, whatever that entailed.

'Sometimes labels can help. Once you know what's going on, you know how to support somebody.'

'I support him just fine. He's never wanted for anything, has he? He's always had food in his belly and clothes on his back, and how many other children get to have a home like this as their playground?'

'You know full well that's not what I mean, and I'd say he's rather beyond playgrounds now, wouldn't you? He's nearly an adult, and you need to start treating him like one.'

'Joel is who he is. The lad is absolutely fine! He likes helping out here, and on the farm down the road, what else does he need? It's a shame he started fucking his stepsister—'

'Don't be disgusting. And he is not "absolutely fine". You might have been able to pull the wool over my eyes because I moved in here during the summer holidays, but I've found the letters from his school. He didn't sit his exams, did he? You made him lie when I asked what results he got. His attendance at school was barely ten per cent.'

'And it wouldn't even be that if I had any say in it! What is the point? He can't sit exams if he can't write his answers. The boy's not all there, but it's not his fault—'

'Not all there? Can you *hear* yourself, Howard? You can't talk about people like that!' she paused, and when she continued her voice had calmed down a little. 'It's easier for you to just dismiss him, isn't it? It's easier than supporting him. Easier than talking to Joel himself. Easier than talking to his school and finding out what they could offer. Don't you think they'd find some way of accommodating him to sit exams? He could have learned to type if you'd got a computer earlier than this summer – it was like the bloody dark ages in this house before I moved in! It was one thing when Linda was homeschooling him, but you haven't been teaching him anything, have you?'

'School is just brainwashing, anyway,' Howard said stubbornly. 'If he wants to know something he can look it up. He can read just fine.'

'You are impossible!' Theresa yelled at him. 'The books here are all ancient. Only a handful are from this century, and those are the ones Linda bought when he was primary school age! You'll say anything, *anything* to try to justify it, won't you? Hiding him away here like you're ashamed of him, claiming you're doing it for him—'

'I'm not ashamed of him.'

'But you're ashamed of *yourself*, aren't you? And you know that if you try to get any support for him, people will start asking questions. *Joel* will start asking questions.'

'None of this is my fault!' Howard bellowed.

'No, it's Linda's!'

Drawing in a breath, Joel tried to calm down, but his pulse was racing. His mother? So, it really *was* all to do with the curse. Her illness had changed his brain, just as he'd always thought. He clutched at one of the staircase spindles, his knuckles white. *Is my baby going to be ill?* Would it die? After all, the curse had started affecting him far younger than it had his mother, so perhaps it was becoming more aggressive. Tears pricked the backs of his eyes at the idea of anything hurting the baby, but he leant forward to concentrate on Howard and Theresa's conversation. He had to know as much as he could.

'Linda was an amazing mother to him!' Howard said. '*She* knew how to get through to him. I don't! The boy doesn't want to learn anything anyway. Why try and change things? His life is how it is. I'm fine with that, he's fine with that.'

'*Is* he fine with that?'

'It's his choice.'

'Choice is when you know what your other options are. Joel has never been given any other options, has he? You've stopped him getting a proper education, stopped him having any proper chance to make friends. You've never been honest with him about anything.' There was a pause. 'And now this business with Marigold… have you ever bothered to tell him about relationships, contraception? Or did you just assume he'll never need to know that, either?'

'I'm not listening to any more of this.'

'You need to have a proper conversation with him. Tell him the truth. Let him figure out what he wants to do with his life. Keeping him hidden away here – he thinks he doesn't deserve anything else. I can see in his face that he blames himself for how he struggles at school. He feels embarrassed and ashamed, and it's not right. The only person who should feel bad about anything, Howard, is *you*!'

Joel got unsteadily to his feet. What the hell was all this?

'Will you shut up?' Howard's voice boomed. 'I am not dragging him off to some busybody to start casting judgments about him—'

'Oh, for Heaven's sake.'

'He is who he is, Theresa. And that's final. I'm not going to start confusing him with all this stuff about his past. How is that going to make him feel any better?'

Joel started to scurry away, sure the conversation was over, and that the door would soon swing open, but Theresa's next words to his dad stopped him in his tracks.

'You know as well as I do why he has brain damage, Howard. If Linda—'

'Don't you dare.'

'He ended up with parietal lobe damage because of something *entirely* avoidable!'

The living room door opened, and Joel just about managed to get away before his dad could spot him darting up the dark staircase.

...

'Brain damage?' Morwenna said quietly.

Joel nodded. He'd given her a simplified version of the conversation he'd overheard when he was sixteen, omitting any mention of "fucking his stepsister", or his mum's illness.

Morwenna had listened wide eyed, and now they were making their way out of the pub, into a bright spring day. The kind where the lawns at Vineworth Manor would have looked spectacular with their broad swathes of daffodils, and the apple trees in the small orchard would be festooned with blossom.

'So… do you know what caused it?'

The Curse. What other explanation could there be? Theresa couldn't have been clearer that it was down to his mother. 'No,' he answered. He'd never managed to ask Howard or Theresa about it, and he'd never spent more than a few minutes looking up Gerstmann's syndrome himself. As far as he was concerned it was as his dad had said. He was who he was. Soon after he'd overheard Theresa and Howard talking, everything had blown up with Marigold and her pregnancy, and the last thing on anyone's mind was talking to him about anything.

'So… that's what causes the fainting as well, is it? The brain damage that gave you the Gerstmann's syndrome makes you pass out as well?'

'I guess so,' he said uneasily. It was sort of true, wasn't it? When he'd been in hospital, the doctors had talked about wanting to do more tests. Blood tests, an ECG, but he'd said no. Just like his parents had always said no to trying to find out more about his mum's illness. What was the point? Why did he need them to tell him what he already knew in his heart?

'But it's not serious? I mean… it is *serious,* obviously, but it's something you live with, not something that will get worse?'

Joel couldn't meet her eye.

I have to tell her now. I have to tell her I'm dying.

Tell her. For God's sake, just tell her the truth.

He opened his mouth. The words were on the tip of his tongue. The family curse. *Just say it.*

Morwenna's face was open, kind, willing him to be honest, but he faltered. 'No,' he found himself saying. 'It's not getting worse. I'll be okay.'

Chapter 36

15 years ago

Hand in hand, Joel and Marigold made their way back to the house from one of their favourite spots – a grassy clearing in the woods where the sun spilled through the leaves so that their bodies would be warmed by the dappled light. Their time there had always been a blur of bare skin and breathlessness, while afterwards they would lay and talk for hours as he stroked her soft hair. Today, though, they'd been talking about their plans to flee Vineworth, and day-dreaming about the future they would have together once they left Howard and Theresa behind.

Their conversation had been so intense that it was later than they had realised, and if they weren't back soon, Howard or Theresa would most likely start looking for them.

As if on cue, the voices of their respective parents drifted to them from somewhere up ahead. Immediately they froze, then they crept through the undergrowth to try to get a little closer and listen in on the conversation.

'We can tell them until we're blue in the face,' Howard was saying, 'but two teenagers cooped up together in this house in the middle of nowhere, we should have realised the pair of them would spend every spare moment at it like rabbits, no matter how much we try to stop them. And Joel, well, he's a Shakespeare lad all right, I know what I was like at his age.'

Stepping just a little closer, Howard and Theresa came into view through the leaves of the bush he and Marigold were hiding behind. They were sat together on a bench in what Joel's mum had called the "baby's garden", on account of the fountain in the centre of the grass which featured a chubby stone cherub. The fountain was, of course, now long defunct, yet another relic from those days with his mother that barely seemed real any longer.

'Yes, but, they're not just any old pair of teenagers, are they?' Theresa was saying. 'And Marigold is about to start university. I just know that at any moment she's going to tell me she's not going because she doesn't want to leave Joel. She could wreck her whole future and for what? A love affair that is doomed from the start.' She sighed. 'Even besides their… family relationship to one another, they're hardly compatible, are they? Marigold sailed through her A levels, and Joel—'

'Can't string a sentence together?'

Joel's cheeks started to burn. He'd not mentioned to Marigold the argument he'd overheard between Howard and Theresa about the brain damage that was apparently his mum's fault. He didn't know where to begin talking about it. Perhaps it would be better if he tried to forget ever hearing the conversation at all – what good would it do to dwell on it? He certainly didn't want to blame his mum for anything, she'd been nothing but kind to him as far as he could remember, and her illness was hardly her fault. Theresa had been cruel to imply that it was. Marigold gave him a squeeze. 'Ignore your dad,' she whispered. 'He doesn't know what he's talking about.'

Theresa was similarly disgusted with Howard's statement about Joel's writing ability. 'That is *not* what I was going to say.'

'It's what you mean though.'

Theresa heaved a huge sigh. 'We need to keep them away from each other. I think we both agree on that.'

'I—'

'And I don't mean by giving him another smack. I don't know what you were thinking. If you ever raise your hand to that boy again…'

'It was the shock,' Howard groused. 'He knows I didn't mean it.'

Joel could tell that Marigold was bristling with anger at the reminder of the awful day they were discovered.

'Well,' Theresa said finally, 'I've decided I'm going to take Marigold away with me. Tomorrow. Then, once I'm confident she's moved on, I'll come back to live here again.'

'That could take months!' Howard protested, as Joel and Marigold stared at each other in horror. 'Years! We've only been married a few months – you can't just leave! And besides, Marigold's eighteen. She can go wherever she wants. You can't stop her coming here and seeing him.'

'Not if I tell her the truth.' Theresa said. 'All of it. I'll tell her and then I will take her away while she processes it. Maybe she can delay starting university for a week or two and I'll take her on a nice long holiday, somewhere hot. Once some time has gone by, she'll understand, and she'll forget him once she has a whole new life ahead of her. As for Joel, well, he's not even seventeen yet. He probably doesn't even know what he feels. The pair of them have only known each other for one summer. It's not love, is it? It's just infatuation. It'll pass.'

There was a long silence. Neither Joel nor Marigold knew what to say to each other, though any curiosity they might have over what Theresa wanted to tell Marigold was far overshadowed by their horror at the thought of being apart from each other. If they wanted to leave, they had better be quick about it.

Chapter 37

'It feels so real now,' Morwenna said as they stepped outside from her final wedding dress fitting. 'This time last year I'd never even met Joel, and in a couple of weeks I'll be marrying him!'

Though Stacey tried to force out a positive reply to this statement, the words died on her lips. How could she possibly pretend to be happy?

'So, Joel really is okay, is he?' she asked as they made their way to the café down the road, hurrying to avoid getting caught out in the spring downpour that was threatening. As if the fitting hadn't been bad enough, she had ended up agreeing to go for a coffee and help Morwenna perfect the speech she had her heart set on giving at the wedding.

Morwenna gave Stacey a sharp look at her question about Joel's health.

'With the fainting, and everything…' Stacey trailed off, letting the searching tone in her voice do the work.

Please, for goodness' sake, let him have told her the truth.

But Morwenna's reply came as no surprise.

'Yes, I told you about all of that. About the Gerstmann's Syndrome.'

'That doesn't cause fainting, though, does it?'

Morwenna's eyebrows knitted together as they stepped inside the busy café, and Stacey knew it was hopeless. Her friend had already told her the spiel Joel had come out with; saying he had brain damage that caused *all* of his symptoms, rather than coming clean about the illness that would sooner or later claim his life. Morwenna, of course, had believed him without question. How on earth had it ended up this way? How had Joel created a situation where his lies were believable, yet her truth about him wasn't – that the people she was closest to found it easier to imagine she was delusional, than that Joel was anything less than perfect?

'Sorry,' she said quickly. 'I'm only thinking of you – of you both – with the wedding coming up. I want you to have the best day, that's all.'

...

Stacey sat quietly and listened to Morwenna chattering about wedding plans until it was getting late in the afternoon, and they had long since finished their drinks. Would this day never end?

Offering to get a second round of coffees, Stacey was on the verge of panic as she reached the counter, taking deep breaths to steady herself. Memories flooded in of the time she'd sat at the very same table in the very same café not long after Kirkbride first contacted her, making her heart rate spike again. Back then, the biggest drama in Morwenna's life had been looking after her dad and enduring cringeworthy dates. Now she was about to marry Joel.

Joel. Just the name made Stacey's skin crawl. Why on earth hadn't he seized the opportunity his spell in hospital had given him to tell his bride-to-be the truth?

'So,' Morwenna said once Stacey sat back down. 'I haven't even got to the main reason I wanted to talk to you.'

The speech. My God, how would she sit here and listen to this?

Taking a folded sheet of notepaper from her pocket, Morwenna opened it out carefully and Stacey braced herself.

Everything she thinks she knows about Joel is a lie.

But what could she do? She'd tried everything. She'd found out about Joel's past, but learning that Marigold was Joel's stepsister, that they had had a baby together – a baby which had died, breaking Marigold's heart – didn't make any difference to anything. It was an awful thing to happen, of course, and Stacey was sorry the pair had been through something like that, but did Joel really think getting her to confess the truth about the book would make him feel any better? Did Joel even remember telling her about his baby? He'd been barely conscious when he'd said it and thought she was Morwenna. He probably had no recollection of the conversation at all.

Morwenna had started to read. The speech was every bit as torturous as Stacey feared; an outpouring of love and happiness. Reaching for her latte to try and hide her discomfort, her unsteady hands almost knocked the mug over.

I can't do this. I can't. I can't let her go through with it!

But if she'd thought the start – and middle – of the speech were unbearable, it was nothing compared to the surprise announcement Morwenna had snuck in at the end.

Chapter 38

Stacey stared at her. 'You're pregnant?'

Her friend nodded, joy radiating from her face. 'I'll be having my first scan the day before the wedding. Not the best timing, I know, but—'

'So, you're… how many weeks?'

'Nine. I didn't think to do a test until a few days ago – with Joel in hospital and everything, I didn't realise straight away that I was late.'

Stacey could feel the colour draining from her face. In addition to his own deteriorating health, Joel's condition, whatever it was, must be genetic. Had he started trying for a family without telling Morwenna the truth?

'Does Joel know you're pregnant?' Stacey asked. 'You're not going to surprise him with the news in your speech, are you?'

'I was considering it, but I can't bear keeping it from him, and besides, I wouldn't want him to miss the scan. I'm going to tell him tonight.'

Stacey couldn't help but put her hand up to her mouth as fear for her friend engulfed her.

She thinks Joel is going to be there for her and their child. She thinks it'll be a family of three, when really it will be a family of two.

Then an even worse thought struck her. Joel and Marigold's baby hadn't made it. If that was to do with Joel's condition, would it happen again? Would Morwenna lose everything; her husband *and* her baby? Her friend was staring at her, and Stacey began to shake from head to toe.

'You need to talk to Joel,' she choked out, 'and as soon as possible. And, please, Wenna, ask him to tell you the truth. That's important. Really important.'

'Why? The truth about what? I don't understand.'

Pushing her chair back, Stacey got to her feet, and having stammered out that she needed to go, she rushed away without a backwards glance.

Joel. Fury at him consumed her. He couldn't carry on as he was. She would have it out with him, once and for all.

…

'What is this about?' Joel said, as he opened the door and she burst into his house.

'I already knew you were a coward,' Stacey said. 'But even *I* didn't think you'd go this far.'

'I don't know what you're talking about, and you need to go,' he said, trying to usher her towards the door. The smell of cooking – Bolognese, maybe – drifted from the kitchen, along with music she couldn't quite make out. It would have been the most ordinary domestic scene, Joel preparing a meal for himself and Morwenna, but there was nothing ordinary about these circumstances. One way or another, this had to end. Tonight. 'Morwenna will be back soon,' Joel continued, 'and Grant was coming round to talk about—'

'No, you are talking to *me.*' She took hold of his arm. 'You're not waiting to be bailed out by people you've fooled with your Perfect Joel act, making me look crazy, *again.* You are going to face up to your stupid, selfish, *reckless* actions.'

Shaking his arm free, he faced her levelly. 'Is this about Morwenna?'

'You're damn right it's about Morwenna! What the hell were you thinking, trying for a baby with her? I know how much she wants children but letting her think she's going to have a family when you're about to drop dead is…' she searched for words strong enough. 'It is *cruel,* Joel. It's cruel. And all because you're too scared to tell the truth.'

His forehead creased. 'We're not trying for a baby. She's said she wants a family, and I admit I've not really committed to it one way or the other…'

'Well, you're committed to it now. She's pregnant. Nine weeks. And you need to tell her the truth now, or I swear to God, I will.'

Chapter 39

Joel gaped at Stacey. Morwenna was *pregnant*? Pain surged through him, and he couldn't bear to stand in the hall looking at Stacey any longer. But she followed him as he made his way shakily to the living room, taking hold of his shoulder to force him to face her.

'Did you hear what I said?' she demanded.

'Yes, but we were being careful…'

'Not careful enough!' After a pause, she said, 'You're the love of Morwenna's life, do you know that?'

'I don't deserve to be.'

'No, you don't!' she pointed her finger at him. 'No matter what you think about me, what you're doing is ten times worse! You should never have let things get this far with Wenna without telling her exactly what she was getting into! She might have still wanted to marry you anyway – probably would, in fact – but you never gave her a choice. You've reeled her in further and further and now her entire life is all about *you*!'

Stacey's cheeks were red with outrage, her eyes blazing at him, and all of a sudden anger engulfed him, as well. 'I would never have done any of this if it wasn't for you,' he flung back at her. 'You could have ended this a year ago. You could have ended it when we were at the retreat! You want to know whose fault it is that I came here and got involved with Grant and Morwenna – look in the mirror!'

With that, Stacey screeched and gave him a shove, catching him off balance so that he stumbled and collapsed onto the sofa, but she was on him straight away, clawing at him and screaming with rage. But then hands were pulling her away. Two pairs of hands, and he found himself staring up into the faces of the very people he'd just admitted to using as pawns in his game.

Chapter 40

'I warned you that you couldn't trust him,' Stacey said, as Grant and Morwenna looked between her and Joel, who was getting unsteadily to his feet from where he'd been slumped on the sofa. She'd caught his face with her nails when she attacked him, and there were streaks of blood on his cheek. But the tides had turned. Grant and Morwenna had heard clear as day what Joel had said; that he was only involved with them because of *her*. Joel had lost their sympathy, and she seized on it. She seized on it with all her might.

'I told you he was at that retreat, Grant,' she said. 'He… he's been stalking me.'

Grant stared at her before choking out, 'Stacey, I—'

'Tell them why!' Joel said desperately. 'Tell them why I was there!'

'He claimed he was a fan of my book,' she lied. 'But he was obsessed with me!'

'It's okay, it's okay,' Grant said to her, holding his arm out to block Joel from coming near her. 'You're safe now.'

'I thought he would attack me while I was at the retreat,' she said, her eyes meeting Joel's. 'I was so afraid of him.'

'No, it wasn't like that,' Joel said to Morwenna, who was standing motionless at his side, one hand on her stomach as if she was trying to shield the tiny baby from the awful scene unfolding. 'Please let me explain…'

'You've been lying from the start,' Morwenna breathed. 'None of this is real, is it? She's been telling the truth all along and you made us think she was crazy!'

'No, she—'

'Get out!' Morwenna exploded. 'Get out! Get out! Get out!'

…

'You're okay now,' Grant said softly, stroking her hair, 'I'm here. I'm here now. Joel's gone.'

Resting her head against her husband, Stacey closed her eyes, but tears spilt out from under her lashes.

'That man, Dante,' she said, 'I didn't know who was sending me messages and leaving notes in my room at the retreat to begin with. I thought it was him, that's why I threw the paperweight at him; because I wanted to scare him off. But I had it all wrong. *Joel* watched me attack Dante. He filmed it and tried to blackmail me, threatening to share the video.'

Grant's face twisted through several emotions as he tried to process it all. 'I'm so sorry,' he croaked out at last.

'I thought it was over, but then he was in Wrexton and I came face to face with him at Morwenna's Christmas party. He made friends with you, getting everyone to trust him. I tried and tried to tell you both!'

'I'm going to kill him,' Grant burst out. 'When I get my hands on him, I'm going to fucking kill him.'

'I *told* you what he was doing to me!' she said, shaking violently. Why did she feel so awful? She'd done what she'd been desperate to do for months. She'd got rid of him. But she was anything but relieved. It felt like her body was breaking into pieces.

'Wenna…' she said faintly.

'She's gone upstairs to lie down, I think. We should check on her, she's—'

At that moment the sound of desperate sobs reached them from the top of the stairs, and when Stacey looked down at her hands, she recoiled at the sight of Joel's blood under her fingernails.

'I need this off me,' she said, her voice cracking. 'I need his blood off me, Grant, I need it off me!' Her voice had risen to a cry, and she ran to the kitchen, turning the tap on full and scrubbing away at her nails so hard that her skin turned pink and the pain made more tears spill down her cheeks.

'They're clean now,' Grant was saying gently, turning off the tap. 'They're clean.'

Her phone began to ring, and she froze, drying her hands hastily on her jumper. Joel.

Grant swiped her phone from her hand and answered it, calling Joel every name under the sun and demanding he come back and face him, until eventually he realised Joel had hung up. Stacey took her phone back from him with trembling fingers and a message came through.

You win Stacey. Consider this goodbye.

Every hair on her body stood on end. *Consider this goodbye.* A wave of startling emotion shot through her. She'd gone too far. Morwenna was still sobbing, and Grant's face was white with anger.

Joel's going to kill himself.

She knew it with absolute certainty. She'd got Morwenna and Grant to believe he was stalking her and that was something he could never come back from. It didn't matter what he said or did now, the people he cared about most in the world would never trust him again. She'd crushed him. She'd crushed him so badly that he thought his life – whatever he had left of it – wasn't even worth living.

'Let's get you home,' Grant said. 'We'll see if Morwenna wants to come back with us, too. She probably doesn't want to stay here on her own, not now.'

'No, Grant, this is all wrong. Listen to me. You have to listen to me—'

'We can talk later, but first we need to get out of here. I can't stand even being in his house.'

'No, you don't understand!' She let out a cry. 'I made it up! He wasn't stalking me! I made it up.'

'What?' he said, staring at her incredulously. 'He said himself he was at the retreat—'

'I made it up!' she said again, almost screaming the words. Darting up the stairs, Stacey knelt beside her sobbing friend. 'Morwenna, I'm sorry,' she said. 'Joel wasn't stalking me. I mean, he kind of was, but not how I made it sound. I lied to stop him…' she gulped in some air, and Grant appeared at the bottom of the staircase. 'To stop him telling everyone I didn't write *Two Lost Souls.*' A kind of elation flooded through her. 'I didn't write it,' she cried. 'I stole it. I stole it from Marigold, and I pretended it was mine. Joel wanted me to confess and I wouldn't. But now I have.'

'Stacey,' Grant said gently, trying to take hold of her as she ran back down towards the front door. She shook him away, flinging the door open. He was running after her, but she sprinted towards her car. Joel was going to kill himself. That was all she could think about. 'Get Morwenna to call Joel,' she told Grant. 'Get her to call him and say that I admitted the truth about the book.'

'What the hell are you talking about?' Grant said, stopping and shaking his head in bewilderment. 'I don't understand what's happening.'

'I think Joel…' she sagged against the car briefly. 'I think he's going to try and kill himself. And it's my fault. It's all my fault. He's not a bad person, Grant. But I am.'

She shook herself and sprang into action again, getting into the car and speeding off down the road. *Think.* Where would Joel go? The end of *Two Lost Souls – The Darkest of Paths* – flashed into her mind; the flames leaping, devouring Hillcroft Manor and taking the lives of Carl and Marigold.

There was only one place he would go.

Chapter 41

Joel's heart was breaking. All he could see was the look on Morwenna's face, the way she'd screamed at him to get out. He swiped at some tears that had fallen onto his cheek.

Was nothing sacred to Stacey? To lie that he was some deranged fan of "her" book, that he'd been stalking her, rather than facing up to stealing someone else's work? A couple of cars sped past, startling him, and a wave of such total hopelessness engulfed him that for a moment he wanted nothing more than to swerve off the road and into the nearest tree. He wanted oblivion.

I've failed. I've failed Marigold. I've failed Morwenna, I've failed my baby – both of my babies – and I've failed myself.

He shivered. Everyone was always one step ahead of him. His dad and Theresa with Marigold: he'd not known how to fight for her. His dad had thrown him out of the house and even then he'd been hopeless, so completely unfamiliar with the way things worked in the real world that he had been stupidly trusting, so unused to being around people that he made all sorts of mistakes. He thought he'd got past that. He thought he understood the world now; that was until Stacey, who he couldn't understand at all. How could a person be so consumed with how the world saw them? He would have pitied her if she hadn't just done what she did. Nobody would believe him about the book now, and as for marrying Morwenna, well, he'd probably never see her again, let alone his child that she was carrying.

It doesn't matter any more. He told himself. *You tried. You really did try, but you failed. Let yourself stop now. Soon it will be over. Soon it will all be over.*

15 years ago

The commotion outside startled him and he ran to the window. Marigold, Theresa and his dad were all out there on the drive in the rain, and Marigold was screaming his name. He tore down the stairs, bursting out of the front door yelling, 'Get the hell away from her!'

Neither his dad nor his stepmother listened to him and continued trying to get Marigold inside Theresa's car.

'Joel, they know,' she said. 'My mum found out.'

Joel stopped in his tracks. *They know*. It was the day they had planned to run away; he had been busy packing. In just a couple of short hours they were planning to sneak out of the house and walk the three miles to the nearest village where they could get a bus to the train station. They had it all planned out, every step of the process – every step up to getting on the train, anyway. The details of how exactly they'd live were still hazy.

Leaving Marigold for a moment, his dad strode over to him, a nightmare looming over him in a rain-soaked, scruffy shirt. 'You proud of yourself?' his dad shouted. 'Getting your own stepsister pregnant?'

Joel ignored him and tried to get to Marigold, who was being bundled into the car by Theresa, but before he could take a step his dad grabbed him and held him back. Fighting madly, Joel eventually broke free and tore towards the car.

'Joel!' Marigold cried out to him, but before he could reach her, Howard made a grab for him again and he lost his balance, sprawling face first into the wet gravel which grazed his skin. He scrambled back to his feet, but Theresa had somehow managed to shove Marigold into the car and the engine had started.

'Let her go,' his dad said to him, calmer now. 'It's for the best.'

'No, it's not!'

He sprinted over to the car and threw himself in front of it, but at the last moment Theresa managed to swerve around him, leaving him calling Marigold's name over and over, even when the car had long since disappeared.

...

Jolted back to the present by a sudden junction with a busier road, Joel took several deep breaths. *I'm so sorry Marigold.* If only they'd left a day earlier. They should have run as soon as they'd overheard Theresa plotting to take Marigold away, even if they had to go with nothing but the clothes they stood up in.

He'd known when Theresa drove off with Marigold that she'd be gone for good. In fact, that hadn't turned out to be entirely true, but the version he saw of Marigold the final time many months later wasn't the same one that had left that day. In many ways, that day her mum had driven her away from Vineworth Manor was the day that Marigold had died.

And now it would come full circle. He'd end it where it had all begun. Perhaps, like Marigold, he had really died that day too.

Chapter 42

'Grant, what is it?' Stacey asked distractedly when she answered the call. She needed to concentrate on driving. It was evening now and Vineworth Manor was the other side of the country. She had no time to lose.

'Joel's phone is off,' he said.

Her blood ran cold. 'Off?'

'Yes. You told Morwenna to call him, and she's tried over and over, but he's turned it off.'

Blind panic overtook her. *Please let me be right about where he's going. Please let me be right.*

He had a bit of a head start, but she was only about thirty or forty minutes behind him.

'Stacey, what on earth were you talking about? You said you didn't write *Two Lost Souls*? You said Marigold wrote it. Do you mean that character in the book? You're not making sense—'

'The book isn't fiction,' she said. 'Some of it is, some of it isn't. Joel is Carl. Marigold is Marigold.' For God's sake, she didn't have time to explain it to him right now. 'Has Morwenna left him a message?' she asked quickly.

'Uh… yes, I think so,' he said.

'Make sure she does. If he turns his phone back on, he needs to know that everything is okay.'

'Where are you? Where are you going?'

'Vineworth Manor,' she said. 'It's Hillcroft Manor, from the book.'

'Stacey…'

'I don't have time for this!' she said and hung up. She just had to keep going. *Please Joel. Please be okay.*

…

It was the early hours of the morning when she finally reached the turning for Vineworth Manor, the first light of dawn in the sky as she made her way up the drive. Lined with overgrown bushes, even the drive felt utterly abandoned and derelict, and a moment of doubt chilled her. Had Joel definitely come here? Perhaps she'd got it all wrong. She was in the middle of nowhere, trying to find a man who, let's face it, could be anywhere.

He's going to die because of me.

The words kept swirling around. She'd also been trying to call him, but his phone remained off – so as far as he knew everyone was still furious with him. He would think Morwenna hated him.

Suddenly, she was in front of a large house that looked as though it had once been grand but was now decidedly neglected and covered with ivy. She got out quickly, pulling her jacket around her body against the early morning chill. There were no signs of life. No one else was here! She cursed herself. She'd been so sure, but she'd got it totally wrong.

Wait. She turned towards an area off to the side of the house where there was a sound. Joel's car! It was outside an old barn. She crept towards it, initially not wanting to startle him, but then she changed her tactics. Startling him was exactly what she wanted to do. She *needed* to startle him. She needed to help him.

At that moment he burst out of the barn, a fuel container in his hand, and her breath caught. She could have been looking into the pages of *The Darkest of Paths*. Joel – Carl – it was all real now. Her hunch had been exactly right. He was going to do it. He was going to burn down the house and take himself along with it.

Joel stopped in his tracks, staring at her in complete shock.

'Joel—'

'Just leave,' he said, as he brushed past her towards the main house. 'This is nothing to do with you.'

'It's everything to do with me!' she said. 'This is ridiculous. You need to stop.' She was using exactly the same voice she'd use for telling Teddy or Ava off, but that didn't stop her. Joel needed to get a grip. Nothing was worth all this!

He paid no attention to her, and picked up a rock from the ground, using it to break one of the downstairs windows. 'Joel!' she cried, as he managed to swing the window open and began to climb inside. 'Stop it! Stop! I told everyone I was lying. I told them about the book.'

Accepting he wasn't going to listen she took a deep breath and made her own way towards the window, which was hanging wide open and blowing in the breeze. Joel had disappeared from sight. The second she got inside she could smell petrol, though she couldn't see Joel. Fear pulsed through her, but she pushed herself onwards.

This is my fault. I did this to him.

Eventually she found him at the back of the house, sitting on an old dining chair at the kitchen table, his face eerie in the light from one dim bulb overhead.

'You need to turn on your phone,' she said.

'Why?'

'Didn't you hear me outside? I owned up, Joel. I told Grant and Morwenna the truth about *Two Lost Souls*.'

He shook his head. 'You expect me to believe that?'

'Yes!' she cried. 'Morwenna has been trying to call you.'

Joel took his phone from his pocket and set it down on the table in front of him, but he didn't turn it on.

'You're lying,' he said to Stacey. 'You would never confess. Why would you? You've got exactly what you wanted. Nobody will believe a word that comes out of my mouth ever again, while you… you get to carry on being Stacey Cockle, the woman who wrote *Two Lost Souls*.'

'I have told the truth,' she repeated. 'And Morwenna loves you. Please don't leave her like this.'

'Maybe she did love me,' he said, 'but not after the things you said tonight. I know you haven't confessed. If you were ever going to tell the truth, you would have done it already.'

'I…'

'You're what? You're sorry?'

Pulling out another dusty old chair, Stacey sat down opposite him. 'I was desperate. I wasn't thinking straight and I'm so, so sorry. *Please* Joel, listen to your messages.' She tried to grab his phone herself, but he swiped it onto the floor where the screen cracked on the tiles.

Picking up the box of matches from the table in front of him he said, 'Please, just go. I want to be on my own.'

He began to take a match from the box, and Stacey snatched it from his hand. 'No!' she said. 'This is… this is *stupid.* I have told Grant and Morwenna the truth, whether you believe me or not. And *The Darkest of Paths* is words on a page. It's not Marigold. It won't bring her back. Wherever she is now, she wouldn't want you to do this. Imagine what she'd say if she was here.'

That made him pause. But not for long. 'She's not here, though, is she?'

'What happened to her?' she asked softly. 'I know the book says she died when she tried to save Carl from the fire. But there was no fire, was there?'

He shook his head.

'Tell me what really happened,' she pleaded. 'You might as well.'

Chapter 43

14 years ago

Joel stared at Howard in astonishment. Had he heard his dad right? Marigold was coming *here* to the house? In all these long months he'd not had any communication with her at all. He'd done everything he could to try and discover where she'd gone, but it had been completely hopeless.

'Theresa wants to pick up some of the things she left here,' he said, stopping in the middle of his task of shifting by wheelbarrow a load of paving slabs that had been delivered. For some reason or other he'd decided to build a patio near the barn and had roped Joel in to help. 'Theresa feels – though I can't say I agree – that it would give Marigold some closure to say goodbye to you properly, that's why she's bringing her.'

'Goodbye?'

'Yes, goodbye,' his dad said as he started trundling across the lawn. 'Why? Were you hoping to get your leg over again?'

Joel wanted to pick up a paving slab and smack his dad over the head with it, but he took a deep breath. He needed to stay calm and try to understand. He'd been using the time since Marigold had left to put in as many hours as he could on the farm down the road in the hope that when he eventually found her, he'd be in a better position to provide for her and the baby. There was only so much time they could afford to pay him for, but often he'd stay and help even when he wasn't getting any money. He liked to be there away from his dad, with the sheep and the chickens. He wasn't squeamish, even when he helped with the lambing several months back. It had made an uncomfortable parallel to his thoughts of Marigold though, since the baby was due in the spring. Would everything go okay for her? Was she scared? Did she need him?

Joel grabbed his dad's arm. The baby!

'Will the baby be coming?' he asked urgently. 'She's had it now?'

His dad laughed at him. 'So, you're smart enough to make a baby but you don't know how long it takes before it's born?' he said. 'Women don't stay pregnant for a year.'

Joel's hand itched to grab one of the slabs. Of course he knew how long pregnancy was. He knew she'd have had it back in the spring, and it was autumn now, but no one had bothered to tell him when his own child was born, so how else could he have phrased that question? He'd asked his dad about it on and off for months. He wanted to buy things for his baby and send them to Marigold, or give her the money if she preferred. He wanted to know if she was getting on okay, and whether she'd had a boy or a girl. A wave of anxiety washed over him.

I want to know if it's healthy. Or whether the baby is ill because of me.

Didn't his dad get that he cared about his child? Did he really think all he wanted when Marigold came was to "get his leg over". If Marigold was coming, he needed to speak to her properly, to find out what she needed from him, to know if she still wanted to be with him. His dad might be claiming Marigold wanted to say goodbye, but most of what his dad came out with was bullshit.

'Ah, here they are now!' his dad said, as the sound of tyres on gravel reached their ears.

Now? Right now? Joel tried to compose himself. He needed to be calm when Marigold arrived, especially if she had the baby with her. He had to make sure she got a chance to speak with him properly, without their parents interfering.

But when the car door opened and Marigold got out, Joel couldn't help but take a step backwards. She was so colourless and drained, dressed in faded jeans and a baggy grey t-shirt. There was no baby with her. He went to put his arms around her, but she pushed him gently away.

'This is for you,' she whispered, pressing something small and hard from her pocket into his hand. 'Don't let them see,' she said.

He looked down discretely. A flash drive. He frowned and put it in his own jeans pocket. He'd hide it in his room as soon as they went inside.

'It's our story,' she said.

'Are you okay?' he asked quietly. 'Where's the baby?'

She shook her head. 'I'm sorry, Joel, but how could we have looked after her? We can't be together. It's too… difficult.'

'You don't mean that!' he said. *Her*. She'd said "her"! He had a daughter. Staring at Marigold, he tried to make sense of what she was saying. She really didn't mean a word of it. He could see it in her eyes. She'd been told to say these things. She'd been bullied and beaten down. 'Of course we could have looked after her! Where is she?'

He was aware of his dad's and Theresa's eyes on them. 'Let's talk somewhere else,' he said, but she wouldn't budge.

'I gave her up for adoption, Joel. She's gone.'

…

'For what it's worth, I think you would have been a fantastic dad,' Stacey said to him, as he stumbled to a halt in his story. 'But I thought you said she had died – your daughter.'

For a long moment he sat still and unmoving. Why, of all the people in the world, did he have to be sat here with Stacey? With the woman who had trashed and cheapened his time with Marigold by stealing the book and milking as much money out of it as she could? She didn't deserve to know any of it. He wouldn't give her anything more of himself. He grabbed another match and held it to the side of the box. 'Get out,' he told her.

'I'll confess properly,' she said.

He paused. 'So, you admit you never told Grant or Morwenna, then?'

'No, I did tell them! I mean I'll admit it publicly. I'll do the video you wanted in the first place and post it everywhere. I'll do it right now.'

'You won't,' he said. 'It's empty promises. Besides, I don't even care any more. You were right all along. What does it matter? It won't bring Marigold back, will it?'

She came around to his side of the table and sat beside him, holding her phone up in front of her. 'Look, Joel, I'll live stream it right now.'

He put the match down and sat listening to her spewing out her confession. The words washed over him. *I was sent the manuscript by a person I met on a writing critique group online.*

That's how she got hold of it! Marigold had *sent* it to her.

As soon as I read it, I realised how much better it was than anything I could do.

A few comments appeared at the side of the screen. People were watching it. An extraordinary feeling surged through him. *I've done it. I've actually done it. I've got her to admit it.*

Chapter 44

Stacey's phone began to ring not long after she finished her confession, Morwenna's name on the screen.

'I'm going to answer it,' she told Joel gently. 'I'll tell her I'm with you, and you can talk to her.'

He nodded, and listened while she outlined the situation to Morwenna, before holding the phone out to him.

'Joel?' Morwenna's voice was panicky. 'Oh my God, Joel, what is going on? Are you okay? Stacey seems to think… I'm on the way to the house, but I'm still an hour away yet.'

'Stacey told you I wasn't just some stalker?'

'Yes, and I'm so sorry that I didn't even give you a chance to explain—'

'I understand,' he said, his voice shaking. 'And Morwenna, I know that you're pregnant. Stacey told me.'

'Yes, I am. And everything is going to be all right.' Her voice was warm and reassuring. 'Whatever is going on we can sort it all out, together.'

'No, we can't. I'm dying, Wenna. I've known I was dying nearly the whole time I've been with you, but I kept it a secret. You… you'd have been better off never knowing me.'

He ended the call and gave Stacey her phone back before putting his head in his hands.

'Joel, you still haven't told me what happened to Marigold. I know I'm not your favourite person, but I think you need to say it. You can tell me. You're not betraying her by talking about it – I think she would want everyone to know the truth. I think she would want the world to understand. Why else would she have written that story, if not to share her feelings with the world?'

'She didn't know she was going to die, though,' he said. 'But the thing is, I think part of her wanted to. I feel like part of her wanted it all to end.'

'Tell me,' Stacey said. She reached out for his hand, and he let her take it.

14 years ago

'Please, just let me speak to Marigold on my own before she goes,' Joel pleaded with his dad and Theresa. Marigold herself was sitting, wraith-like, on an armchair in the living room, staring listlessly out of the window. A storm had started, and the wind was hurling rain against the glass. The temperature had dropped, and it was obvious Marigold was cold in her t-shirt, but it was as though she couldn't feel it.

'I don't think that would be appropriate,' Theresa said.

Joel pushed past the two of them to reach Marigold, but his dad grabbed him.

'What have you done to her?' Joel yelled at him and Theresa, trying to struggle out of his dad's grip. 'Look at her! She needs me. She wouldn't have given up the baby if the two of you hadn't forced her somehow. I know you made her do it. Where is our daughter? Tell me, what have you done with our daughter?'

There was a long silence. Marigold wouldn't meet his eye, and the only sound was rain hammering against the windowpanes. 'Will somebody just answer me!' Joel cried. 'Why won't you let me speak to Marigold—'

'Your daughter's dead,' his dad said suddenly. Marigold sat bolt upright. 'What?' she breathed.

'Theresa told me on the phone yesterday. The baby died just a couple of days after being adopted.'

Marigold let out a high, keening cry, and Joel tried to run to her, but his dad was gripping him too tightly. In a furious rage he shoved Howard so hard that he fell, and Joel sprung free, but it was too late. Marigold was already on her feet, still making that awful, haunting cry.

'See what you've done?' his dad said. 'This is what comes of having sex with your stepsister! You think a healthy baby is going to come out of such a perverted relationship? This is *your* fault, Joel. Yours!'

Joel ignored him and chased after Marigold who was disappearing out into the hall. 'Stop!' he called to her. 'Stop! Please…'

But she was wrenching the front door open, and before he could reach her, she plunged out into the storm.

'Marigold!' he yelled into the rain, darting this way and that to try and catch sight of her. 'Marigold! Come back! Please… come back.'

…

'Your dad was a monster,' Stacey said. 'To tell you it was your fault about the baby because you were stepsiblings – you know it wasn't, don't you? You weren't blood relations so the fact she's your stepsister would make no difference.'

'It *was* my fault. It was the illness that killed our daughter. I know it was. There were times I doubted it, that I've wondered if I really have what my mum suffered from, but since I've started fainting, I know it's true.'

And now it might happen to Morwenna's baby too. It was more than he could bear.

'So… Marigold, did you find her?' Stacey asked at length.

He closed his eyes. He could still see it as clear as day. He could remember his frantic search, scrambling through the undergrowth as the rain came down in sheets and the wind nearly blew him off his feet. Hours and hours he searched, until he was shivering and going around in circles. It was as though she had disappeared off the face of the earth. But then he'd looked down the steep bank that once, a long time ago, had been part of a large rockery but was now overrun with weeds and brambles.

'She was dead,' he told Stacey flatly. 'She'd fallen down a bank, and landed on a big, jagged rock at the bottom. She looked like a rag doll. Like she'd been chucked there by a child throwing a tantrum.'

'Oh my God,' Stacey said.

'I ran down to her, but her body was so… I think she'd broken her back. I sat there with her until Theresa eventually found us – God knows how long it was. Apparently, I was completely incoherent by the time she got to us – I'd been out in the rain so long I had hypothermia.'

'I'm so sorry,'

'Before she died, while she was away with her mum, Marigold had finished the story. Our story. That was what was on the flash drive she gave me. I couldn't bring myself to read it for years, and then after I did, I happened to be in a bookshop and *Two Lost Souls* caught my eye. I don't know why it grabbed my attention; but it did, and when I started flicking through it…' he sighed. 'I never knew she sent it to *you*. To *you*, of all people.' He couldn't bear to look at Stacey a moment longer, and pushed his chair back, before striding out of the room.

Chapter 45

The sun was fully up, and as light streamed through the windows, the familiar rooms filled his vision. The people the house had been sold to had made some changes, but it seemed they'd given up halfway through. He'd heard it had changed hands again since then, but the current owners must have been overwhelmed by the work that needed doing, or run out of money, because it was empty and abandoned once more. He'd looked it up just a few weeks back and saw it was up for auction.

'Let's go outside,' Stacey said, appearing next to him, and he followed her reluctantly, relieved to take a breath of fresh morning air once they stepped into the sun. She led him over to a tree to the side of the house with a rickety bench underneath, and she sat down. 'Your dad disinherited you,' she said. 'I did some research when you were in hospital and I saw that the house went to your stepmother after he died, not to you. That's how I figured out who Marigold was.'

'What does any of that matter now?' he asked as he sat beside her.

She was silent for a while. 'Well, there's something I don't understand.'

'What's that?'

'If your dad disinherited you, why do you have so much money?'

He glanced round at her. Money. Of course she'd ask about that. All she'd seen when she read Marigold's work were pound signs, so why should he be surprised that that was her one question after all he had said?

'He and Theresa never actually got divorced, though they separated after he told Marigold her baby had died. Marigold would still be alive today if he hadn't said that. Theresa must have blamed him for her daughter's death. I think that's partly why he left everything to her in his will; out of guilt, not solely to spite me.'

Stacey didn't comment so he continued. 'My dad died about two years after Marigold did,' he said. He threw me out just a week after her death, and I had no further contact with him. I didn't even know he'd got ill. But then Theresa called me out of the blue and asked if I could help her go through the house and pick out anything I wanted to keep, and what I thought we should get rid of, or sell, or give away. I said no to begin with, and that I couldn't care less about anything in the bloody place, but she was desperate. She said she'd make it worth my while, and I did take a few things that were my mum's.'

'And?' Stacey pressed him.

'And what?'

'The money!'

He made a sound of disgust and snapped, 'She said she'd give me half of what it sold for, if you really have to know.'

'*Half?*' Stacey breathed. 'For helping to clear the place out?'

'It wasn't only that – I think she did feel bad that my dad didn't leave me anything. I said it didn't matter to me and that I didn't even want anything from the old bastard. But she was adamant she wanted me to have half the money, even when I said I'd never touch anything that came from *him*.'

'How much did it sell for?'

He glared at her. 'Is this all that you're interested in?'

'Please, tell me.'

'Eight and a half.'

'Million?' she clarified. 'Eight and a half million pounds?'

'There's a load of land that housebuilders were interested in. And a couple of cottages as well; holiday rentals.'

'Your stepmum gave you over four million pounds?' she pressed him.

'There was inheritance tax,' he said, 'but… yeah, essentially. And I left it sitting in the bank and didn't touch a penny until I bought the house in Wrexton and invested with Grant. Well, and I used it to pay for the retreat, not that that exactly made much of a dent in it.'

Stacey was frowning and she gave him a long, searching look. 'No,' she said finally. 'It doesn't add up.'

'You're an accountant now?'

'I don't mean the maths! I mean Theresa. Your stepmother. That's not "feeling a bit sorry for you" money. It's not "thank you for clearing out the house" money.'

'I don't know what you're talking about,' he said, but then the conversation he and Marigold had overheard between Howard and Theresa popped into his head. *I'll tell her the truth,* Theresa had said. *All of it.* At the time he and Marigold had brushed it off; all they'd cared about was the fact they would be forcibly separated – what did it matter what nonsense Theresa was going to fill Marigold's head with to justify it? But now he could think of nothing else. What *was* the truth? More of Theresa's words flooded in. *You've never been honest with him about anything.* That's what she'd said when she confronted Howard about his brain damage. But what did that have to do with Marigold? None of it made any sense.

'Joel, listen to me.'

'No,' he said, shaking off the memories. 'You listen to *me.* I'm done with all of this. I've told you what happened to Marigold, and that was enough. What's the point in opening old wounds? It's over now. I just want to see Morwenna and explain everything.'

'And you can, soon. But first, you have to listen to me about this. What did I do at the retreat when you messaged me about posting a confession video? What did I do to try and make it all go away?'

'You said you'd give me money,' he said.

'Exactly. Guilt money. This four million from your stepmum, it's *guilt* money, Joel. There's something more to this, and you need to find out what.'

Chapter 46

He stared at her. *She's right. You know she's right.* 'Well, I guess she feels bad that she took Marigold away and made her go through with the adoption without giving me any say in it,' he said weakly. 'She stopped me from ever setting eyes on my daughter.'

'No,' Stacey said. 'It's not that. It's something else.'

'Then… what?'

'I don't know. But there's more to it, I know there is. And you know it too, I can see it in your face.'

A shiver went through him. *I don't want to know. I don't need to know.* Clearly if Theresa had thrown so much money at him to ease her guilt it was something horrible, and he'd had enough of horrible. Morwenna and their unborn child were his priority now. 'There isn't anything else,' he said, more to convince himself than her. 'There really isn't. I've told you exactly what happened.'

'Oh, come on, Joel. This whole thing stinks. Your stepmother is hiding something. I mean, how *did* she pressure Marigold into the adoption? Marigold must have been nineteen by then, it's not like she was so very young, surely if it really hadn't been what she wanted she would have stood her ground over something that important? And Marigold could have found a way to contact you, if she'd really wanted to. There has to be something else going on that we're not seeing.'

He was silent for a long while. He'd never thought to question the money at the time. Theresa's explanation had seemed entirely reasonable to him. She believed he'd been wronged when he didn't inherit and had wanted to be kind. Perhaps she thought it was what Marigold would have wanted.

'Take it from one who knows,' Stacey said softly. 'She wasn't trying to make *you* feel better. She's trying to make *herself* feel better. And for that amount of cash, she is feeling pretty bad about something. Mark my words.'

Stacey

'Here we are, then,' Stacey said, as she took in the house in front of her. Though not on the scale of Vineworth, Joel's stepmum's home was impressive nonetheless; a pretty barn conversion enveloped by a garden bursting with spring flowers.

'I don't know how you talked me into this,' Joel said, stopping in his tracks and staring at the house. 'It's ridiculous.'

In fact, he'd been so resistant that Stacey had virtually had to bundle him into her car to stand any chance of getting him here. 'I'm not knocking on her door at seven in the morning asking her ludicrous, offensive questions—'

'Then don't,' she said, frustrated by his attitude. 'After the night I've had, asking some woman I've never met ludicrous and offensive questions before breakfast sounds positively tame to me. *I'll* do the talking.'

'That makes it even more bizarre.'

She turned to him, taking his arm when he tried to look away. 'Joel, please, you have to trust me,' she said softly. 'I know you're nervous, but I'm here.'

'Trust *you*?'

'Yes, I know how it sounds, but let me do this for you.'

'Even if… *if* there is something, I'm not sure I want to know what it is. Perhaps it's better to leave it in the past.'

'Don't let her get away with it,' she said, sensing he was on the verge of walking away. Did he really not want to know a family secret worthy of a four-million-pound payout? 'She took Marigold away from you. And your daughter.'

'It's over a decade ago. And she lost a daughter too – Marigold's death devastated her.'

'And it devastated you too. And for someone claiming things that happened over ten years ago don't matter, you were pretty fired up about *The Darkest of Paths*.'

He let out a long breath. Had she gone too far? She wasn't trying to mock him, but he had to stand up for himself. Losing Marigold and his child had wounded him deeply, that was clear, but there had to be some way of him finding peace, and if he couldn't do it himself, well, she was going to help him.

'Come on,' she said, sensing him beginning to come round. 'I'm right here by your side. And I've already messaged Morwenna and told her to come and find us here.'

He took a step, but then swayed on his feet, and she steadied him. 'And the next thing you're doing is going to the doctor,' she said. 'Screw this family curse nonsense. You need to find out exactly what is going on with you.'

'I'm fine,' he said, disentangling himself from her. 'And if we're doing this, let's do it.'

Chapter 47

To say Theresa was surprised to find them on her doorstep at such an early hour was an understatement. Wrapped in a floral silk robe, she took a step back at the sight of Joel; who, as well as having scratches across his cheek, had torn his shirt climbing through the window into Vineworth Manor.

'Joel?' she said finally. 'And…' she glanced at Stacey.

'Stacey,' she said, without any further explanation.

'Why do you smell of petrol?' she asked Joel. 'And you're bleeding.'

'We had car trouble,' Stacey lied, not that that was much of an explanation, 'and we need to come in.'

Opening the door wide she let them step inside, and Stacey took in the homely surroundings. The hall was painted a warm biscuit shade, full of art and colourful wall hangings. They followed Theresa through into a large country kitchen, where vases filled with flowers from the garden sat in a cluster in the centre of the wooden table. Somehow, she'd thought Theresa's house would be cold and forbidding, since that was how she saw the woman who had taken Marigold away from Joel, but the reality was quite different. In fact, she was looking at Joel with eyes full of concern.

'Are you okay, Joel?' she asked. 'And where have you been? It's very early to be—'

'He's just found out he's going to be a dad,' Stacey said. 'And he's supposed to be getting married soon.'

'Oh, that's wonderful! Congratulations to you both.'

'I'm not having a baby with *her*.'

'I see,' Theresa said, flustered. 'Well, this is… it's a bit odd and unexpected, I have to say, but I'm happy to see you. I'll make some coffee, shall I? Then we can sit down and talk about whatever this is. And perhaps Joel can get cleaned up, as well.'

'He wants to know why you gave him half of what Vineworth sold for.' Stacey said bluntly. If she left this to Joel they'd get nowhere. He was making it pretty obvious he didn't like the woman but left to his own devices he'd sit quietly and drink coffee, exchange small talk, and then leave without uttering a word about what they'd come here for. *He's scared,* she realised. He's already been hurt so deeply by what happened back then that he doesn't want any more pain.

'I…' Theresa said, Stacey's question completely catching her off guard. 'I'm sorry, but I don't see what this has to do with you. If you're not even Joel's fiancée…'

'Stacey is my… uh…' Joel started.

'Friend,' Stacey suggested, and Joel shot her a look but didn't contradict her.

'She thinks it's strange that you'd give me that amount of money when you didn't have to.'

Theresa gave a brittle smile. 'Then perhaps your *friend* shouldn't make assumptions about things that are nothing to do with her. I'm sure you meant well,' she said to Stacey, not unkindly, 'but there really is no need for all of this. I felt that as Howard's son, it wasn't fair that Joel got nothing. That old place was worth so much that even with us sharing the money we had enough to set us up for life. Far more, in fact, than either of us would ever need.'

'I'm not buying it,' Stacey said, while Joel cringed. Was she really doing the right thing, forcing him to go through with these questions? What if he found out something that tipped him over the edge again? But she'd gone too far to back down now.

'I think we should go,' Joel said. 'I said there was no point—'

'Look, I know you lost a daughter,' Stacey pressed on. 'And I'm sorry for that, I really am, but Joel is still hurting from what he went through all those years ago. You might think your money made up for what happened, but it didn't even touch the sides. And I *know* there is something else. I know. For God's sake, it's been almost fifteen years. Don't leave it another fifteen. If you have something you need to tell him, then *tell* him…'

All three of them stared at each other for a long moment. Outside the window, trees swayed in a gentle breeze, and a large clock on the wall ticked away the seconds. Joel spoke first. 'Stacey, we need to go. And Theresa, I'm sorry for turning up like this. You won't see me again, don't worry.' He began to make for the door, and Stacey gazed after him hopelessly. What should she do? She hovered on the brink of telling Theresa what Joel had been about to do to himself, but the woman's eyes were already on her step-son, and her arm twitched as though she wanted to run after him and grab him to stop him leaving.

'Wait!' she said finally, as Joel's hand rested on the door handle. 'Joel, come back. Sit down. I'll make coffee, and I should get dressed; I feel ridiculous talking to you in my dressing gown. Your friend is right. I don't want to leave it another fifteen years, or twenty, or thirty. I don't want to leave it unsaid. You have a right to know.'

Theresa disappeared off for a few minutes, to return in a brightly patterned skirt, paired with a simple cream jumper. She placed a first aid kit down in front of Joel, along with a mirror, and while he dabbed antiseptic onto the cuts on his face, Theresa fiddled about with a fancy coffee machine. 'Here we go,' she said, finally placing three cups down on the table as Joel finished cleaning the dried blood from his cheek. Theresa sat opposite the two of them, folding her hands – which were shaking slightly – on the table in front of her.

'Joel,' she said. 'I'm just going to come right out with it. It's about your daughter.'

'What about my daughter?' he breathed.

'She didn't pass away a few days after being adopted. She is alive, and she's a teenager now.'

Chapter 48

Joel stared at Theresa. What the hell had she just said? Had he started hallucinating as well as his fainting and dizzy spells? Perhaps it was the petrol fumes from his clothes making him hear things.

'Do you understand what I said?' Theresa was asking, reaching across the table for his hand. He snatched it away.

'No,' he said. 'No, I don't understand. *You* said—'

'I didn't,' she said, her voice soft.

He shook his head, lost for words at her audacity. Was she seriously going to *deny* it? Deny that she'd told Howard the baby had died?

Theresa must have sensed the tirade he was about to hurl at her because she quickly continued. 'It was your dad that said it.'

'Yes, because you told him on the phone about the baby.'

Theresa put her hand up to her forehead for a moment. 'I know what a nightmare that whole day…' her voice cracked, and she looked down at her coffee cup, struggling to regain her composure.

'The day Marigold died,' he said coldly.

'Yes.'

'Why did you even come to the house? You'd taken her away, taken our baby away, what more did you want? To rub our noses in it?'

'Marigold was worried about you being left there alone with your dad, and I must admit I was as well. I told Howard I'd left something at the house, and that Marigold wanted to say goodbye to you properly, and I eventually got him to agree to let us come and see you.'

Joel struggled to focus. As well as checking on his wellbeing, Marigold had clearly been desperate to give him the flash drive with *The Darkest of Paths* saved on it. His mind was reeling. His baby – was she really alive? He had a daughter out there somewhere that he'd never met! What did she look like? Did she know anything about him and Marigold? Did she know she was adopted? His mind raced. Would he be able to meet her? But then anger filled him again. Why – *how* – could they have said the baby had died? It was evil. It was unforgivable.

'When you kept trying to talk to Marigold that day, when you were demanding for me and Howard to tell you where the baby was, he just saw red. He lied. I'd never phoned him to tell him the baby had passed away. But the two of you were young and you believed him without question.'

'And you didn't think to say anything?' Joel shouted. He was on his feet now. 'You just let us believe it?'

'No!' she cried. 'No, Joel; Marigold ran off before I could get a word out. We all went after her, but it was that terrible storm—'

'You don't need to remind me about the storm!' he said. 'I *know* it was a storm. I know…' he jabbed his finger at her weakly, and then he turned towards the door. He couldn't listen to any more of this. He hated his dad. He hated Theresa. His whole body was boiling inside, but before he reached the door the world turned black.

…

'Joel?' Stacey was saying. 'Joel? Can you hear me?'

He rolled groggily over onto his side. He'd been dreaming they were in his stepmother's house. She'd been saying all sorts of crazy things—

He blinked. The woman herself had loomed into his view, kneeling down beside him. 'Were we…' he frowned. 'We weren't talking about the baby, were we?'

'Yes,' Theresa said, her face etched with lines of worry. 'Just stay down there. I'll get you some water, and I'll make you something to eat.'

She rushed off, and Stacey stayed by his side. Were there tears in her eyes? 'I'm sorry,' she said. 'You're not well. I shouldn't have made you come here.'

'They lied to me,' he said, sitting up slowly as the conversation came flooding back.

'You have to hear her out,' Stacey said. 'Don't run off in anger, although God knows I can't blame you for wanting to.'

'Here,' Theresa said, placing a plate down on the floor next to him. Propping himself against the wall, he reluctantly took a few bites of the toast spread thickly with butter and jam. He felt like he'd been hit by a bus. Yet he also felt the most alive he had in ages. His daughter was out there somewhere! He could barely believe it.

'If Marigold hadn't died,' Theresa said shakily, 'then I would have told you both. But – Joel – I was in hell. I'd lost my only child.'

'So, you just let me think…'

'I'm so sorry.'

For a moment there was only silence, and Stacey encouraged him to carry on eating, though his stomach was tying itself in knots. How could Theresa have kept it a secret for so many years?

'You could have told me after my dad died,' he said. 'I was with you for days, helping you clear out the house. You've had years… so many opportunities.'

He got to his feet with Stacey's help and made his way back to the table, the two women doing the same. He drank half his mug of coffee in one go, the toast and the warm drink bringing a bit of life back to his body. How could Theresa have kept it a secret from him? How could she treat him like that?

'The thing is,' Theresa said, 'I wasn't sure whether it would be good for you to know.'

'You mean, *you* didn't want to go through the pain of talking about it,' Stacey burst out. 'How could it not be good for Joel to know his child had lived?'

There was a long silence. 'Perhaps you're right,' Theresa admitted. 'All I wanted was to get that house sold and move on. There were no happy memories for me there; all I felt when I thought about that place was pain. I just wanted to forget about it; everything that happened at Vineworth.'

'Why did he do it?' Joel said, anger bubbling away. 'Why did he have to say it? If he hadn't, Marigold would still be alive. We could have been together! I know she was my stepsister, and I know it's not… it wouldn't have been ideal, but we weren't related by blood. My dad carried on like it was incest or something—'

Theresa put her coffee mug down on the table slightly too hard and he glanced up at her. His dad's words were spinning in his head. *She is your sister! Your sister!*

'Theresa, she wasn't…' He shook himself. No. Surely not. But the doubt nagged at him. *You've never been honest with him about anything.* It all made sense! *This* was what she told Marigold that made her give the baby up for adoption! 'She wasn't…' he started, horror flooding his body. 'Were you and my dad together before he married my mum? Was Marigold—'

'No!' Theresa said. 'No, Joel. God, no. She wasn't your half-sister if that's what you're thinking. It wasn't that.'

'But there is something,' he pressed her. 'There is something that made my dad so angry, isn't there? Something beyond us being stepsiblings? That's why Marigold had our daughter adopted. That's why you forced us apart from each other.'

Abruptly, Theresa pushed her chair back and stood up, looking like she was about to be sick. 'Look, Joel, perhaps you should get some rest. You look exhausted and so does your friend. And I need… I need some fresh air.' With that, she ran towards the French doors, fumbling with the key and disappearing out into the garden, while he stared after her blankly.

Chapter 49

'Come on,' Stacey said, grabbing his arm. 'You're not letting her wriggle off the hook now.'

He got to his feet, following Stacey out into the garden. Theresa had made it to the table and chairs on a small patio beneath an apple tree, and she had her head in her hands.

'Joel,' she said, looking up as he drew near to her. 'You really should get some rest after fainting. Go back home to your fiancée, she must be worried about you. You don't want to be hanging around here with me.'

'He collapsed because he's ill,' Stacey said. 'He's got whatever it was that his mum died of. And now he's going to have a baby, and he's worried he won't even live to see it.'

At these words, the colour drained from Theresa's face. 'Why did they tell you?' she breathed.

'Why?' Joel said. 'What do you mean, why? How could I not be told about *the family curse?*'

'Have you spoken to a doctor about it?' she asked him.

'No.'

'Why not?'

'Because he thinks there's no point,' Stacey said. 'He ended up in hospital one of the times he fainted, but he discharged himself without listening to what the doctors had to say. He's given up. You want to know why he smells of petrol? He was going to burn Vineworth Manor down and take himself with it.'

'Stacey!' he said. 'Please, I don't want her to—'

'Is that true?' Theresa asked him.

'Don't you think he's been through enough?' Stacey continued. 'How can he move on if he doesn't even know what really happened?'

Joel sat down opposite Theresa, and Stacey plonked down at his side once more. 'Please,' he said. 'What did you mean by, "why did they tell you"? Why wouldn't my parents tell me?'

'Listen to me,' Theresa said, reaching across to take his hands. 'If you're worried about your health, talk to a doctor. But don't press me to tell you this. You'll wish you didn't know.'

Joel pulled his hands away from hers. 'You thought it would be better for me not to know my child was alive.'

'I know, and I'm sorry. I'm so sorry for how I handled all of that. Do you… Joel, do you really believe that you're dying, like your mum? Is that really what you think?'

'Of course I am,' he snapped. 'You know I am! I heard you talking to my dad about the Gerstmann's syndrome. Saying how it was my mum's fault I had brain damage. Blaming her for something she had no control over.'

Theresa let out a long, shaky breath. 'You heard all of that?'

'Yes, I did. It's not my mum's fault. She passed her illness on to me. It wasn't *deliberate*, like you made it sound.'

She was shaking her head. 'You've got this all so wrong. And to think it was because you overheard me talking to your dad…' her voice cracked.

He stared at her. What was happening? How could he have got it wrong? He'd overheard their conversation as plain as day.

'Listen to me,' Theresa said at length. 'Forget this "family curse" nonsense. Go to the doctor, let them run tests so you can find out why you're fainting. But please believe me when I say you're better off leaving now. You're about to get married. Just enjoy it. Your dad has gone, and the past is in the past. Maybe one day your daughter will want to meet you. *That* was worth knowing. But to hear any more… just let it go. It doesn't matter and no good will come of it.'

Joel hesitated. If she said no good would come of it, perhaps he didn't want to know whatever it was. And was she saying the doctors would be able to help him? Did he and Morwenna have a future after all? His life wasn't bleak like it was just a few short hours ago. Why throw himself back into despair, if that's what Theresa's secret would do to him?

But it's the reason, his mind nagged him. *It's the reason my dad said the things he did. It's what drove him to tell such an awful lie – a lie that sent Marigold to her death.*

'I get what you're saying,' he told Theresa calmly, 'but I have to know. I need to understand why my dad behaved like he did. I need to understand why you said I have brain damage because of my mum.'

At that moment there was the sound of a car door. 'It's Morwenna,' Stacey said. 'I'll go and find her.'

'There's a gate just round the side there,' Theresa told her, and Stacey scurried off in the direction she had pointed.

'Is Morwenna your fiancée?' Theresa asked him.

He nodded.

'I really wish I'd known you overheard that conversation,' she said, but before she could say any more there was a burst of shouting from the direction of the drive, before the two women appeared in the garden.

'Morwenna, please, listen to me,' Stacey said, but instead of replying, Morwenna slapped her, and Stacey cried out in shock. 'Don't you *ever* speak to me again!' Morwenna shrieked. 'Lying and making accusations about Joel when I'd just told you I was pregnant! You make me sick!'

Clutching her cheek, Stacey tried to reason with her, but Morwenna ran towards him, wrapping her arms around him and pressing her cheek against his. 'Joel, oh God, Joel, I thought I'd lost you. What on earth is going on?'

'Stacey found me,' he said shakily. 'She… I guess she saved me.'

Morwenna let go of him and pointed her finger at Stacey. 'That *bitch* did not save you!' she said, 'if she hadn't said what she did, you'd never have run off and tried to…' her voice broke.

'I'm so sorry,' Stacey said, having made her way over to stand beside them.

'For what?' Morwenna turned and shouted at her. 'Telling lies about Joel? Making me and Grant hate him? *Or* are you sorry for stealing *Two Lost Souls*? The book about *Joel's* life, written by *his* girlfriend?'

'I didn't know when I took it,' Stacey said, 'I didn't know any of it was true.' Tears began to spill down her cheeks, and Theresa stood up and led her away. 'Let's let them talk,' she said to Stacey. 'They need some space.'

Sitting with Morwenna at the table beneath the apple tree, Joel took a deep breath. 'This mess isn't entirely Stacey's fault,' he said. 'I've been lying, too. I never meant to hurt anybody, but it was like I kept digging myself into a bigger and bigger hole and I didn't know how to get out.'

She nodded. 'Then tell me, Joel. Tell me now.'

...

By the time Theresa came back out of the house, Stacey trailing along behind her, he had managed to explain everything to Morwenna up to the point of Theresa dangling the family secret in front of him that she claimed would do him no good, and Morwenna was struggling to take in everything he had said, shaking her head as she tried to make sense of it all.

'I'm very angry with you,' she said at last, her voice unsteady. 'You've told so many lies. Caused so much damage.'

'I know.'

'But I'm going to put that to one side, for now. Just tell me, *are* you dying?' Morwenna asked, as Theresa and Stacey made their way across the lawn towards the table.

'Honestly, I'm not sure I know,' he said.

Morwenna looked up at Theresa as she reached the table. 'You're Joel's stepmum?'

'I am.'

'Morwenna,' Stacey cut in desperately. 'Please hear me out—'

'I wasn't talking to you,' Morwenna said coldly.

'Joel, do you still want to know?' Theresa asked. 'Do you still want me to tell you everything?'

Morwenna was holding his hand in her lap and gave it a squeeze. 'Yes,' he said. 'Yes, I do.'

Chapter 50

Joel shook his head. What had he just heard? 'What do you mean, Marigold was my cousin?'

Theresa was being absurd. Of course Marigold wasn't his cousin. It couldn't possibly be true.

Morwenna was quiet at his side, the world completely still.

'She was.' Theresa paused, as if still unsure whether to continue, but then she nodded. 'Marigold *was* your cousin. And, Joel, this condition your mother had – it's a rare heart condition. It can run in families, and that's why some other members of your mum's family died suddenly. They can do ECGs and other tests now to see if you have the same condition. They can't cure it but there are things that can help if you have it.'

'What's that got to do with Marigold?' he asked helplessly. None of it felt real. Theresa's voice seemed to come from a great distance.

'I'll get to that in a moment. But first, please listen to me. You should get your symptoms checked out, like I said before, but they're extremely unlikely to be caused by this same condition that your mum had. And it's certainly not why you have Gerstmann's syndrome. This "family curse", as your mum insisted on calling it, it wouldn't affect your brain like that. It affects your heart rhythm. It can cause fits, dizziness and fainting, things like that. And yes, it can be fatal.'

'What are you getting at?' he asked. 'Why would it be so unlikely that I have it? It's the *most* likely cause, surely, if it's genetic?'

Theresa was curling and uncurling her fingers on the table, struggling to meet his eye. 'I'm not doing a good job of explaining this, I know—'

'Please,' he said. 'Just say whatever it is you're trying to say. Just tell me.'

'Okay,' she said, letting out a long breath. 'Your mum…' Theresa shook her head sadly. 'She's not your biological mother.'

His head began to spin. It was like he was floating, looking down at himself. This was nonsense. This had to be nonsense. 'Then… who…' he managed to say.

'My sister,' Theresa said. 'My sister was your mother.'

…

'No,' he said. 'No. Linda and Howard Shakespeare were my parents. I don't understand why you're doing it, but you're lying. This is a lie.'

He got up from the table and made off towards the gate out onto the driveway. Theresa was twisted and cruel to be saying these things. Maybe she was even lying about his baby. He couldn't trust a word that came out of her mouth. Stacey's feet were pounding after him.

'Joel, stop—'

He glared at her, and at Theresa, who was following him with Morwenna in tow.

'I don't want to talk about this,' he said. 'There's something wrong with you, Theresa.'

'Joel!' Stacey pleaded with him.

'No,' he said. 'Why am I even here? *She*—' he gestured at Theresa, 'talked Marigold into giving our baby away with these vicious lies, and as for *you*,' he turned to Stacey, 'why the hell did I let you bring me here? Why did I listen to you for even a moment? You don't care about me. I don't know what you're getting out of all of this.'

He turned his attention back to Theresa. 'Did you not hear how Stacey *stole* your daughter's life's work, or do you not care?'

'I wasn't sure what you were talking about, if I'm honest,' Theresa said.

'You don't even know, do you?' Joel said. 'Marigold wrote a book.'

Theresa's eyebrows drew together. 'She did say something about writing,' she said. 'She didn't say *what* she was writing, and I just let her get on with it. It seemed to help take her mind off of everything while she was pregnant.'

'It was a book called *The Darkest of Paths*,' he said. 'It was our story – mine and hers. Changed a bit, but it was her feelings about the whole situation she'd been put in.'

'I didn't realise.'

'Do you want to know what happened at the end of it?'

'I—'

'They both die. Me and her. *That's* what was going through her head when you forced us apart.'

'I just told you; she was your *cousin*!'

'I don't believe you. My mum wasn't your sister. It's all lies. And anyway,' he threw at her, 'even if you're telling the truth, cousins can get married. It's not illegal. We could have been together.'

'For God's sake, Joel!' Theresa cried.

He stared at her, his body flooded with rage, horror, despair. Why was she doing this to him? Trampling on his memories, rewriting his history? Was nothing sacred to her?

'What were you saying about this book Marigold wrote?' Theresa asked eventually. 'You said Stacey *stole* it?'

'She did,' Joel said, controlling his emotions with difficulty. 'She stole it and published it. *Two Lost Souls*, she renamed it, and slapped her own name on the cover. I take it you never read it.'

'No,' Theresa said, 'I'm not a big reader.' Her eyes strayed to Stacey. 'Is this real?' she asked. 'Did this really happen?'

'It was a bestseller,' Stacey said, her voice almost a whisper.

'There you go,' he said. 'The pair of you have plenty to talk about. But I'm leaving with Morwenna. I don't want to hear any more of this bullshit.'

...

He sat in the car, with Morwenna waiting silently by his side, while Stacey and Theresa left him alone. Out of the window, he saw Stacey place her hand on Theresa's arm, clearly trying to apologise, or explain, but Theresa shook her away. Raised voices floated to him but he couldn't hear the words. It didn't matter anyway. He closed his eyes, letting the sound wash over him. He was dimly aware that Morwenna was saying something, but the words didn't register. *Theresa's lying. There's no way it can be true.* The thing was, he and Marigold had always known their relationship might never be able to be formal. The rules around stepsiblings marrying were complex – they'd spent ages trying to research it – and as they had, however briefly, lived in the same house being brought up together, their relationship might never have been recognised. *Was it wrong, me and her?* Whether it was or it wasn't, stepsiblings was one thing, but the idea they could have been related by blood disturbed him. He couldn't believe it. He *wouldn't* believe it.

He jumped at a knock on the window, and turned to find Stacey and Theresa, the latter holding some paperwork.

He lowered the window. 'I'm not interested,' he said.

Theresa thrust the papers at him, and he took them. 'What is this?' he asked her.

'Read it.'

With a sigh, he glanced down at what was in his hand. A birth certificate.

William Christopher Brown

Mother's name: *Susanna Brown*

Date of birth: *5th May 1992*

He stopped reading. 'Why are you showing me this?'

'That's your date of birth, as you well know. And your middle name.'

'So? My name isn't William.'

He knew exactly what she was trying to insinuate. Brown was Theresa's maiden name, and so too was it her sisters. He shoved it back at her.

'Joel, your name isn't William because of the new surname you were going to have after the adoption. They had to change it.'

He let out a humourless laugh. Now he knew it was a joke. 'Right, because if they didn't change it, my name would have been "William Shakespeare", that's what you're saying?'

'Read the other document,' she said.

He forced himself to look down – quite sure the second document, whatever it was, wouldn't be worth the paper it was written on.

Name and surname of child: Joel Christopher Shakespeare

Name and surname of adopter or adopters: Howard Shakespeare, Linda Shakespeare

Date of adoption order: 16th June 1992

The paper shook in his hand. 'Why do you have this?' he asked her. For some reason it was the only question he could think of.

'I took it from the house when we cleared it out,' she said softly.

'To stop me from finding it.'

She nodded.

'My dad told me he'd lost my birth certificate.'

'And you didn't think that was strange?'

'Of course I didn't!' he blustered, trying to think of anything other than what he'd read. 'You know as well as I do what a shambles that house was. There was paperwork strewn about all over the place. He said the only people who cared about keeping paperwork organised were busy-bodies—'

'Or do-gooders,' Theresa finished for him. She gave a sad smile. 'I remember what he was like, and the daft things he used to say. I remember them both; Howard *and* Linda.'

'You didn't know my mother.'

'I did,' she said. 'Please get out of the car. Let's sit down and talk about this properly. There's so much more to say, and perhaps then you'll understand why it ended up such a mess.'

He wanted to ignore her. He wanted to start the engine, drive off with Morwenna and leave Stacey and Theresa behind – to leave all of it behind. Yet for some reason he reached for the door and stepped out.

Chapter 51

Back inside the house, Theresa made more coffee and placed down a large biscuit tin. She and Stacey had apparently reached an uneasy truce, though he could sense the tension between the two women, as well as between Stacey and Morwenna.

'Now,' Theresa said as she sat down. 'I'll tell you first about my sister, your birth mother, if that's all right?'

He nodded. The whole thing was still entirely surreal to him. Stacey reached for a shortbread biscuit and nibbled at it.

'Susanna – well, nobody actually called her that, it was Susie – she was very troubled.'

'Troubled?'

'She was an addict, and in the end… well, she died. Of a heroin overdose. Not intentionally, we don't think, but, still.'

'Right.'

Morwenna touched his hand. 'Are you okay?' she asked him.

'Why wouldn't I be? I don't know her, and she didn't want me, what difference does it make to me that she's gone?'

Somehow, though, it did. A dark, yawning hole was opening inside him. The whole thing was so… big. His whole life, nothing, *nothing* was what it had appeared.

'I don't know who your father was,' Theresa continued, 'but one thing I do know is that Susie loved you.'

'Yeah, it really sounds like it.'

'She did a brave thing,' Theresa said. 'She didn't have you adopted because she didn't care about you. She did it *because* she cared. She wanted you to have the best life possible, and she didn't feel that she could give you that, no matter how much she wished she could. I know that she missed you and that she thought about you. In fact, initially she asked *me* to adopt you, and I agreed, but my ex-husband – Marigold's dad – he was completely against it. He said it would be far too messy. Linda – your mum – she was a close friend of mine, and that's why I suggested to Susie that Linda and Howard could adopt you. She liked that idea, because although she didn't know your mum, she trusted my judgement. It wasn't easy, though, being friends with Linda once she'd adopted you, but I'll get to that later.'

'You fell out?' he asked. 'Because I don't remember ever meeting you as a child.'

'You did meet me, when you were little,' Theresa said, 'but then… the friendship ended.'

'And Susie? When did she die?'

'When you were about twelve.'

'Did she know my mum had died?'

Theresa nodded. 'Yes. It affected her badly, finding out you'd lost the only mum you'd ever known. I think, probably, it would have been better if you'd been adopted by strangers and we had never known anything about your life, though on the other hand I did like having some contact with you when you were little, and when I married your dad.'

'And to think you criticised me and Marigold. You married your friend's husband.'

She shook her head. 'It wasn't the way you make it sound. I went to your mum's funeral, and I saw that Howard was struggling, so we met up a couple of times, but then I didn't see him again for years. Then Susie died, and a year or so after that I got divorced. I was feeling lonely, and I got in touch with Howard again; only to check how he was and how you were getting on. But then things just grew from there.'

Joel swirled his coffee around in its mug. What a strange web of relationships made up his history. His head was beginning to ache. Stacey was on her fourth biscuit. They had been awake for over twenty-four hours now, and exhaustion was filling his body, though his mind was still working overtime. He picked up a biscuit and ate it slowly, while Theresa stayed silent. 'Do you want to ask me anything, Joel?'

'Yes,' he said. 'I want you to tell me why you fell out with my mum. And why you said it's her fault I have brain damage.'

'Okay,' she said heavily. 'And believe me, the last thing I want to do is start criticising her, but I'm just going to have to say it like it is.'

He nodded, and after a deep breath, Theresa began.

…

'I met Linda at university,' Theresa said. 'She was… well, I liked her because she was so different. Always in outfits that were every colour and pattern under the sun, and she never cared what anybody thought of her. "People can take me or leave me," she told me once, "either way is fine with me."' Theresa smiled wistfully. 'The thing I liked about her the most was that although she was so independent, she cared so fiercely about the people she allowed in. If someone she loved was upset, or needed help, she would drop literally everything to be there for them. That was more important to her than anything else.'

Joel nodded. That sounded like his mum.

'The thing I didn't understand about her straight away was how much she was affected by this *family curse* business. It was like she wanted to cram all of her life in as quickly as possible. She married Howard straight after she graduated, and the pair of them together—' she shook her head. 'Your mum was always very open-minded; she'd believe in anything and everything. Ghosts, UFOs, she loved the unexplainable. And your dad loved his conspiracy theories, he was always spouting some new plot he thought he'd uncovered. It was harmless enough though, and they were obviously happy and in love. They didn't have a lot of money back then, of course, it was before your dad inherited Vineworth Manor. Your mum started working at a little farm shop, and your dad didn't stick at anything much, he'd do a bit of this and a bit of that. Then, his parents died, and he got Vineworth Manor. He and Linda had all sorts of ideas about turning it into a farm and some sort of commune; I lost track of it all, to be honest. Then I got married, and when I was pregnant with Marigold, Linda said how she and Howard wanted to settle down. They wanted to try to get some income from Vineworth Manor, the place was a money pit when they weren't making it earn its keep – and, well, she wanted a baby. But she was scared if she had one, the child would have this "curse" hanging over them just like she did. Of course, I told her to go and speak to her doctor about it, but they weren't even registered with any doctor's surgery. The pair of them seemed convinced all you needed to be healthy was to eat their biodynamically grown vegetables and steer clear of anything that had any medical or scientific basis. I think to your mum the curse really was a curse, no matter what anyone said to the contrary, so medicine had nothing to do with it in her mind. I don't know if she even knew what it was, medically speaking, I only found out it was a heart condition after she died, and I spoke to some of her relatives at her funeral.'

Joel frowned. He could remember his mum's funeral; there were a load of people there he'd never seen before, and Howard kept him apart from all of them. He couldn't recall seeing Theresa there, but then, he'd been too upset to take in names and faces.

'When Marigold was only little,' Theresa continued, 'we found out about Susie's pregnancy. Linda was talking a lot about how much she wanted a baby, but she never asked to have Susie's baby when I explained the situation. It was *me* who suggested she adopt you, and as soon as I did, she jumped at the chance. The thing is, I knew how much she would love you. That's why I suggested it to her. It made absolutely no difference to her that she wasn't the one who had given birth to you; a baby was a baby, and she loved you from the moment she set eyes on you.'

Theresa sighed heavily. 'In a way, that was the problem. I don't know if it makes sense to say she loved you *too* much, but it wasn't what I would call an entirely healthy relationship. She would never let you out of her sight. You always stayed in that big house or in the gardens, and you almost never saw any children your own age, though I did bring Marigold to the house when you were toddlers.'

'I saw Marigold when we were toddlers?' he asked – the idea was very odd.

'Only a handful of times, but yes. In fact, one day I managed to coax Linda to take you out to a soft play with me and Marigold. But I didn't realise she had never taken you to get your vaccinations, and because she kept you cooped up, you'd never been exposed to any illnesses.'

Theresa paused for a moment. 'It was incredibly unlucky, the chances of it happening the one time you went somewhere busy like that…'

'What happened?'

'You got measles, and you were ever so ill. But then it spread, and you got meningitis.'

'She never told me… and I don't remember.'

'You were too young to remember. You were very, very sick and in the end your mum did take you to hospital, but not as quickly as she should have. But your mum never forgave me for making her take you out that day. She said it was all my fault, but of course it wasn't.'

He ended up with parietal lobe damage because of something entirely avoidable. 'That's why I have Gerstmann's syndrome, isn't it?' he said. 'Because I had meningitis and it damaged my brain.'

Theresa nodded. 'From what I can understand, you were lucky to even survive. It could have been much, much worse.'

'That's why you said it was my mum's fault; because she didn't want me to have any vaccinations, and then she waited too long to take me to hospital when I was ill. You said it was all avoidable.'

'Well, yes,' she said. 'I was angry that day I was arguing with Howard, and I probably didn't phrase things the best way. Obviously, your mum never meant for any of this. She really did love you and wanted what she thought was best for you, but… I told you I'd say it like it is, and the fact is if you'd had your vaccinations, you'd never have got measles that day. And if she'd been quicker to take you to hospital, you wouldn't have become so unwell. Because *she* was the one who wanted to wait, not Howard. He would have taken you, or called an ambulance, but your mum was scared of hospitals – she said they would make you sicker. She was convinced she could save you herself and didn't accept she was out of her depth until it was almost too late.'

'So, did you ever speak to my mum again after I had meningitis?'

'No. I tried, but she would have nothing to do with me, and after a while I gave up. I'm surprised Howard even invited me to her funeral, to be honest, but perhaps that was more because he wanted my support than because he thought she'd want me there.'

Stacey had taken a fifth biscuit, but she dropped it. It broke in half, spraying crumbs across the table. 'Sorry,' she muttered.

'I still don't understand why you're here!' Morwenna exploded at Stacey. 'This is *nothing* to do with you! What's the plan? Looking for inspiration for another book, is that it? Oh no, I forgot, writing books *yourself* isn't really your style, is it?'

'Just let her be,' Joel said. 'If it wasn't for her, I suppose I'd never have found out any of this.'

Morwenna backed down, but not before fixing Stacey with an icy glare.

'So, you told Marigold all of this,' he said to Theresa. 'You told her we were cousins, and that's why she gave up our daughter?'

'Yes. The thing was, your dad never wanted you to know you were adopted. He felt that you discovering the truth would be the ultimate betrayal of Linda's memory. That's why he reacted so violently to the fact you and Marigold were seeing each other. He was terrified that the truth would come out – that we'd end up being forced to tell you that you were cousins. That's why I took her away, and she agreed not to contact you and tell you any of what I'd revealed to her. I might not have agreed with all of Linda's choices, but I didn't want to rip your world apart by revealing the truth. We thought with some distance you and Marigold would forget each other.'

'But we didn't.'

'No. I should never have brought her to the house that day… the day she…' she took a breath. 'We were both so worried about you. I could never have imagined Howard would say what he did about the baby. To lash out in such a cruel way…' she closed her eyes for a moment and silence fell, until Stacey's phone began to peal and she rushed outside. 'Grant?' he heard her say before she shut the door and her words were snatched away.

'So,' Theresa said. 'I don't know what else I can say. Except that I'm sorry. The way things ended up – I could never have foreseen it. But I regret all of it. The pain you and Marigold ended up going through, I wish I could have spared you both that. I wish everything had been different. I wish everyone had just been honest with each other right from the start.'

'Joel!' Stacey burst back into the room. 'I need to go back. Grant is in a right state, demanding to know what's going on – I need to talk to him.'

He turned to Morwenna, and she smiled at him reassuringly. 'I think it's time for us to go too, now, don't you think? Or do you want to talk to Theresa a little longer?'

'No,' he said, as his body was filled with a strange lightness. 'I think I've heard all I need to hear.' He smiled back at her. 'Let's go home.'

Epilogue

Taking in the sight of the tree-lined gravel driveway, Stacey's heart pounded. The large, red brick house, those beautiful lawns spreading out either side like a lush green carpet. The gardens beyond, where she and Joel and the other writers had once walked, enjoying the pretty rose garden and the wildflower meadow.

She got out of her car tentatively. She must be out of her mind, coming back. Some of the other writers might be here – the ones she had spoken to before, when they'd believed she'd written *Two Lost Souls*. She put her shoulders back. There was no helping that. She was owning her mistakes, and she wasn't going to hide away forever.

She paused as another car pulled up beside her, and its occupant stepped out. For several seconds they simply stared at one another in astonishment.

'Joel?' Stacey said.

'Stacey.'

'What are you doing here?' they both asked simultaneously, before giving an uncomfortable laugh.

'Come on,' Joel said, once they'd got over their initial shock, 'why don't we walk for a minute or two?'

They strolled along in silence for a little while, until they reached the rose garden, which was just entering full bloom. Stacey couldn't help but stop for a moment to admire the riot of flowers. 'So,' she asked slowly, 'what *are* you doing here?'

'Well, I really did like the food,' he said.

She laughed. 'I'm sure it's no better than what Morwenna cooks. She's always had a way with flavours.'

'That's true,' he agreed, and then paused for a moment. 'I came because I've got some ideas for a children's book. Esther – that's our daughter, she's two now – she inspired me. I came to brainstorm and draft, and see how I get on. I've been working with a writing tutor, and I can type quite well now if I get my ideas planned out first. Morwenna pushed me to come; she said she didn't mind staying home with Esther, and we won't have much time on our hands soon with our second on the way.'

'Morwenna's pregnant again?'

'She is. The baby's due in a few months – Esther will have a little brother.'

Stacey felt a pang. She'd never even met Joel and Morwenna's baby Esther. Once upon a time she would have been one of the first people to meet her. She would have been one of the first to hear that Morwenna was expecting again, and they would have chatted together excitedly.

'Congratulations,' she said. 'I'm happy for you.' She paused. 'Did you find out why you kept fainting?'

'Emotional stress,' he said. 'It was because of everything that was going on with you, and the lies, and all of it.'

'I'm sorry,' she said quietly. 'I should have told the truth about the book straight away. I should never have let things go so far.'

'I don't think I exactly did myself any favours,' he said. 'I made a real mess of things for myself, for everyone, in fact – and I'm sorry for the pain I caused you and your family. I'm lucky Morwenna still wanted anything to do with me – not that things were easy between us, at first. I really hurt her with all the lies, and it took a while to earn her trust back. I wish I hadn't gone about things the way I did – I thought I was justified, when I started out, but I think I was in pain and couldn't see how to make sense of anything. It was easier to put my energy into hating you than it was to ask questions about my past.'

They fell into silence, before he said, 'How are you, anyway?'

'Oh, you know,' she said, at a loss how to sum it all up. 'I'm okay, I guess.'

'And Grant?' he said, as they sat together on a stone bench under a rose arch. The same bench where she'd once sat desperately trying to find words to write in her notebook. 'How is that going?'

She sighed. 'We're getting there. But he's finding it hard to process it all – how I stole the book and lived a lie so much of my life, how reluctant I was to own up and take responsibility.'

'I'm glad he gave you a second chance. If I'd broken the two of you up for good, I'd never have forgiven myself. I wish he'd let me talk to him so I can say how sorry I am, but I understand why he doesn't want anything to do with me.'

'I feel the same about Morwenna – I wish I could talk to her properly. You know, once she started seeing you, I used to hate every moment the four of us were all together. But now the truth is out in the open I long for those days. Being friends with Morwenna again, you working with Grant. There's nothing I'd want more.'

'You never know,' he said. 'Things have a funny way of turning out. If anyone knows that, I do.'

She turned to Joel and saw the difference in him. He was at peace, now. Or certainly far more at peace than he was before. 'Now some time has passed, how do you feel about what Theresa told you?' she asked him.

'I'm still not completely sure,' he said. 'I've met her a couple of times and she's told me more about Susie, but I don't know what I make of all that. The thing that really matters to me is the child I had with Marigold. Theresa said that Marigold named the baby Daisy, and she wrote her a letter, which mentioned me. I hope that when Daisy is older, I can meet her, but it's her choice, I suppose.'

'I hope you do meet her,' Stacey said. 'You deserve to know each other.'

'Are you hoping to start writing, then?' Joel asked her.

'Well, I'm not here to throw more paperweights around,' she said, and then she turned to him. 'I actually did write a book, all those years ago. That's why I was in the writing critique group. I sent my manuscript to Marigold – not that I knew her name back then – and she sent hers to me. *One Winter in Paris,* mine was called. I read it again recently, and it wasn't quite as bad as I thought it was.' She smiled. 'I've decided to dust it off and start work on it again, try and write a second draft.'

'That's great,' he said. 'I never knew that you'd done that – you actually had written something.'

The sound of voices drifted to them from the car park; more writers were arriving and chatting before they went inside.

'We should probably head over there,' Joel said. 'Otherwise, all the cakes will be gone.'

'You know what's ironic?' Stacey said, as they began to make their way back out of the rose garden and across the lawn towards the house.

'What's that?'

'I think out of everyone caught up in this mess, *you're* the person who's the least angry with me.'

Joel gave a laugh. 'I'm not angry with anyone,' he said. 'Not any more. Not even my dad, though I'll never forgive him for what he said about the baby. And Stacey, not everyone is angry with you. Morwenna isn't angry any more, even if she's not ready to speak to you.' After a brief pause, he asked, 'How does it feel, anyway? To be ordinary Stacey Cockle, not Stacey Cockle who wrote *Two Lost Souls*?'

'Honestly?' she said, linking her arm with his. 'It feels fantastic.'

If you liked The Fake and you're keen to read more of my books, I invite you to subscribe to the LK Chapman newsletter to make sure you never miss a new release from me. Visit my website, **www.lkchapman.com** to sign up, and you will also be able to download a free short story!

Thank you so much for supporting me by buying my book, it means a lot to me, and I hope you enjoyed reading The Fake.

Instagram: **instagram.com/lkchapman**
Facebook: **facebook.com/lkchapmanbooks**
X: **@LK_Chapman**

Other books by LK Chapman

No Escape psychological thriller series
Worth Pursuing (short story)
Anything For Him
Found You
Never Let Her Go

Psychological thrillers/suspense
The Stories She Tells
Into The Lake
No Safe Haven

Short Stories
The Storm

Anything For Him
(Book 1 of the No Escape trilogy)

Felicity is at her lowest – vulnerable and emotionally numb after her parents die in a house fire, she is attracted to volatile and troubled Jay like a moth to a flame.

Allowing herself to be drawn in to Jay's twisted revenge plan against his former best friend, Felicity soon learns that no matter what she does, it will never be enough for Jay. As his jealousy and insecurity tip him into escalating violence against her, Felicity questions everything he has told her about his past and his former girlfriend, Sammie, and hatches a desperate plan to escape...

No Safe Haven

Will she ever escape her past?

Poppy's life has never been easy. Becoming a mum at sixteen, falling out with her family and being abandoned by her boyfriend has left her feeling lost and alone, but her son is a ray of light in her life and the pair form a strong bond: It's the two of them against the world.

Many years later, with her son grown up and away at university, Poppy arrives desperate, exhausted and half-starved to a pretty doorstep, hoping to find sanctuary in the home of her old school friend Harriet - and it is clear things have gone horribly wrong.

Finding Harriet living with her sister Jessica and nephew Reef, Poppy soon settles into a comfortable life in their rural village, helping Harriet in her delightful fabric shop, and believing the sisters have offered her a way to start again with a clean slate.

But as the hardships she has fled catch up with her, and cracks in the sister's strange relationship begin to show, Poppy is suspicious of Harriet's true motivations for helping her and fears her only option will be to flee once again.

With bonds between the three women tested to breaking point, and dark secrets revealed, will Poppy find safety and happiness, or has she simply fled one nightmare to end up in another?

No Safe Haven is a twisty tale of friendship, family and loyalty in a world where everyone has something to hide.

The Stories She Tells

A heartbreaking secret. A lifetime of lies.

When Michael decides to track down ex-girlfriend Rae, who disappeared ten years ago while pregnant with his baby, he knows it could change his life forever. His search for her takes unexpected turns as he unearths multiple changes of identity and a childhood she tried to pretend never happened, but nothing could prepare him for what awaits when he finally finds her.

Rae appears to be happily married with a brand new baby daughter. But she is cagey about what happened to Michael's child, and starts to say alarming things: that her husband is trying to force her to give up her new baby for adoption, that he's attempting to undermine the bond between her and her child, and deliberately making her doubt her own sanity.

As Michael is drawn in deeper to her disturbing claims, he begins to doubt the truth of what she is saying. But is she really making it all up, or is there a shocking and heartbreaking secret at the root of the stories she tells?

The Stories She Tells is a powerful psychological suspense novel that explores the impact of a traumatic childhood. It contains some emotive scenes and sensitive topics.

Acknowledgments

Thank you to my family who are always there for me and support me as I work on my novels.

For my amazing cover thank you to Dissect Designs.

And of course a big thank you to my readers!

About the author

LK Chapman writes psychological thrillers about relationships, family drama, secrets and lies – from dark and disturbing tales of obsession and jealousy, to twisty thrillers with a dash of romance – her passion is creating characters that get under your skin and stories that keep you gripped.

Chapman's books are inspired by her studies in psychology, and she has always been fascinated by the strength, peculiarities and extremes of human nature. As well as working as a psychologist, Chapman volunteered for mental health charity Mind before starting her journey as an author. It has been an incredibly exciting journey and she is so grateful for the support of her readers.

When she is not writing, Chapman will usually be found in her garden or getting out and enjoying the outdoors – immersing herself in nature and giving her mind a chance to work on her next story!

Subscribe to the LK Chapman newsletter by visiting
lkchapman.com

Printed in Dunstable, United Kingdom

68334823R00139